GREED

GREED

JOHN FENNELL

Greed

Copyright © 2021 by John Fennell. All rights reserved.

No part of this publication may be reproduced, stored in a retrieval system or transmitted in any way by any means, electronic, mechanical, photocopy, recording or otherwise without the prior permission of the author except as provided by USA copyright law.

This novel is a work of fiction. Names, descriptions, entities, and incidents included in the story are products of the author's imagination. Any resemblance to actual persons, events, and entities is entirely coincidental.

The opinions expressed by the author are not necessarily those of URLink Print and Media.

1603 Capitol Ave., Suite 310 Cheyenne, Wyoming USA 82001
1-888-980-6523 | admin@urlinkpublishing.com

URLink Print and Media is committed to excellence in the publishing industry.

Book design copyright © 2021 by URLink Print and Media. All rights reserved.

Published in the United States of America

Library of Congress Control Number: 2021900667
ISBN 978-1-64753-638-1 (Paperback)
ISBN 978-1-64753-639-8 (Digital)

06.08.20

DEDICATION

I dedicate this book:

To my grandmother and my step-brother who have both passed away during my incarceration. R.I.P. Autherine Joyce Butler and Lael Omar Wagner.

To my wife Catrina Fennell. Thank you for being so supportive and understanding. Thank you for being by my side and for always believing in me and my talent. I love you!

Thank you to Erlinda Santoy for her hard work and dedication to the ***Greed*** manuscript. It is much appreciated.

Thank you Kelly Allen for stepping in to help with last minute editing of Greed. You always come through.

Last but certainly not least, I thank the good Lord above for sustaining me and giving me the strength every day to endure. Thank you for the many blessings, talents and gifts you have given me.

Thank you for taking out time to read and explore my thoughts, there will be more to come. Stay tuned...

ELEVATION

Have they all lost it, is what I ask myself…

…Or is it me…

That's what they say… "J" you've finally lost it…

How can I have lost what I never had, or did I once have "it"…

Let's talk about "it"!!

Not little "it"…we're speaking of capital I.T.

Do they even know what capital I.T. is? Maybe and Maybe not…

My little "it" may be capital I.T. to small minded people (they)

What if I were so above the rest (they)

That capital I.T. Never was in their little world… Then maybe I have lost "it"

I have exceeded their thinking.

JMF 19

GREED

MAK and Tim, two young thieves, stole the wrong truck and found out it was loaded with drugs. The Cuban drug lord was shipping the truck to Cuba from California. The drugs were going to Florida and the truck was heading to Cuba. Stashed in the dashboard is a 50 million-dollar worth of diamonds.

    MAK has no idea about the diamonds when they unload the drugs. Tim finds the diamonds but never says anything. The truck is found in San Antonio, TX. The drug lord has connections in San Antonio with other gangs and crooked law enforcement. He makes a few calls and once he puts out the word that it's million-dollar reward for anyone who finds and brings him the people or person who has possession of the contents of the vehicle. Money makes things happen and Greed takes over everyone, and San Antonio has never seen mayhem like this before as gangs, laws, and money hungry people tear the city up to find and get MAK and Tim back to California. And, for one million dollars everything goes.

CHAPTER 1

San Antonio, TX 9:20pm

The moon was full and the rain was just starting to come down MAK and Tim had been out all night looking for someone to stick up for a few bucks. Rent was due and MAK's soon-to-be-mother of his son has been raising hell all week about him and Tim getting jobs. MAK and Tim are best friends and been getting in trouble together since they were 12 years old. MAK is engaged to Tim's little sister. Tim and Vanessa are one of the few Mexican families that were relocated to the Rigsby Courts when the Victoria Courts were torn down.

As it got later, MAK and Tim thought they'd go out to the truck stop and catch one of the truckers stumbling out of the bar or bathroom and hit for a few hundred bucks. "Man, nobody's going to be out here dawg it's raining", Tim said to MAK with a Newport in his mouth. "Look, we need to get something. I'm tired of hearing your sister's mouth every day" MAK said, grinding his teeth at the thought of Vanessa bitching. "Well, slap the hoe in the mouth fool. That's what my dad uses to do to my mom's."

"Fuck you stupid? That's my baby in the stomach niga, you know if I hit Nessa, she going crazy in that bitch and I can't take no chance of her losing this baby again."

MAK and Vanessa have been together for years and have had 3 miscarriages because of their constant fighting. Vanessa gets made and starts serious fights. MAK doesn't hit her, but he pushes her around to keep her from hurting him too badly and all this has been too much during past pregnancies.

"Come on, park right here", MAK told Tim as they pulled to the far end of the "Flying J's" Truck Shop… "MAK look, man, don't shoot nobody we just here to get some money"… "Alright, chill, let's go so I can get home and put this dick on your sister", MAK laughed but Tim gave him a fuck you look, cause the truth was when they got home he probably was going to do exactly what he said. They walked around for a few minute until the saw a tall Mexican man checking his tires and trailer lock. "Les get them" was the only words MAK said and they marched over to where the man was with his back turned to check the lock. As they approached, Tim pulled out his brand-new Glock 17 he got from another lick they hit last week. MAK pulled out a snub nose 357 he's been having for years. With their hands in their jackets, MAK asked, "Excuse me, sir! Can you spare some change? We're trying to get something to eat." "What you guys doing out in the rain so late?" the man asked. "Getting money", Tim said as he pulled out the weapon. As if by nature, MAK drew his weapon. "Fuck some change. Give us everything or its lights out old school". The old man panicked and fell to his knees. "Please don't kill me. It's in the truck." It's all in the truck, please don't kill me."

The old Mexican man was a truck driver for a furniture store in California but was paid to move a special load for a new company. All they told him was "Here's $20,000. Take this load to Miami, Florida. It's packed with a new product. They'll give you another $20,000 once the load is delivered." He agreed with no hesitation. They loaded his trailer-up with the product; the boss paid him and he left. He'd only stop in San Antonio, TX to get a bite to eat and a few minutes rest. "Where in the fuckin' truck?" Tim yelled. "In the glove compartment, but it's locked/ Here are the keys." MAK took the keys and went to the front while Tim watched the old man.

When MAK climbed in the truck, sitting on the front seat was a sawed-off shotgun. "Damn glad he ain't have that with him," MAK said to himself. He found the key to the glove compartment, opened it and saw a brown envelope. A box of the shells for the shotgun and a mapquest destination print out. He grabbed everything in the front seat, jumped out and grabbed the shotgun and went back to the trailer. "Jackpot homeboy," MAK told Tim. "Come on. Let's go" Tim said. "Hold on, hold on. Hey, what's in the trailer old man?" MAK said, making the old man raise his head to look in his eyes. "I don't know." "You don't know?" Tim said with frustration in his voice. You're hauling the shit and you don't know?" "I swear I don't know. I'm just taking it as a favor for a friend. I don't know," the old man said almost in tears.

"Well, let's see what you and your friend are taking to…let's see."

MAK looked at the destination sheet. "Oh here we go, Miami huh?"

"Get the fuck up." MAK pointed the shotgun at the old man's head and threw him the keys.

"Here, open the trailer," MAK said shoving the old man into the back of the trailer. "What the fuck you doing?"

"Let's go, you tripping fool." Tim said to MAK while looking all around for any unsuspected eyes.

No one was in sight. The rain had everybody inside Flying J's. Plus, today's special was good ole 3 for one taco with a free soft drink and 25-cent coffee. All the truckers loved it. They talked about it over the CB's "3 for 1 in the 210" could be heard in all surrounding cities by truckers.

MAK ignored Tim and hurried the old man to open the trailer. "Hurry the fuck up motherfucker before I shoot your stupid ass," MAK said, then stuck the gun in the old man's back.

"Please don't shoot. I do what you say, sir," the old man mumbled with rain falling off his lips.

The old man was terrified and was having trouble putting the key in the lock because of his shaking hands. MAK got mad and hit the man with the butt of the shotgun and knocked the old man to the ground.

He grabbed the keys and asked, "Is this the fuckin' key?"

"Yes, that one right there." The old man stayed crouched in a ball on the wet ground.

MAK unlocked the lock and opened the trailer. He couldn't really see anything but a bunch of chairs, tables, computers and lots of boxes with red tape on the sides with fragile written in bold letters. MAK looked through the boxes with his light from his cell phone. The box he opened had a marble tabletop with black pepper sprinkled everywhere in the box.

Tim yelled, "Hey stupid, it's raining out here. Let's go before somebody comes."

"Hold on scary ass nigga. Let me see something right quick," MAK said not looking back at Tim.

MAK moved the table top and saw something under it wrapped in plastic. He took the package out and blew the black pepper off. He sneezed a couple of times then tore the package open. A tan powder spilled out on his hands and on to the floor of the truck. MAK looked back at Tim and the old man.

Tim saw the look on MAK's face and said, "What you find? I see the look." MAK took the package to the back and showed Tim. "What the fuck is this? Tell me this ain't what I think it is," MAK said, with a hint of excitement in his voice.

Tim looked with wide eyes and said, "Let me see? Where did you get this?" "I just made it," MAK said being a smart ass. "I found it in the box in the trailer".

"That's not mine. I swear to you that's not mine. I'm hauling for a friend," the old man pleaded.

"Shut the fuck up, and tell us how much is in there!" MAK said pointing the shotgun at the old man. The old man threw his hand in front of the barrel as if that would stop the blast if MAK decided to shoot.

"I don't know how much. I only haul for a friend. I swear to you. They don't tell me what I haul. I just pick up the truck, get money and I leave"

MAK hit him with the shotgun again and said "How much motherfucker?"

"I don't know. I swear I'm not telling you a lie".

Tim told the old man to taste it and tell him what it was. MAK said, "Here, let me taste it"

Tim said, "Stupid, what if this shit is poison?"

"You're right. Let him taste it first." MAK corrected himself.

The old man hesitated but the shotgun aimed at his head was a big threat. He took a little powder chunk in his hand and put it in his mouth. Instantly, his tongue went numb and he spits it out. His whole mouth started numbing and he looked to MAK and Tim and said: "It's cocaine".

They both-smiled. MAK told him to stand up. "Please don't kill me. I'll do what you say. Please don't kill me".

MAK told Tim to go get in his car and follow them.

San Diego, CA

Up in his 10th-floor office, Rudolfo "Rico" DeLuna laughed over the speakerphone with his best friend and loyal personal bodyguard Hector "El Torro" Martinez, as his assistant brought in a hot coffee and a client list. Rico was working late tonight catching up on back orders. Rico owned a number of import companies in and around the California area. Hector runs the street side of Rico's business, which is uncut cocaine and weapons. Rico met Hector in a Mexican jail, while they were both doing time. Rico was a coyote when he was young. He'd help illegals get into the U.S. undetected and safely to California. He was caught once and was placed in custody. The guys he was transporting got mad that they got caught, blamed him and they started jumping on him. Rico was good with his hands but he's no match for the 6 adult men in the cell. Hector jumped in for Rico, not much help but he still helped none the less. Rico took that as a blessing and when Rico's connection came to get him out Rico took his new buddy with him. They stayed close through the years as Rico worked his way to his current position.

"We'll discuss that tonight over dinner, my treat," Rico said to Hector and they hung up.

"Whatcha got for me Stephany?" he said to his assistant. "We have a big one coming in from China. Plus, there's the rest of the Hawaii shipments," his beautiful assistant answered.

"Well, let me get all that so we can finish and get the hell out of here."

Stephany was a young knock out blond with many talents that helped keep her job and her pay pretty high for an assistant. Her tight skirt fit nice and snug around her thighs and butt area. Her breasts were a perfect handful; Not too much and definitely not too little. Rico had his way with her at least 3 times a week if not more. His wife had no idea since she wasn't allowed to the office. Before he left, he went to his safe and grabbed a black box, powered it up and checked its GPS coordinates. He tapped it, checked his watch and then placed it back in the safe.

Rico and Stephany went downstairs and on the way out he waved to Jake the security guard. When they got to their cars, Rico hugged her with his hands on her ass and she tiptoed to reach his lips. After they kissed she got in her white Lexus GS300 and Rico got in his all black BMW 745i. Rico raced down Commerce heading for the expressway when his cell phone rang. He recognized the overseas number and answered "Hola my friend."

"Hola Rico" the voice on the other end said in broken English. "Ju know why I call you right?" said the caller.

"Yes of course and don't worry. Everything is going smoothly and your shipment will be delivered on time as we agreed," Hector said. "Okay good. There is a lot riding on this one," Rico said.

"Yeah, I know. Don't worry. My man's handling everything. We have a drop in Miami, Florida and then I have a guy that will take your part of the shipment the rest of the way across the water to you."

"Can I trust him, Rico?" That's $500 million worth of diamonds we're talking about."

"He doesn't know that. He thinks he's moving the furniture to my Tio's house on the other side."

"Okay. Call me if anything goes wrong."

"Nothing's going to go wrong. "Call me. You understand?"

"Yes, sir." They hung up and Rico dialed Hector "Hola" Hector. Meet me at my house."

"I'm on my way, Sir. I'm not too far away. I'll be there in a few." Rico picked up some roses on his way home for his wife.

At Rico's house, his wife answered the knock at the door in nothing but a large bath towel. Her hair was a little past her shoulders, dark black w/ blond streaks and curly. She was a perfect build, 5'5, 137lbs, nice C-cup breast and athletic body, even though she never worked out. Nice ass and her walk would make a runway model die from envy. When she opened the door, Hector stood there with a devious grin on his face. Hector was 6'4 229lbs, dark-skinned Hispanic with very small accent.

"Hi, Hector. It's been a long time."

"Yes, it has Nora."

"Come in. Rico's not home yet, but he'll call any minute if you want to wait."

"I just spoke with him. He's on his way."

"Well make yourself at home. You know where everything is."

Before she went to the other room she said "An old friend can't get a hug? It's been forever."

As Hector approached her, she let the towel drop to the floor, revealing her nude but beautiful body. Hector smiled and said "Nora, please go put on some clothes. I don't want Rico thinking anything, please"

"So I guess no hug nuh?" Nora said as she walked to the bedroom biting her bottom lip. "Maybe when you're fully clothed."

She bent over to pick up the towel and called Hector's name. He turned to look and she was spreading her ass cheeks exposing her pink shaved pussy. She laughed and went into the room. Hector said to himself Rico would kill us both if he knew. Then he thought back to the vacation they all went on a couple of years ago.

HAWAII, 7 years ago

The music was loud and everybody was getting wild and wasted. Rico, Hector, Jesus, Lil' Freddy, and the rest of the family were having the time of their lives. Rico just offed 10 million dollars in diamonds and with the help of Hector and the team he unloaded 3.5 million in cocaine and guns all over the United States.

"I'd like to make a toast to us" Rico said.

Everybody raised their glasses and bottles. Just then, the women came into the room.

"Come out here and party. Everyone's looking for Y'all," Nora said.

She had a group of female friends with her. All of them drunk and full of some of Rico's best cocaine. Rico said he had to make a quick run to the other side of the island to make sure the shipment would be delivered on time tomorrow.

"Want me to go with you?" Hector said.

"No, I'm good. Keep the party going for me."

"Cool, I got it."

"Hector, while Rico's gone, come dance with me," said Nora.

"I don't dance Nora."

"Come on homeboy, it's a party. You're supposed to dance." Rico encouraged.

Rico was in a rush to get to the hotel where he had Stephany waiting. No one knew Stephany came because she came on an earlier flight. Rico left and Nora continued to pull Hector to dance with her.

She said, "Fine, you don't have to move just stand there. I'll do all the work."

"Okay we can do that but I'm not dancing," Hector said.

She started dancing on Hector, grinding and bouncing. As she's grinding her ass on Hector, she felt his manhood rise. She kept her focus on that area, letting Hector know she felt it. She turned around and smiled. Then, put her arms around his neck and she continued her grind. She placed his hands on her ass, and then licked his chin. It would've been his lips if he weren't so tall. The drugs and alcohol had everybody in a zone so no one was paying any attention. Hector squeezed Nora's soft ass and she bit his chin lightly and turned around and started grinding her ass in his dick again. Hector started to really enjoy it and put his hand on her slim waist. She lifted her hula skirt and he could see her thong bikini and her caramel toned ass cheeks. She took his hands and slapped it on her ass, then slips it between both cheeks and bent over and touched her toes. Hector slid his hand to her wet pussy. As soon as he touched it, she flinched and came up. She turned, faced him and grabbed him hard-on.

He stuck his hand under her skirt and rubbed her clit till she moaned. "Let's go, Hector." "Go where?" he said, with that grin. "Walk on the beach"

Hector told the fellas he was walking with Nora and he'd be back. They walked till nobody was in sight and Nora turned and kissed Hector. They both were wasted. Nora went down on Hector right there. Her warmth mouth sucked him and licked his dick till he almost fell to his knees. She laid in the sand and Hector climbed on top of her... he slid her bikini bottom off and entered her. Nora bit down on her lip as Hector dove deep into her over and over. They made love for 30 to 45 minutes. When they finished, they hurried back to the party and everyone was still going strong. Nobody noticed they left.

Present

The slam of the front door brought Hector back to the present. "Hey Hector, what's going on brother," Rico said.

"Hola, what's going on homeboy? How's business world?"

"Oh, it's great. How are those streets today?"

"Same ole, same ole" "Where's Nora?"

"Oh, she's in the room, I think. She let me in and headed in that direction."

"Well, let me take her these roses and change. I'll be right out." "You look like you put on a few pounds Hector. You better slow down." Rico said half joking because he knew Hector pride himself on staying fit.

Rico went to the bedroom and find Nora in bed doing her toenails with her favorite black nail polish. She had on black shorts and one of Rico's muscle tee. "Hi babe", she said as Rico walked through the door. "You're early. I thought I'd have to call you."

"No, I missed you," he said as he handed her the roses.

"Thanks, Papi. They're beautiful. What did you do?"

"Ha ha...nothing. Can I just be nice?" They kissed and he changed. He went to the front with Hector.

"You want a drink Torro?" Rico asked.

"Yeah! Something strong." Hector replied.

Rico went to the bar and poured then both drinks. "What's the status on your dude with the shipment?" Rico asked as he gave Hector his drink.

"I haven't heard anything, so I'm assuming everything is okayay, you know? Why do you ask? Are you worried or something?"

"No. Carlos called asking questions about the guy. You know how he is. Plus, this is a big one. Nothing can go wrong you understand me? We can retire off this one Torro."

"Well, I'll give him until tomorrow and I'll call him and check on his status," Hector said then took a sip.

CHAPTER 2

San Antonio, TX 9:45pm

MAK forced the old man back to the truck's front. "Get in and drive where I say or boom, you hear me?"

"Yes, please, just don't shoot. I'll do what you say."

"Good, cause if you don't, I'll kill you, dumb motherfucker" … MAK said mocking the man's accent.

They started up and pulled off. MAK's phone rang, it was Tim… "What the fuck dawg, you losing your fuckin' mind? Now where are we going?"

Tim said, "To my Aunt Paulette's house. Now get off the phone and watch for the law," then MAK hung up. Paulette was MAK's Aunt on his father's side. She raised him on his little sister after their parent's died in a house fire when MAK was 6 years old and his sister was 4 years old. Paulette took them in so they wouldn't have to go to child protective services. Paulette was a heavy drug user and the money the state was giving her for the two of them came in handy for drugs. MAK fell in love with the streets, unlike his sister who promised herself she wouldn't be anything like Aunt Paulette and her drug addict friends. Tameca, MAK's little sister, graduated last year and now attends the University of North Carolina. She calls MAK and Aunt Paulette almost every day. MAK unlike his baby sister dropped out of school in the 10th grade and steals for a living. He took after Paulette

They turned down the long dirt road leading to Aunt Paulette's mobile home in the country a couple of miles outside San Antonio. They pulled up, all the lights were out, but Aunt Paulette was sitting next door with the neighbor on the porch. MAK yelled for Paulette to come to the truck. "Come here Paulette."

"Who is that?" Paulette said.

"It's me MAK."

"Boy, who are you with?"

"My homeboy."

She got up and started across the driveway…MAK told the old man "Play along and you'll be on your way in 30 minutes you understand?"

"Yes, I do what you say, please."

"Yeah! Yeah! I know, you'll do what I say. Please don't kill you." MAK mocked the man's plea.

MAK took the keys from the man and told him to smile when Paulette came to the truck. Paulette got to the truck and said: "Who is this nephew?"

This is my homeboy. He gotta use the bathroom. "What he smiling at? You alright?"

"Si, I have to use the restroom."

"Well here go the keys. Take him in the house. Ima be at Debra's. You got some weed?"

MAK shook his head 'no' and hurried out. Tim got out of the car and spoke to Aunt Paulette. "What's up, Aunt Paulette? You been alright?"

"Yeah, Tim baby. I'm good. What y'all up to? I know when y'all get together, it's trouble."

"No, we chillin' getting fucked up, rolling, you know how we do."

"Getting fucked up on what?" she asked.

"Here, check this shit out." He gave her a little block of the cocaine MAK gave him back at Flying J's. All the way to Aunt Paulette's house, Tim was snorting small bumps of the cocaine.

He was high and his face shows it. MAK looked at him and said "Come on fool." with an aggravated tone.

Aunt Paulette said, "Oh, you weren't going to even tell me huh? See how my nephew do me?" She said to the MAK.

She took the dope and went back to Debra's house and they both went inside to get high.

MAK said, "Why you tell her that shit man?"

"So she won't bother us." "Let's go inside nigga." They went inside and soon as they got in MAK hit the old man with the shotgun and this time it knocked him out. They dragged him to the back room, tied him up and put him in the closet.

"Man, you gotta try some of this shit fool. It's better than that shit we are getting from Ricky."

"Bust some lines down and hurry up so we can check this truck." Tim wasted no time getting a couple of lines made up while MAK grabbed two beers from the fridge. He sat down and splits the $20,000. They both laughed 'cause they were happy they got money and lots of it. MAK rolled up a $100 bill and snorted a fat line, let it sit for a few seconds and then snorted up the other nostril.

"Good, right?" Tim said.

MAK's eyes were full of water and he just leaned back and felt the drain. "Say something, nigga" ... Tim said

"Yeah! It's good…real good. Now let's go check this truck out."

"Let me get some and we can go."

Tim snorted the other two lines and they went outside to the truck. MAK got a flashlight out of his trunk and they climbed in the trailer. MAK went straight to the box the package came from and pushed it to the edge of the trailer, opened it and took the table out and set it to the side. He found nine more packages exactly like the first one. He looked at Tim and they smiled.

He told Tim "I'll slide the boxes to you, you stack 'em on the ground so we can take em inside"

MAK pushed 12 boxes to Tim. Once those boxes were out of the way there were crates…pretty heavy crates.

"A, it's something else in here too but we going to need a crowbar to open the crate it's in."

"I think it's one in the trunk," Tim said.

"Well, we'll get it later. Let's get everything inside first." MAK told him.

It took half an hour to unload the boxes and crates and get them inside. When they got the last crate in, they heard the old man kicking on the closet door.

"I'll kill him," MAK said.

"No fool, let's go talk to him."

"Niga you high for real. Talk to him about what, the Spurs? No I know, the river walk" MAK said in his usual smart-mouthed tone.

"No shit. I don't know. Just to calm him down."

"Let's go," MAK said. They went in the room, threw open the door and MAK pointed the shotgun at the old man.

"Shut the fuck up! Didn't I tell you you'd be gone in 30 minutes? Now any more noise and I'll pop your ass." Then he slammed the door back. They took all the dope out the boxes and it came out to 120 blocks. MAK told Tim to go take Aunt Paulette some more dope so they won't come over there while they had everything out. Tim went to Debra house to give them the dope while MAK got the crowbar from the trunk.

He told Tim, "When you come back, get my gun out that truck. It's on the front passenger seat."

"Alright, I got you."

Debra and Aunt Paulette were in Debra's back room smoking when they heard the knock on the door. Debra went to answer it. She looked out the peep-hole.

"It's your nephew's homeboy"

Debra opened the door and said "What you want? She's busy."

"Tell her I got something for her"

"Some more of that dope"

"Yeah! that shit good right?"

"Yeah, baby come in."

She moved so Tim could come in. "We're sitting at the back." They walked to the back room where Paulette set in a cloud of smoke, eyes wide open like she was surprised.

"Here Aunt Paulette. This is from MAK"

Paulette took the dope and said, "Where y'all get this shit from?" … "From that Mexican man, he hooked us up" … Tim lied to blow her off.

"Well I'll go. Y'all enjoy that shit."

Tim left and stopped at the truck to get MAK's pistol. He climbed in the truck and saw the pistol and started looking around in the bed area of the truck. He found two pornos and a bottle of Wild Turkey in a small backpack. He also found a cell phone. He turned it off and stuck it in his pocket. As he was getting out, he got his foot caught on the wires from the truck's CB. He yanked and kicked, and the CB's box fell out the dashboard. In the back of the console, he saw another box with a small lock on it. He reached back there and grabbed it. He shook the box and heard what sounded like marbles or something small. He tucked the box in his pants and went inside.

"Did you get my gun?" MAK asked as soon as Tim came through the door.

"Yeah! I got you fool"

"What Aunt Paulette say?"

"Nothing. She took the dope and I left"

"Okay. Look what was in the crates?" MAK opened one of the lids and there was brand new sub machine guns and a lot of them, enough to fight off a small army.

MAK looked at Tim and said "whoever this shit belongs to is going to be mad about this shit fool. This is a lot of stuff to lose. What you think?"

"I don't give a fuck. Finders keepers loser's weepers." Tim said in a joking kid voice.

"Don't tell me you're scared now Mr., Shut up and follow us"

"Hell no, I ain't scared. I'm just saying this is a lot of shit. He working for somebody."

They hid the stuff in MAK's old room, then went and got the old man out the closet.

"Come on, let's take a ride old man" MAK told Tim

"Follow us"

"Here we go again with this shit…Where are we going?"

"Back to the truck stop and drop this old fuck off. I made him a promise"

They locked up and left. MAK knew Paulette would be busy all night so she won't need the keys. MAK told the old man, "You won't see me no more."

On the ride, Tim pulled out the box and tried to open it but it wouldn't budge. The little lock held good. As they pulled into Flying J's, the old man parked down on the same end he was on. There were other trucks but no one outside. Tim parked down on the side of the streets. He could see the truck's trailer. He kept messing with the lock on the box. MAK told the old man to turn the truck off. As the man reached for the keys, MAK opened the door and boom.

Tim heard the sound and saw the bright flash. He stuck the box under his seat, pulled his gun out and ran towards the truck.

All he could think was "How am I going to tell Vanessa MAK got shot and I didn't help him?" Just then, he saw MAK running from the truck.

"Let's go. What the fuck are you doing?"

"Man, I thought he..." Tim couldn't even finish.

"MAK grabbed him and pushed him to the car.

"Let's go" MAK told Tim.

"What the fuck happened man? Tell me you didn't fool."

"Okay, I didn't fool. Now just drive."

"Drop me off at home and you stay at Paulette's tonight and watch the stuff," MAK told Tim.

"Alright, you're a crazy motherfucker but you need to get some help. And wipe your face you got blood on your damn forehead and cheek".

They pulled up to the apartments and Vanessa was sitting on the stairs alone and mad as hell. As soon as she saw the car, she got up and went inside but left the door open.

"Here we go" MAK said.

"Slap her in the mouth. I'm telling you my pop does it all the time to my mom and it works" Tim said. Then he pulled off laughing. MAK walked inside and Vanessa was on the couch.

"Hey baby. What's wrong?"

"What's wrong? You ain't called or answered the phone. That's what's wrong." Vanessa said instantly and viciously.

"Well, look what I got?" MAK pulled out the money and showed her as he flipped through the bills.

"I don't care. I was worried about you stupid and where's my brother?" Vanessa said rolling her head back and forth as she spoke.

"He's staying at Aunt Paulette's tonight. He didn't feel like hearing your mouth" MAK said sarcastically.

"Fuck you and him. You plate in the oven, I'm going to bed." She wobbled down the hall then turned and said "Oh yeah, give me that money with her hand out"

MAK handed her the money and she disappeared into the room and screamed "I love you and I got a doctor's appointment in the morning".

Tim pulled up to Paulette's house, got out grabbed the box, the house keys and started for the door until Paulette called him.

"Wait for me Tim, baby" Paulette said.

Tim tucked the box, she came over, they went inside together. Once they got in, she ran to the restroom. Tim tucked the box under the couch, he grab his now hot beer off the table. He needed it, the cocaine had his throat numb.

Paulette came out the restroom and said, "You got some more dope, Tim?"

He pulled it out and started making lines on the table. He snorted some. When Paulette sat down, he let her snort some. She said, "I'm going back over to Debra's, let's me get some and I'll be out your way. The house is all yours tonight" she said with the look of a true fiend on her face.

Tim gave her some dope and she said, "Lock it, I won't be back tonight as she ran out the door".

Then she was gone. Tim remembered the box. He went to the kitchen and grabbed a knife. He popped the lock, opened the box and when he saw the contents he almost flipped out. He poured ice cold diamonds on the table and sat back in shock.

CHAPTER 3

SAN ANTONIO, TX NORTHEAST SIDE 7:15AM

Ring…ring…ring…ring…boom…boom…ring… "What, What, What Solis? I know it's you. Today is my day-off so go away", Detective Adams said through the door of his one-bedroom apartment on the cities northeast side. Detective Adam is with the San Antonio Police Department's Special Units Detectives. He's been on the force 10 years but moved up fast through the ranks. Being a white officer in a mostly Mexican and black environment sometimes proved to be very frustrating…but thanks to his partner Soli he held his temper to a minimum. He was transferred to S.A.P.D. 3 years ago from Kerrville County after he shot and killed a 14-year-old kid. The incident bothered him daily, he blames himself. Solis tells him he's being too hard on himself.

"Open the door Super Dave or I'll be forced to kick it in" Solis told Adams.

"Solis you're waking my neighbors please go away"

"Oh, I get it; you got one of those Broadway hookers in there well buddy that's probable cause"

"Solis okay, okay I'm opening up" Adams opened the door, she stood there with her hand on her hip and blowing a huge bubble with her gum. Officer Solis was full blooded Hispanic and spoke no Spanish. She stood 5'7" 139lbs, kept her haircut short and dyed reddish brown. Light brown eyes with long flowing eyelashes. She was tom-boyish built, not really curvy but had sex appeal and a beautiful smile.

"So, where is she?" …she said as she pushed passed Dave. "She's in the bedroom but she's not dressed so stay in here will you"

"If she's a hooker I'm taking her ass to jail. I fuckin' swear Dave" Solis knew all the local hookers. She used to work undercover as a prostitute and has busted hundreds of them. "They" Dave said with a smirk "are not hookers"

"They? What do you mean they?"

Dave whispered "I had my first three some last night"

Dave was smiling like a 12-year-old who lost his virginity. "You're sick you know that AND THOSE BITCHES TOO" Solis yelled.

"On the way we're stopping to get you a shot. I hope you fuckin' bathed" she said sniffing the air.

"Wait out! "What do you mean out?"

"I'm off Solis, and I still got four more Viagra left please don't do this to me".

"Oh, fucking well happy dick, that's got to wait. We got ourselves a 187 and could possibly be a capital. So, throw the whores out, throw some clothes on, and let's go. They're waiting for us".

Adams slid down the wall put his head in his hand and said "God do you hate me?"

In the car Adams ask Solis for the details of the new case. "All I know is the manager called 911 and said one of the truckers noticed blood all over the windshield of another rig as he walked to his own truck around midnight. The manager went out to the rig, noticed the blood, knocked on the driver's door. When there was no answer, he checked the door. When he climbed up and looked, he saw a body and he called the police. Sherman from Eastside patrol was the first on the scene and that's about all I got as of now happy dick."

"Come on Solis, are you going to keep that all day?"

"Yes asshole. I can't believe you, that's so nasty"

"Hey, don't knock it until you've tried it…it did get kind of nasty through" ha! ha! Adams laughed. Solis punched him in the arm and headed for the expressway.

Upon arrival, they could see police cars, news vans and plenty of on lookers.

"Look at this shit. It's a fuckin' circus out here" Adams said to Solis who was staring in disbelief.

"Why are they so hyped up behind a trucker's death? He must've been famous like that 50 Cent guy you want to fuck huh?" Adams joked.

"Fuck you! Happy dick…and you suffer from erectile dysfunction" Solis asked with a serious look.

"Hell no. Why you ask me that?"

"Because you said you had four more Viagra pills. Those are for mean whose" she giggled then continue "whose you know…car won't start"

"Solis that comment right there just fucked our friendship up. We use to be like cloak and dagger now you went and said some shit like that to me…its' me man Super Dave"

"Do you or don't you suffer from erectile dysfunction?"

"You swear you won't tell?"

"I swear" she said with a smirk.

"Yes, I do…. there, you happy?"

"ha! ha! Ha!" Solis laughed so hard tears came to her eyes.

"Adams, are you shitting me? The Super Dave can't get the ole Chevy started…that's crazy"

"Solis" Adams said with a look of regret "you're not going to say nothing right?"

"No Dave but your new name is unhappy dick" she laughed some more and pulled into Flying J's Truck Stop.

SOUTHEAST SIDE 7:45 AM

"Get up and call Tim before we be late. You know how traffic is going downtown this time of the morning" Vanessa said to MAK from the bathroom. Vanessa went to the bed and pulled MAK onto the floor "Get up. We need to get ready"

MAK hit the floor and looked up at his pregnant girlfriend and said "I don't think giving you a black eye will affect the baby"

"I wish you would fucker. I'd cut your fuckin' dick off" … "I'll ask the doctor if I just bust you in your mother fuckin' eye, will my baby live or will he be cock-eyed like your ugly ass daddy"

"MAK don't talk about my Papi. He's not ugly, just special." They both laughed. He got up and kissed her, grabbed the phone call Tim.

"Turn the TV on please babe." MAK looked at her with a yeah-right look and walked to the living room. Vanessa turned on the TV in the bedroom put it on FOX and sat on the bed.

"Today on the city's Westside, police arrested a man in connection with a string of home invasions" The news anchor woman said… "Wait, this just in. Police are now on the scene at the Flying J's truck stop where a Mexican man, police believe to be in his early 50's, has been shot and killed. Police believe it to be drug related. We have no further details at this time." "That is fuckin' sad" Vanessa mumbled to herself.

"I hope they catch that motherfucker" "What are you talking about Nessa?"

"Some shit on the news"

"What did Tim say?"

"He's already on the way so hurry up."

✦✦✦✦✦✦✦

FLYING J's 8:03 AM

Detective Adams and Detective Solis flashed their badges and made their way through the crowd and passed the carlon tape.

"Hey Dave. How's it going?" Officer Mitchell said as Adams and Solis came up.

"Oh, I'm good. I love coming in on off days"

"He's a little bitter this morning Officer Mitchell"

"Solis, I told you, you can call me Sherman"

"Oh really! How bout I call internal affairs and tell them you're dirty and you sexually harass old women on the eastside"

"Okay Mitchell Officer. I mean Officer Mitchell is fine with me"

Detective Adams said "you two are a match-made-in-heaven"

"Mr. Unhappy" was all Solis had to say and Adams shut up and apologized.

"Adams and Solis, where the hell you two been?" Chief Garza inquired.

Solis said "his motor don't work"

Adams elbowed her. "Stop clowning around and get over here. This is your mess clean it up and fast you hear me. This shit is ugly, come on look. Looks like a revolver to the head… Knocked half the poor guys face off. No wallet. We got prints all over the place so you guys got your work cut out here. But look at this."

They went to the trailer and climbed up. Forensic technicians were in the trailer along with Narcotic's agents.

"What are they doing here?" Solis asked about the Narc's.

"Two kilos of cocaine were found in the back of the couch over there, plus this residue was found on the floor. That's not it, check this out."

Chief Garza went to another couch and pulled out an all-black AKSU-74 sub machine gun, with high capacity magazines. The AKSU-74 is the shortened version of the AK-74 which was the replacement for the AK-47.

"Looks familiar?" Chief said.

Adams and Solis both said "No" at the same time.

"That's because they're only for military troops. They're not even allowed off base without special clearance."

"Well how the hell did they end up in that couch?"

"That's you job, no, no that's your life as of right…"

Chief looked at his watch for a few seconds and said "3-2-1. Now"

"How the guns got in that couch? How that couch got in this truck and who took the rest of it? That should bring our shooter a little closer to us. You'll be working with Cantu from narcotics."

"Chief, come on let us work alone. You know I hate that fuckin' racist piece of shit" Adams said.

"Okay look, I'll see what I can do but for now make it work." "What do you mean make it work? The guy is a…"

"Adams shut up. I said make it work for now or would you like to work with Sherman on Eastside patrol?"

Solis spoke, "We'll make it work Chief. Adams is having a bad morning. He drank last night and woke up with some…I mean in some trash."

"Well, get to work"

Solis looked at Adams and said "look Super Dave, you better get your head together…fuck Cantu. We got a job to do so let's do it and get whoever did this shit. We need to get those guns before they get spread around San Antonio. If this was done with a pistol, wait til' this asshole starts using those souped-up AK's"

"Yeah! I hear you Solis. I'm sorry, you're right. Let's get this shit wrapped up before bodies start popping up everywhere."

Little did Adams and Solis know this was just the start of their troubles.

CHAPTER 4

San Diego, CA

Hector opened the sliding back door to his three-bedroom condo and stepped onto the patio for a nice morning smoke. Hector only smoke Cuban cigars. He grabbed his phone to check for any missed calls. He has 3, one from Rico and two from one of his local workers. He knew what Rico wanted, so instead of calling him back he went ahead and made the call to Jose. Jose was a local truck driver Hector met through one of his workers. He called the number, the answering machine picked up on the first ring, so he hung up. He went back in, sat on the couch and turned on the TV…. he flipped through the channels for a while, found Pulp Fiction and stopped. He went to the kitchen, opened the refrigerator and got out some weed from his stash spot. He sat back, got high for close to 30 minutes then called Jose back.

San Antonio, TX

"Man, what the fuck is that noise my nigga?" MAK asked Tim
  "What noise?"
  "It's sound like something's buzzing"
  "I don't know nigga. This y'all car." Tim said as he turned into the Nix hospital.

Vanessa said "Let us out right here and go park. We already late."

MAK and Vanessa got out and Tim went across the street to park. He found a spot right in front. When he turned the engine off, he now heard the buzzing sound MAK was talking about. He looked under the driver's seat and saw the phone he stole last night. He forgot he turned it on before he left Paulette's house. He used it to call Paulette's phone so her caller ID would pick up the number and he could give the number out to chicks. He picked up the phone looked at the number and said to himself "Sorry, but he won't be available for a while." Then laughed to himself.

San Diego, CA

Hector hung-up the line and clicked over to line two. "Hola."

"Hola Torro, this is Rico. You asleep?" Rico spoke into the receiver.

"No Rico, I'm up. I just called my guy. I got no answer but I'll keep trying. What's up with you?" Hector said then inhaling more smoke.

"I'm on my way to the office. I woke up late this morning keep trying your guy and get back to me ASAP" Rico said with a hint of urgency in his voice.

"I got it. You'll hear something in the next hour. You got my word" Hector promised.

"I trust you brother but can you trust this guy? Remember you picked this guy" Rico said.

"Yeah! I remember. I'll get on it, Rico." Hector insured him.

Then Rico hung up. Hector looked at his phone then sat it down.

He thought to himself "If this fucker Jose is trying some funny shit with this load, I'll kill his whole fuckin' family, cause, Rico and Carlos are going to have my damn head on a got damn stick"

San Antonio, TX

"Baby after we finish, we're going to get a new car. I'm tired of driving that bucket, you hear me?" MAK said to Vanessa while they sat in the crowded waiting room.

"Okay, but don't forget we need to get some stuff for the baby, plus the cable is due next week."

"Well you keep two grand and give me the rest."

"Damn how much money was it all together?"

"Shit close to ten G's" …. "Where you get it from?"

"Me and Tim hit a lick last night…caught some body slipping and made them drop out."

"Who the hell walking around with 10 G's on them?"

"Shit, you be surprise what people got on them now days."

Tim came into the waiting room. "A, how long we going to be here? I want to go get me some wheels."

Tim said "Shit that's what I just told Nessa. I'm ready to clown. We shouldn't be here too much longer. We had an appointment. We are late. He should be calling us in a minute."

"There he goes right there babe."

"Vanessa Macias"… the doctor called Vanessa to the door and said "I didn't think you were going to come so I took someone before you. You can wait or come back tomorrow at 3:30pm."

"Hold on. Let me ask John."

She went over to MAK and relayed the message. MAK said he'd rather wait. She went and told the doctor he told her she'd be next give him 30 minutes. They went downstairs to the cafeteria. Vanessa was hungry.

Tim told MAK "A, let's go smoke a cigarette while she eats."

"No, he's staying with me. You go and smoke by yourself."

"I'm not even talking to you Nessa. I'm talking to that grown ass man that can speak for himself. MAK, do you want to go smoke a cigarette?" "Nah, I'm good. Ima chill."

"Man, you know what? You can't let her run your life my nigga. She's the devil and she want you to be glued to her ass all the time. Be a man and say, 'Nessa fuck you'. I'm going to smoke with my nigga and if you say something, I'm going to slap your ass in the mouth like what your daddy does to your momma" then they all laughed.

The phone in Tim's pocket started buzzing again. He pulled it out and looked at the number and ignored it. Nessa said "Whose phone is that?"

"Who got the motherfucker?"

"I hate your smart-ass mouth. Whose phone is it?" "It's mine. I bought it from one of Paulette's friends."

"Well why you won't answer it?"

"Because I don't want to."

"You probably stole it knowing your ass."

"I don't steal shit. I bought this hoe."

"Let me use it to call mommy."

"Alright but don't be all day on it."

He gave her the phone and went outside to smoke. She called her mom.

"Hola, Mami, it's Nessa. What are you doing?"

"I'm cleaning. Nessa, where are you? This is an out of town number."

"Out of town? Tim said he bought this phone from one of John's Aunt Paulette's friends."

"Oh, you know Paulette's friends. There's no telling baby… Did you see the news this morning? Some poor old man was killed over drugs again."

"Yes, I saw Mami"

Beep…Beep…

"Hold on, Mami. Tim's other line is beeping."

"Okay call me back when you finish."

"No, Mami just hold on."

Vanessa answered the call "Hola who's this?"

"Can I speak with Jose?" The caller said into the phone.

"I'm sorry there's no Jose at this number. Are you sure you dialed the right number?"

"Yes, I'm sure, who is this?"

The caller said with a hint of anger in his voice.

"Who I am is none of your business. But I think Jose sold this phone to my brother last night. So, it's not his no more. So, try not to call no more okay? Good bye and Vanessa hung up the line and got back to her mother. The line beeped again but Vanessa ignored it and kept talking…

San Diego, CA

"All the shipments from China are 10 minutes away" Stephany told Rico.
"and Hawaii is going to be delayed until Thursday Mr. DeLuna"
"What's the delay for? Did they say?"
"No, they just called and said to let you know and to deliver their apologies."
"When you get time, call them and see what the delay is. Then call the shops and tell them."
"Anything else sir?"
"Yeah! But that'll have to wait until lunch" Rico said and then sipped some coffee. Stephany left and Rico went to the wall safe, grabbed his GPS and brought it to his desk. He turned on the box, it beeped twice and he sat there a minute. He put the coordinates into his computer when he saw the position, he thought for a second and said to himself "It was in the same spot as yesterday night."
"This fucking guy is playing with my time." He picked up the phone and dialed Hector.
Hector was dialing out when Rico's call came in. Hector ignored it, he had problems right now. Hector dialed Jose again, no answer.
"I'm going to kill this motherfucker and his fucking…" Hector mumbled to himself, then his phone rang. Hector thought about answering but used better judgment and ignored it.
He called Li'l Freddy. Two rings and Freddy picked up. "Hola boss what's up?" Freddy said in a deep voice that didn't fit his in-person look.
"I got problems. Get to my spot now and bring that bastard Jesus with you."

Hector said almost yelling... "What's up Torro? You sound upset."

Freddy said feeling nervous not knowing what to think of the phone call. "Just fucking hurry. It's important" Hector said then hung up and started pacing the condo. "What the fuck am I going to tell Rico?" Hector thought to himself.

Rico thought to himself "Why the fuck is Torro not picking up his fucking phone?" "Never mind, he'll call" Rico said to himself looking at the phone.

No time to panic, Rico went on with his everyday activities but kept his GPS on his desk to keep an eye on the beep on his screen.

Li'l Freddy and Jesus arrived at Hector's within 20 minutes. Hector was dressed and sitting at his bar drinking when they knocked on the door. He opened it and grabbed Jesus around the collar, threw him to the dining room floor.

"Where the fuck is your friend?" Hector yelled then grabbed the cup he was drinking from and smashed it in Jesus' face.

Li'l Freddy was still standing in the door way, stunned at what was going on.

"Close my fucking door and get in here." Hector told Li'l Freddy without looking back.

Li'l Freddy stepped in and closed the door. "Torro what's up man? What are you tripping about?" Li'l Freddy said.

"This motherfucker said that son of a bitch Jose was cool and he could be trusted and he ran off with Rico and Carlos' whole damn truck load. Do you know what the fuck they going to do to us if we don't find that truck?" Hector yelled.

Jesus started scrabbling away trying to get up and out of Hector's reach. Blood dripping from his face he stood up and pleaded with Hector. "Come on Torro it's me man Jesus chill out man." Jesus pleaded.

"Chill out, you stupid fuck. You just cost Rico over 50 million fucking dollars. You think he's going to chill out when I tell him we lost the god damn shipment?" Hector yelled at Jesus.

Hector threw another punch in Jesus' direction that dropped him to his knees. Hector grabbed him around the throat, dragged him to the kitchen sink, turned on the garbage disposal and told Li'l Freddy to hold Jesus.

"Come on Torro." Freddy said hesitant to join in.

"Grab him now!" Hector yelled. Jesus was kicking and yelling. Hector punched him in the stomach and knocked the air out of him. He tumbled over. Hector kicked twice and told Li'l Freddy to grab him. Li'l Freddy grabbed him and took Jesus' hand and stuck it halfway into the garbage disposal.

"You got 30 minutes to get me the location of his family or I'll kill you myself." Hector told him while inching his hand further into the sink.

"I know where they live Torro. Please man don't do this." Jesus said through tears.

Hector let his hand go and said "Go clean your fucking face and let's go." He never seen Hector so paranoid. This was serious.

CHAPTER 5

San Antonio, TX

Detectives David Adams and Petra Solis were back at the office going over paperwork and statements they got at the scene. They had county inpound enroute to pick up the truck from Flying J's truck stop to get it tagged in at the police evidence yard to be inspected.

"We got nothing David, what are we going to do?" Petra said over her computer screen.

"I think we should start with the guns… Find out where they came from. The trucker was coming from somewhere and going somewhere. We can start there first, and maybe something will arise until those fingerprints come back." David said to Solis.

"Okay, I'll locate the deceased family when we get an ID on the poor guy." Petra said.

Just then Detective Mario Cantu came into their office. Detective Cantu was in narcotics. He had a team of tough officers under him that played by a different set of rules but got the job done. He and detective Adams hated each other for reasons of their own. Cantu was assigned to the case to assist Adams and Solis.

"Don't you knock Cantu? Oh yeah that's right you're so used to illegally kicking in doors with your no-knock-warrants you probably forgot how to knock." Petra said as Cantu stepped in.

"Look Dike, I don't know why you feel like you can speak out of turn if I don't press your button. Stay quiet or I'll show you what your pussy made for." Cantu shot back.

"You probably couldn't get it up on a good day, boy lover." She said standing up.

David felt that one hit home so he jumped in "Hey, you two save that for later. We got a serious case here."

"It's not your turn gringo. I'll tell you when you can pop out your box okay." Cantu said and looked back at Petra.

"All of you shut the fuck up" the Chief said as he stood in the door way. "You all better get along. The press is all over this drug deal gone bad thing. Cantu stop with your stupid remarks and get on this drug thing. Get your team and find out if there were more of those drugs and where they are. You better keep Adams informed. He's the lead on this one, got it?" Chief said looking Cantu in the eyes.

"Got it Chief, but tell the dike stay out of my way. I smell her unshaved pussy way over here" Cantu said then laughed.

Petra threw a hole puncher at his head. He ducked and it broke the window. Cantu waved, blew her a kiss and stepped out the office.

"See what the fuck I mean Chief? We can't work with that motherfucker." David said.

"I'll take care of him. You two get to work and control her will you." Chief took Cantu into his office.

"Sit the fuck down you crazy mother." He yelled to Cantu. "Look, I don't care what your beef is with Adams and Solis but you better saver it. You hear Cantu?" Chief scolded then flopped down into his chair.

"Come on I'm just giving them a hard time you know how it is man." Cantu said.

"Do you hear me? I'm not smiling and they're not either. Just grow the fuck up and do your damn job. Do I make myself clear?" Chief said.

"Yeah, loud and clear Julio." Cantu shot back the Chief's first name.

"That's Chief Garza asshole." Chief said.

Detective Adams entered the truck license plate into the data base and got the info he was looking for. "Petra, I got it... Mitchell's Furniture Supplies, San Diego, CA 1921 Barks Ave. Phone number and area code 261-504-6911. Call them and ask who was driving the truck #694-4 and you know the rest of the routine."

Petra grabbed the phone and got right on it.

"I'll be right back. You want something to drink?" Adams said to Petra.

"No, I'm good thank you." Petra said not looking up.

Adams left the office, down the hall he ran into Cantu coming out of the Chief's office. "Adams, hey man no hard feelings huh? I'm just a joker man but I'll be more professional on this case okay?" Cantu said with a hand on Adams' shoulder. Adams didn't know if he was being for real or being Cantu but he agreed and they shook hands.

"Tell Solis I'm through with the dike jokes until this case is done." Cantu said. "Speaking of which, what you guys got so far?" he asked David.

"Give me an hour or two and we'll meet. I'll give you what we got and we can go from there." Adams said to him.

"Good, because I already put the word out for my informants to be on the lookout for anybody acting all of a sudden like Tony Montana with the dope." Cantu said to him.

Back in the office Petra was making progress on the truck. She found out who the guy was who used the truck. His name was Jose Vasquez. He's been with the company for years. He lives in San Diego and his address was there along with a home and cell number.

"Hey, Super Dave. Check this out, our guy from Cali. I got an address and a number." Solis told him pointing at the paper.

Adams looked over the info and told Petra to type his name and number in and get a face to go with the name. She did it and printed the sheet out.

"I'll see if this is our guy. Anything else?" Solis asked.

"No, I'll check with impound on our truck, meet me back here in an hour." He said then he left. Petra took the picture to the coroner's office to see if they could match the face of Jose to the corpse on the table.

"Here are his finger prints Detective. That should make it easier to ID." The coroner said to Petra, as she looked at the picture of Jose. Petra took the finger prints to the tech and asked for and ID ASAP. Then she asked about the prints from the truck.

"Those will be ready first thing in the morning." The tech said.

"Thanks a bunch. I'll be here first thing to pick them up…can you have this back too?" Solis asked.

"I'll have them all for you." The coroner assured her.

"Thank you, Joy." Solis said shaking her hand and leaving.

Southwest/ San Antonio, TX

MAK, Vanessa and Tim looked at the used cars on the car lot ready to drive away in something different. MAK decided he'd get a 2007 Dodge Intrepid, Time picked him out a 2006 Chevy Impala. They test drove them and paid in cash. Their first stop was a Gill's on San Pedro Ave. to put new rims on their cars. While the shop was putting the rims on, MAK asked Vanessa about him starting to sell dope from Paulette's house. "Look baby I can make a killing. Paulette know all the fiends." MAK said to her trying to convince her.

A useless argument because no matter what she said he'd do it anyway. "Babe just be careful okay" was all she said.

Tim was in the restroom on the phone with a friend of his that worked at a pawnshop in the rich part of town. "Eddie, man can you get off some diamonds? I'm talking real fucking diamonds." Tim said in a whispered tone.

"I'll have to see them first and tell you then." Eddie told him.

"Okay tonight at 8:30. I'll come by and holla at you…but this is between us don't tell nobody specially my brother-in-law and sister." Tim asked him.

"A, you got my word kid." Eddie said. Tim hung up and went back outside with MAK and Vanessa.

The cars got finished and they headed back to the apartment. "Baby, we got some shit to do, I'll be back in a little bit. Here's the keys to the other car." Vanessa gave MAK the keys to the new car and gave her the old car keys.

MAK and Tim left to Paulette's house. MAK had a plan on his mind. They got to Paulette's, went inside, got a package out of the stash spot, then went cross to Debra's house where Paulette always was. Before he could knock she opened the door. "What's up nephew?" Paulette said.

"I got a deal for you: Let us hustle here and I'll keep you high. No charge." MAK said to Paulette.

Paulette looked and Debra and they both said "Hustle what?"

MAK pulled the package out and their mouths hit the floor. "Can you cook half of this for us and get all your friends to start coming over here?" MAK asked her.

Debra and Paulette both got to work cooking the dope up for MAK and Tim. While MAK made a couple phone calls. He called a couple jack boyz he knew that were always looking to buy guns. He then called some local dope boys to kind of get the ball moving. Within a matter of 3 and ½ hours, he had 3 guns sold for $1200 a piece. He just had to drop them off. A couple coke heads he hung with were looking for some coke. He let them know he came across some blow better than any around town.

Once the dope was cooked, he got Paulette and Debra busy cutting, chopping and weighing. He and Tim bagged it up.

Detective's Office SA, TX

Adams, Solis and Cantu sat in the office and weighed their options. Solis was to locate the family of Jose and inform them of the tragedy. Adams and Cantu were trying to figure out how they were going to track down the guns when the only leads as of now is California.

"We're pretty much at a standstill right now. I think I'm going home for the rest of the day and get started fresh in the morning." Adams said to both of them.

"I agree" Cantu said.

"See you guys in the morning. I'mma make these calls and I'll call you later Super Dave." Solis said as Adams and Cantu walked out of the office. Solis called the first number for Jose which was his home phone.

Paulette's House

After all the drugs were bagged up, MAK gave Paulette and Debra their share, he and Tim went back across the street to divide the rest between them. "We are finally going to be rich men" Tim said.

"Are you ready? Because I know I am" MAK said.

"You stay here. Paulette's going to make some calls and send some sales by. So, one of us needs to be here. I'm going to drop these guns off and couple powder packs. I'll be back." MAK climbed into the Intrepid and left to make the drop.

Tim looked at his watch, he had a few hours to burn before he had to meet with Eddie.

MAK pulled up to a house looking like no one lived there and got out. He knocked on the door and a skinny dark-skinned guy, everybody know as, Daz answered the door.

"What's up MAK?" Daz said pants sagging low exposing his boxer shorts.

"Nothing what's up? Where's Flesh at? I just talked to him about buying some guns. MAK said shaking hands with Daz.

"Oh yeah! What you got?" Daz asked.

"Some new shit from my homeboy in the military. Flesh said he knew what I was talking about when I told him" MAK said.

"He in the room…and who car you're in?" Daz asked pointing at the car.

"Oh, that's mine. I bought it today." MAK said.

MAK brought the guns in and went to the back room where Flesh was with three girls and two other guys of the jack boys click. "What's up guys?" MAK said to the crew.

When MAK walked in Flesh said "Let me see those motherfuckers. I read about them in the gun magazine my old man gets. How the hell you get yo hands on these bad boys?"

"Top secret." MAK shot back then handed Flesh one of the AKSU-74's.

"So this is the replacement for the AK huh? You said you had some coke, too right?" Flesh said holding the gun.

"Yeah! What ya'll trying to get?" MAK said pulling out the coke.

"Let me get a half…and here the money for the straps. I'ma try these hoes out tonight on them Northeast side niggas." Flesh said. MAK gave Flesh the drugs and he left. He said he was going to stop by to check on Vanessa before he goes back to Paulette's.

Detective's Office

Back at the office, Solis let the phone ring a dozen times…no answer or no answering machine. She went to the other number then thought to herself, "Cell phone, cell phone? I don't remember a cell phone being on the evidence sheet. If he had one, where was it?"

Before jumping the gun, she checked the evidence log… No cell phone. She called the number and a young voice picked up. "Hello, hello" she said.

"Who is this?" the voice said.

"This is Becky. Where are you?"

"I don't know no Becky"

"Oh, I must've dialed the wrong number, sorry" Solis said.

"What's up Becky? What you looking for? You sound like you look good. You got a man?" the voice said.

"No I don't got a man" Solis played along with him. "Why you ask? You got a girlfriend?"

"No, baby. I'm single" Solis said… Knock… Knock…

His conversation was cut off by a knock at the door. He told Solis to hold on. A neighbor from down the street was there to score some dope. Paulette sent him over.

"Ey, shorty, can I call you right back? I got company" the voice said.

"Sure, how long?" She asked, not really believing what was happening.

"Give me about twenty minutes and call back" he said.

"Okay, twenty minutes, bye." Solis hung up the phone and could not believe her luck. She picked up her cell and called detective Adams.

"Hello?" Adams answered.

"Guess what just happened?" She said almost yelling.

"What?" Adams said.

"I may have just talked to out killer." She said.

Adams was stopped at a red light when she told him this. "What do you mean talked to our killer?" Adams asked now baffled.

"I'm not sure, but remember when you said to call the numbers? Well, I called the house phone and got no one and then before I dialed the cell, I checked the evidence and there was no cell phone on the victim. I thought if he had a cell number listed, it had to be his own. So, I called it and some guy answered. He tried to hit on me." She said.

"And what happened?" Adams asked unaware that the light had turned green.

"Well, he told me call him back in 20 minutes." She explained.

"I'm on my way back right now. Get a trace on that phone. We might be onto something." Adams did an illegal U-turn and gunned it back to the office.

Solis tried the house phone again while she waited, there was still no answer.

Adams called Cantu. "Meet me at the office. We got something; Solis may have just spoken with the killer over the deceased's cell phone." He told Cantu as soon as he answered.

"I'll be there in 5 minutes, Adams." Cantu said. Then they hung up.

Paulette's House

"Hello?" Tim said into the phone.

"A what's up? Anybody come through there yet?" MAK asked.

"Man, it's alright but you need to hurry up. I gotta go somewhere." Tim said.

"Where you gotta go, nigga?" MAK asked.

"I got a hot date with this chick I met a couple days ago." Tim lied.

"When? I'm with you everyday and I don't member you meeting nobody." MAK said.

"You ain't gotta know all my business. Just hurry up or I'm leaving." Tim said in an agitated tone.

"Alright, I'll be there in a minute." MAK said.

Tim hung up and called Eddie to let him know he'll arrive shortly. Eddie told him no problem and he's already called a couple people who might be interested in buying the diamonds if they're good.

"Man, they're good, don't worry." Tim said to Eddie then he hung up.

San Diego, CA

Li'l Freddy and Jesus banged on Jose's door loud and hard.

"Who is it?" said a child's voice.

"Are your parents' home?" Jesus asked.

"Just a minute." Jose's 9-year-old daughter went to the restroom to let her mother know someone was at the door. "Mom, some guy is at the door and he is knocking hard."

"Okay, honey. Tell him to hold on. I'll be out in a minute." Her mother said.

Jose is a father of 3 and has been married for 20 years. Jose's wife came to the door. As soon as she opened the door, Li'l Freddy kicked it. The door hit Jose's wife in the face, instantly busting her nose and mouth. The daughter screamed when her mother hit the floor from the force of the kick. All three men rushed in and closed the door.

"Check the rooms and kill everybody in them." Hector said to Jesus. He told Freddy to get the little girl while he dragged the mother into the living room.

Bang! Bang! Bang! They heard three shots go off and Li'l Freddy ran to the back using the little girl as a shield in case someone in the back came out shooting.

When we walked into the room, Jesus had shot Jose's two sons. One in the head, the other in the chest and stomach. They were listening to the radio and playing video games and didn't hear the commotion. When Li'l Freddy saw his friend was fine, they went back up front where Hector had the wife on the couch waiting on them.

"What was that?" Hector asked.

"Two boys in the bedroom." Freddy said.

"No!" the mother screamed. "What did you do to my children?"

"Listen to me, bitch. Your husband has something very valuable to us. Find him or you won't have any children left, ya understand me?" Hector said to Jose's wife.

"I don't know what you're talking about. Please don't hurt my daughter, please." Jose's wife yelled through tears.

"Find Jose and we'll give her back." Hector said holding the daughter by the hair.

"He's gone to work. He had to deliver some furniture to Florida. Please leave us alone." She cried.

"I know that load was never delivered and his cell phone is not in his possession. So, here's what we're going to do, when you find him, call me. Here's my number. Until then, she's coming with us." Hector told her.

"No please…" Jose's wife cried. "Not my baby please!"

"Oh yeah, if you call the cops, she dies." Hector said.

"No! Fuck you! Give me my baby!" she cried and tried jump up but was met with a smack from Jesus' pistol that knocked her to the floor in tears. The three men went out to the Hummer they were in and drove off.

The lady jumped up and ran outside screaming. "No! Wait, please wait!" Neighbors were staring, then she remembered her boys and ran back into the house. She stepped into the room and saw the boys and let out a yell that brought the neighbors running in.

When the neighbors saw the children, one called the police and the other grabbed the mother from the floor where she fell from weakness. She screamed and kicked and yelled for her children. One neighbor tried to ask where her daughter was, but she was hysterical and couldn't hear a thing.

"Hello, yes police please hurry my neighbor's children have been shot and one may have been kidnapped. Please hurry." The neighbor said to the police operator.

"Lisa, Lisa where is Three? What happened to Three? Three was her daughter's nickname because she was the baby of three children. "Lisa, listen to me. Where is Three?"

It was no use. Lisa was so broken up she couldn't function.

Detective's Office SA, TX

Cantu arrived back at the office before he walked in. "Is it safe?" he asked Solis.

"What do you want?" she said in a condemning voice.

"Adams told me to meet him here. You may have just talked to the shooter." Cantu said in his most humble tone.

"You're not a homicide detective. You work with drugs so go find some drugs and leave murders to us." She said with fire in her eyes.

"Don't you ever stop, Solis?" Cantu said now getting agitated.

"No, I don't like you, never have and never will." She hissed. Just then Adams walked in.

"Hey, what's up? You call him back yet?" Adams asked Petra.

"No, I haven't, but what did you call the drug guy from? He doesn't do homicide or am I missing something here?" She asked Adams.

"Look, Chief said work together and that's what I'm doing." Adams told her.

"How would you like it if I brought a pool guy to fix your roof huh? You get a roof man to fix your roof. Do you get where I'm going?" She said in her most sarcastic tone.

"Petra, please stop." Adams said using her first name. "Let's just make this call, and where are the phone trackers?" Adams said curiously looking around the room.

"They'll be here in a minute. I already told them the deal." Solis said to them.

Paulette's House

"Man, you lucky you pulled up. I was about to leave." Tim said to MAK and Vanessa. He rushed out the door, jumped in the car and left. Paulette came across the street and sat to talk with MAK and Vanessa.

"Hey, Nessa. How you doing? The baby alright?" Paulette said smiling and rubbing Nessa's stomach.

"Yeah, he good. How you been?" Vanessa replied with a smile.

They small talked as Paulette's friends came to the door one by one to see what the new dope was like.

Tim's phone rang.

"Hello... Hello, this is Becky. I just called. You told me to call you back in 20 minutes remember?" Solis said disguising her voice to sound sexy.

"Yeah! I remember what's up? I didn't think you were going to call back." Tim said.

"Why not? I like meeting new people. Besides, your voice turns me on." She said flirtatiously. "I'm glad I called the wrong number."

"Who were you trying to call?" Tim asked.

"My girlfriend. Terry." She said.

"Well, when can we see each other in person?" Tim asked anxiously.

"I don't even know your name yet." She said, hoping he'd bite the bait. Petra and the others listened with note pads ready. The tracker needed at least a minute and a half to track the call so Petra had to stall him.

Cantu whispered, "Talk nasty to keep him on."

She looked at him with disgust, but Adams agreed and whispered, "He's a guy. We'd all fall for it."

"So what's your name?" She asked.

"Tim, but everybody calls me Crazy T cause I be wildin' out a lot." Tim said.

"Oh yeah? Well, Crazy T, I like to have fun if you know what I mean." She said.

Tim looked in his rearview, licked his fingers and rubbed his eyebrows and said "Well shit fun is my middle name baby girl."

"I hope you like sexy Latin chicks with big tit and ass cause that's me." She said with a slight accent.

"Oh yeah?" Tim said.

"And after a couple drinks, I get really friendly papi." She said.

"So what's up? You wanna have a couple drinks tonight on me?" Tim said. "My treat to my new friend Becky."

Tim pulled into Eddie's pawn shop, shut the car down and kept talking. "Can we do that?" He asked.

"Let me think." She said trying to stall. "3-2-1 got him. Edward's Jewelry and Pawn at 21625 South Nueva Avenue." The phone tracker said to the detectives.

"Yeah we can do that, but can I call you back to see if my mom will watch my daughter?" She said, now ready to bust his ass.

"Yeah baby do what you gotta do and call me back. I wanna see how freaky, I mean friendly you can get." Tim said. With that they hung up and everybody grabbed their guns and badges. Adams called in for a unit to go to the location and notify them what they see.

Tim went inside Eddie's with the case of diamonds under his shirt and two diamonds in his hands. The shop wasn't packed, but there were a few people there.

"Hey, Eddie. I see you're still doing good in here." Tim said to the old man. Eddie was an old black man Tim met when he and MAK used to break in houses to steal jewelry. Eddie was the only one who would take stolen jewelry off their hands.

"Hey, kid. Come on in the back and let's see what you got. It's been a while since you guys been in the jewelry game. Ya'll back on?"

"You can kinda say that." Tim fired back.

"Let's see what you got lil buddy." Eddie asked.

Tim pulled out the stones and gave them to Eddie. When Eddie looked at them, he knew that those were the real deal. He's been in the jewelry business all his life. This was his father's store, so he's been seeing gold and diamonds since his earlier days.

Outside a police officer pulled up to the pawn shop, parked, got out then walked around. He got on the radio and said "Bravo 1, I got 6 cars in the parking lot, but no activity. The lights are on and people are inside."

Adams came back and replied, "Bravo 6, stay outside on alert. We may have 187 suspect inside. Let us know if anyone leaves. We're sending you backup."

"Roger that, Bravo 1." The officer replied.

Eddie put the stones under a microscope and said, "Kid, to be honest, I can't afford these but I know someone who can. If you want to wait till tomorrow."

"What you mean you can't afford them?" Tim asked.

"Man, this is some pretty heavy shit you got here. Whoever they belong to has some money and going to be sick when they find them gone." Eddie said.

"Well, what can you give me right now for one of them?"

"All I got is about 12 grand in the safe but you'll be cheating yourself kid." Eddie said to him being honest.

"Look Eddie, give me 10 grand and keep that one. Tomorrow, if you can sell 20 of these bad boys, I'll split the money with you 50/50, but don't try to fuck me." Tim said rushing Eddie, seeming desperate.

"You got a deal kid." Eddie got 10 grand out the safe, gave it to Tim and told him to go out the back. He didn't want anybody seeing him come out the office like that.

The officer was writing down all the license plate numbers of the cars in the parking lot. He was bent down scraping mud off one dirty jeep to read the number when Tim walked out and got in his car. Since he came from the back the officer never heard a thing. Tim jumped in the car, started it and backed out. The officer was on the other side of the pawn shop, so he didn't hear the car pull off.

"Sorry, folks but the store will be closing in 5 minutes. If you're going to buy something, please hurry." Eddie said to the remaining customers.

"Bravo 6, this is Bravo 1. Backup is 2 minutes away. Any movement?" Adams said over the radio to the officer at the pawn shop.

"That's a negative, Bravo 1. Nobody came or left." He responded looking around.

"Good. Notify us about any movement." Adams said.

"Roger that Bravo 1."

Tim drove down the block and made a left turn at the light, noticed 4 police cars coming down the street followed by 3 unmarked cars. "Wonder where they were going, trying to creep on somebody. Let me get from over here. It's hot." Tim thought to himself. He turned and got on the freeway.

Outside the pawn shop, the police set up a perimeter around the parking lot. Petra and Adams went in. The plan was to go in and call the number, see who picks up and grab them. They entered holding hands like a couple walking around to check everybody out.

Eddie walked up to them and said "Sorry folks, we're closing. No more customers."

"Okay, sorry." Adams said.

As they walked towards the door, Solis dialed the number but no one reacted. "Could he know already or is he just not picking up the phone?" She thought. It was only 4 men in the shop and they all looked like they could be Tim. "No answer." She said to Adams.

"Well, let's improvise." He said then yelled "Hey Tim!" Everybody turned around not because their name was Tim but because he yelled so loud.

"Excuse me, you need to go sir." Eddie told them. They pulled Eddie outside. He jerked away in defense until they pulled out their badges.

"We're detectives and we have reason to believe one of those guys in there may have been involved in a capital murder last night and we can't afford to let him get away. It's our only lead at this point." Adams explained to him.

"Well, how can I help?" Eddie said.

"Look, all we know is his name is Tim." Adams said. "We need your permission to question and ID the people in your store." Adams said.

"Yeah, sure go ahead." Eddie gave them permission knowing that Tim just left out the back and he wasn't about to say a word about it.

The detectives went in together and made the announcement. "Everybody, can I please have your attention. I'm Detective David Adams and I need to see everyone's ID. We're looking for a guy who just ran from custody a few minutes ago." He lied not to alert if the killer was among them. Everybody gave their ID's. No Tim among them. Petra called the number again and got no answer.

"Did anyone leave their phone in the car?" Petra asked, everyone said no.

"Well, we'll have to check each car." Adams said. Adams asked the officer for the license plate numbers.

"And you're sure no one left?" Petra asked.

"No, ma'am. No one's left since I've been here." He replied.

"You know I did see a car as we turned the block to get here." Another officer said.

"Fuck. We fuckin' let him get by us." Cantu said running out the door.

"Sorry folks." Adams said giving them back their ID's and running outside the car.

Ring... Ring... Ring... Petra's phone rang. "Oh shit, it's him." She said. "Hello." She said with her accent.

"Can I speak to Becky?" Tim said.

"This is she." She said looking at Adams with the I don't believe this motherfucker look.

"What's up, this Tim. What up? Did you get that babysitter or what?"

"Yeah! We still on for that drink?" She said.

"Yeah meet me at the Office on Rittl'mman off I-35 in 15 minutes. I'm right down the street." Tim said.

"I'll be there in 10." She said, then they hung up. "He's going to the Office on Rittl'mman." Petra told everybody.

"What the fuck is the Office on Rittl'mman?" Cantu said.

"It's a hole in the wall bar. Follow us." Adams yelled out.

Eddie finished with the customers and locked up. He looked at his cell phone and dialed the last number. 3 rings later "What up, Eddie baby?" Tim said with his loud music in the background.

"Say kid, your ass is in big fuckin' trouble. What did you do?" Eddie asked.

"What you mean by that?" Tim said cutting the music completely.

"Man, 2 minutes after you left, cops came crashing in here looking for Tim saying you may have been the shooter in a capital murder." Eddie told him.

"What you tell them?" Tim asked.

"Nothing. They checked everyone's ID then a female officer called some number and was checking everyone's cell phones." Eddie told him.

"Holy shit!" Tim said as he looked at the phone.

"What kid? You alright?" Eddie asked.

"Hell no, I ain't alright. Fuck man! How fast can you sell these diamonds?" Tim asked him in a worried tone.

"I got a couple of people but not till tomorrow. Then I can call a couple more out of town buddies." Eddie assured him.

"Do that and I'll get with you tomorrow." Tim said.

"Alright, kid but if you need me, call me." Eddie told him.

"Alright, bye." Tim hung up. "Fuck…fuck…fuck." Tim banged the dashboard of the car. "Becky must be the police… But how she knew I was over there at the pawn shop?" He said out loud.

Petra looked at the license plate numbers and gave it to everyone and said, "Listen, when we get here, look for the plates. We'll park in the apartments in the back and walk to the bar."

Cantu said, "Adams and I should go in first and order drinks. You call and we'll get a look at him."

"Okay, that's cool." Solis replied for the first time in agreement with Cantu.

Tim pulled into the Church's Chicken parking lot across the street from the Office so he could watch and see who was looking for him. Seconds after he parked, he saw police cars pull to the back of the bar. There were a few guys out front standing around drunk and talking loud. Tim saw officers surround the building, looking at cars, then 2 went in. then the phone rang, it was Becky.

"Hey is this Tim?" She said.

"Yeah, this me." He replied shaking his head.

"What's up?" He saw Becky outside talking on the phone. "I'll be pulling up in a minute. You there yet?" She said.

Tim lied and said, "Yeah I'm out front in a green and black polo shirt and blue jeans." He used one of the guys out front who was on his phone.

Petra looked around. When she saw the green and black shirt she gave the officers the signal and within a second they drew their weapons on the crowd. "Get on the fuckin' ground now!" the officers yelled. The men didn't know what was going on so they ran in all directions. Petra yelled "green and black shirt!" All officers changed their focus on him and went after him.

Tim started the car, hung up the phone and drove off. The guy in the green and black shirt ran through the apartments in the back of the bar. He pulled out a gun, turned and fired at the officers in pursuit. Clap…clap…clap… The officer's ducked behind the cars. "Shot's fired!" blared over the radios. Cantu and Adams heard it and came running out of the bar. "Shots fired!" Screaming through the radios. "Suspect armed and dangerous!"

"Where are you Bravo 1?" Adams yelled.

"The apartments to the rear of the club" … Clap…Clap… Clap…

"Ahh! Officer down! Officer down!" One of the officers yelled through the radio. "Officer down, request backup."

Petra raised up from behind one of the cars and saw the injured officer. "Which way did he go?" She asked.

"Around the corner." She ran over to the officer to see how serious the wound was. The officer took two shots to the leg, one in the knee cap, another in the thigh. Petra got over her radio and called for an EMS unit to assist the officer. Adams and Cantu came running past them.

"Which way did the suspect go?" Cantu asked.

"That way. Hurry, let's go." Petra said.

They ran around the corner in military style. The other officers were standing behind a brick wall pointing at an apartment. Adams, Solis, and Cantu hurried over to where the officers were.

"He ran in there." One of the officers said. Adams told two officers to go see if there's any way out around back any windows or back doors. They broke off and ran around the building.

"Is there anybody else in the apartment?" Petra asked the officer.

"We don't know. We just saw him run in there after he shot a couple times."

"Okay, Cantu. This is your specialty Go get 'em tiger." Adams said.

"Look, follow my lead." Cantu said. They all ran to the door. Cantu put his ear to it checking for movement with his pistol in his hand. He banged on the door. "Tim, come out or we're coming in! Cantu yelled.

"There's no Tim in here." A female voice said.

"Can you open the door miss or we'll kick it in."

"There's no-" Before she could finish, Cantu kicked the door as hard as he could. The door flew off it's hinges and the female ran to the back of the apartment. All officers ran in.

"Tim, make this easy, man. Nobody has to get hurt." Adams yelled through the house. A gun flew in the hallway. All the officers pointed their weapons ready to fire.

"I'm coming out man, don't shoot." A male voice said.

"No! Lay down and put your hands out where I can see them." Adams said.

They saw hands and they rushed him. Cantu kicked him in the mouth. "you piece of shit. You shot an officer!" Cantu said then kicked him again.

Adams grabbed him. "Hey, what the fuck man? Chill." The guy said. Petra cuffed the suspect and lifted him off the floor and walked him out the door.

They got the suspect back to the car and threw him on the hood.

"So, lover boy, guess you and Becky won't be having that drink after all." Petra said with a grin on her face.

"What the fuck you talkin' bout?" The suspect said to Petra.

"Play dumb if you want to, it's cool." She pulled out her phone, pushed redial and let it ring and ring and ring. She looked at the suspect said: "Where's your fuckin' phone?"

"In my fuckin' pocket, bitch." The suspect yelled.

Petra punched him in the stomach and turned him around to check his pockets and found his I-phone. She called the number and let it ring, and let it ring, and nothing. She looked at Adams and Cantu and told them, "Imma let this phone ring. Go back in that apartment and find that phone please."

Cantu went back. Adams stayed and asked Petra, "What's going on Petra?" He said curiously.

"I called the number and his phone didn't ring. I asked him about the drink with Becky and he acted like he didn't know what I was talking about." She said looking worried.

"So what's that mean?" Adams said.

"I don't know. I just feel something." She said looking at the phone.

Adams looked at the suspect and said, "Tim, where's the other phone we talked to you on?"

"What other phone? I ain't got no other phone and y'all ain't talk to me…and who the fuck is Tim?" The suspect said.

Adams went through his pocket and found his wallet and grabbed his ID. It read Derick Walker III. He looked at Petra and told her, "This ain't Tim. His name is Derick Walker the third. Derick, do you have another cell phone anywhere?"

"No, man. Why y'all pull guns on me like that. I thought y'all was trying to rob me, man." He said.

"Shut up. You're in enough trouble already." Solis yelled at him.

"For what?" He said.

"Murder…attempted murder and resisting arrest." Adams told him.

"Man, I ain't murder nobody. What you talking bout?" The suspect asked.

"That's enough, Adams." Petra said. "Put him in the car." Petra told Adams. She looked at the guy's phone and looked at the caller ID. Her number wasn't on there at all. She decided to call Jose's phone from Derick's phone. She dialed the number it rang twice and then she heard "Hello."

CHAPTER 6

San Diego, CA

Rico looked at the GPS and noticed the red light had moved, but it was still in the same city. He punched in the coordinates and realized it was the San Antonio Police Impound.

"What the fuck? This motherfucker got busted with my shit." Rico said, then grabbed his phone and dialed Hector.

"Hello, Rico. I'm really fuckin' busy right now. We need to talk but give me a couple hours." Hector said before Rico could get a word out.

"You damn right we need to talk. Your fuckin' guy got busted by the cops in San Antonio" Rico said.

"What do you mean busted by the cops?" Hector said ardently surprised.

"Yeah! Busted. I put a GPS box in the furniture truck because I didn't trust your guy. I checked it right now and it's at the fuckin' police Impound in San Anto." Rico shouted through the phone.

"Are you sure, Rico?" Hector said.

"Yeah, I'm sure. Why?" Rico asked.

"Nothing. What are we going to do about it?" Hector questioned.

"Don't worry. I got some connections in San Antonio. I can get the diamonds and maybe some of the coke, but that fuckin' guy might start talking." Rico told him.

"Damn. Rico, I'm sorry brother. How can I fix this shit? I'll do anything." Hector told him in a pleading tone.

"You might have to go down there and get those diamonds, but give me a minute and I'll get back with you. What did you want to talk about? Rico asked.

"I called that fucker's phone this morning and some bitch answered and said Jose sold his phone to her brother so I went and paid Jose's wife a visit about an hour or two ago. I got a lil' insurance policy till we get Jose or the shipment." Hector told Rico, referring to Jose's daughter.

"Well, you did good. Hold on to that. We might need it. What is it anyway?" Rico asked curiously.

"His daughter." Hector told him.

Rico hung up and dialed an old buddy he knew down in San Antonio. The line rung 4 times then his buddy picked up and said, "Rico DeLuna, to what do I owe this honor?"

"My friend, how's that rough Texas life treating you?" Rico said.

"oh, ya know ups and downs, the usual. I'm in the middle of a big murder right now but what's going on?" The guy said.

"I got a problem and it's in your city." Rico said.

"What kind of problem?" The guy asked.

"Well, you know I have a lot of traffic going through San Antonio, right? Well, one of my loads have been intercepted by you guys." Rico told him.

"Are you sure it was us?" He asked.

"Yes, I'm positive 'cause I had a GPS on it and it's at your police impound right now." Rico assured him.

"Let me check real quick. What was the shipment in?" He asked looking at his computer.

"An 18 wheeler, hauling furniture from here in San Diego to Florida." Rico said.

"We did have furniture- holy shit! Rico that was yours?" The caller said surprised.

"You know what I'm talking about?" Rico asked excited.

"Yeah, man but to be sure, do you know the trucks number?" The officer asked.

"Yeah, I have it here. Hold on." Rico said. While Rico looked for the numbers, the officer checked the computer for the truck that was taken into the impound. He found it and the rest of the info with it. "Okay, Mario. I found it. It's #694-A. Some fucker named Jose was the driver." Rico said.

"Yeah, we got it, but I got bad news. Buddy, that driver of yours is dead." The officer informed Rico.

"Dead? What do you mean dead?" Rico said in a loud voice.

"I mean dead. He was shot in the head at the truck stop and the load was stolen. It's an open case, right now me and two workaholics are on it." The officer told Rico in an apologetic tone.

"Fuck!" Rico said. "Look, Mario, I need that truck. There's a black box under the dashboard that I need, man. The rest of the load can be paid for, but that box is important to me and a lot of people man. I'll pay you good if you return it to me." Rico said sounding in distress.

"Hey, anything for you Rico. How much we talkin'?" The officer said.

"1 million." Rico said.

Mario heard that and said, "I'll have that box to you in a couple hours."

"I'll send Hector to pick it up and he'll have your million."

"Okay, Rico. I'll call you back."

Rico hung up and called Hector back. "El Torro, it's Rico again. That fuckin' Jose is dead man."

"Yeah, I know. If I get my hands on him he's a dead man for sure." Hector said in an aggressive tone.

"No, brother, he's dead. He got killed in San Antonio. Someone jacked the shipment last night. I got in touch with my guy down there in San Antonio and he's going to get the diamonds. I need you to go with me to pick them up." Rico said.

"Okay, when we leave, Rico?" Hector said.

"Tonight." Rico answered.

"Done. But what do I do with the insurance policy?" Hector asked.

"Fuck man, take her back home." Then Rico hung up.

"Take her home." Hector said to himself "fuck that." "Hey, Jose is dead. He got killed in San Antonio and Rico wants us to go down there and pick up some shit. We leave tonight. So take the girl and go drop her off at the store by her house and make sure nobody sees you." Hector told Lil' Freddy and Jesus.

Rico called Stephany in and told her to call and have a plane ready for him to leave tonight.

"What time, sir?" She said.

"Make it for 8:00." Rico said.

"Do you want me for company?" She asked with lust in her eyes.

"No, this is important. No time for fun." He told her.

"Okay. Is that it?" She asked.

"Yeah. Call my wife and let her know I won't be home tonight. I have business to handle." He demanded.

San Antonio, TX

Adams didn't get any sleep. He and Solis pulled an all-nighter in the office trying to figure out what went wrong with the Tim situation.

"I'm going to question him again." Petra said.

"It's no use. I think he's telling the truth." Adams said.

"What the fuck do you mean telling the truth? He knows something. He knows Tim and he's sitting there telling us stupid lies. Dave, I feel it." Solis said pacing back and forth.

Last night after busting Derick and calling the phone back and hearing Tim's voice, Petra was so mad she threw the phone and broke it. They took Derick in, got him booked and have been questioning him all morning with no progress.

"Look, Petra, we need to try and trace that phone again and pray he hasn't gotten rid of it. After your outburst last night, he may have trashed it." Adams said.

"Somehow, he knew we were at that bar or he would have shown. He set us up to go after Derick. Now, how did he know?" Petra asked Adams. "If he knew we tracked him by the phone, why would he answer when I called from Derick's phone and not mine?" She asked.

Adams replied, "Maybe he thinks we can only track him from your phone. He might not know that anytime he turns it on we track his ass."

"Shit, I didn't even know that." Petra said. "And tell me, why didn't we think of that last night?" Solis asked.

"Too much clogging my memory at the time. Call the trackers back in here." Adams commanded Petra.

Mario walked to the evidence tech with some paperwork and told him he needed to see the truck that was brought in on the murder investigation. The tech knew him, so it was no problem. Mario went straight to the dashboard and saw it all intact. He looked under it, then stuck his arm under and found nothing. He told one of the techs to come take the dashboard off for him. The tech grabbed his tools and got to work. When he finished, there was nothing under it. He got his phone out and started dialing Rico's number.

He stepped to the side to talk. "Hello, Rico. This is Mario. I'm here with the truck and there's nothing under the dashboard."

"Yes, there is. I put it there myself. Look behind the CB." Rico said in an agitated tone.

"Rico, I'm standing next to the whole dash. I had the tech take it apart. There's nothing here, man." The officer said to him.

"Do you think whoever killed Jose found it, Mario?" Rico said.

"Could have. Shit, they took dope and guns. Why not the box? What's in the box, anyway?" The officer asked curiously.

"Something priceless for my wife's father. I was going to surprise him." Rico said disappointed.

"Well, that's not going to happen, buddy." The officer responded sarcastically.

"Look for the motherfucker who jacked that load and I will give you one million dollars, but you have to bring me the box."

"One million? Are you serious, man?" The officer said.

"Do I ever play about money?" Rico said.

"No. You don't." The officer said.

"What do you got on him? Maybe I can send you some help." Rico said.

"All we got as of now is somebody named Tim and that's about it." The officer said.

"Can you keep me fully posted on your progress and any info?" Rico said in more of a demand instead of question.

"I can do that, no problem." Mario and Rico hung up and Mario thought about the million dollars. He thought to himself "we will capture Tim and that million by any means necessary."

The fingerprints came back and were delivered to the office which was packed this morning. Petra looked over the fingerprints and came up with only five matches. Timothy Jimenez jumped out and hit her like a stack of bricks. "Got that motherfucker." She said.

"Who?" Adams said.

"Tim. His real name is Timothy Jimenez, last known address was 1827 Rigsby Ave. Apt # 5. He's been arrested several times for all kinds of crimes from petty theft to aggravated assault and now we got this bastard for capital murder." She said looking at his mugshot.

"Well, let's call Cantu and go get him." Adams said.

Cantu was coming up the elevator when he got Adam's call about Tim. "I'm in the elevator, Adams. I'll meet you downstairs. I'll be in the garage." Cantu said now pushing down on the elevator button.

When Cantu hung up with Adams, he called Rico back. "Hey Rico, it's me, Mario. Get that million ready. We're on our way to the kid's house. His name is Timothy Jimenez. He lives in the Rigsby Courts and is a local gang member." The officer told him.

"Look, Mario, I want this motherfucker for myself. You hear me? He robbed me and he must pay by my hands." Rico said.

"Rico, how am I supposed to get him to you without these people's questions flying off the head?" The officer said.

"I don't care how you do it. You're the cop. I just want him and that box. If you want the money, get it done." Rico said.

"Don't worry, Rico. I'll do it." Mario hung up.

Rico took the info Mario told him and called in a favor down in San Antonio from his worker. The worker usually only transports illegal aliens across the border, but when Rico filled him in on his problem and told him about the one million dollar price he was willing to pay for Timothy Jimenez and the black box, the guy was willing to go all out. Rico told him to do whatever it takes to get the box to him.

By Rico getting the price so high, Mario knew it was the real deal. Mario had done crooked things in the past for Rico for free. A million dollars only pushed him to the limit. First, he had to figure out how to shake Adams and Solis. He knew if they got to Tim, they would take him to jail and it would be hard to get him to Rico.

Cantu met Adams and Solis and a couple more plain clothed officers downstairs. Adams began the plan of entry. "We're going to surround the building just like last night and try to take him easily with no gunfire. Solis, you stay with me and Peck, the rest of you go with Cantu. We'll hit the door and you guys secure the perimeter." As they filed out to their cars, everyone strapped on their vest. Petra wished everyone luck.

Paulette's House

"Babe, I'm ready to go. Can you please hurry up?" Vanessa said to MAK in the shower.

MAK turned the shower off and stepped out. Vanessa stood there holding the towel. "Looking for this?" She said in her sexy voice.

"Yeah, so give it here if you want me to hurry up." MAK said.

"Let me dry you off, babe." Vanessa said.

"Okay, but if you start something, you betta finish it." He said.

She looked at him and said, "Don't I always?" Then she started drying his wet body slowly. When she passed his waistline, she grabbed his penis in her hands and dried it extra slow. She squeezed it soft then started jacking MAK off. His penis got hard and Vanessa got on her knees and licked the tip of the head and in one quick motion, she swallowed half of it. She caressed his balls and sucked it til he was at the point to bust. Then she started jacking him and sucked it as far down her throat as she could fit it and let him bust in her mouth.

"Now can you hurry up?" She said to him.

"Oh yeah, now that's motivation baby. I'll be ready in 5 minutes." MAK said doing a celebration dance.

MAK called Tim when he started to get dressed. He let the phone ring couple times then hung up. "Nessa, have you talked to yo brother?" MAK asked.

"I haven't heard from him since he left last night. Call his phone." She said.

"I did. He ain't answer." MAK told her.

"Oh well, what you gon die if you don't talk to him?" She said.

"Shit, I hope he found a girl so he can move out our apartment." She said, being serious.

"Man, that's yo brother," MAK said to her.

"So? We finally have a baby. We need some privacy sometimes." She told him.

On the I-10 expressway, Adams, Solis and Cantu were on their way to the address listed for Timothy Jimenez. Tim looked at his phone and noticed MAK calling, so he ignored it. He thought to himself "That nigga shot the old man but the police looking for me. I told his stupid ass don't shoot nobody, but no, he gotta be 0-dawg on shit. Well, I'mma cashing in these diamonds and dip on everybody."

He called Eddie to check on the money. Two rings and he picked up, "Hey, Tim. Lil' buddy. What's up?" Eddie said.

"Did you get in touch with anybody?" Tim said sounding anxious.

"Yeah, a guy in Houston wants to see them. He said if they're as good as I say, he'll take 10 of them for us." Eddie assured him.

"Good. When can it happen?" Tim asked.

"He'll be here tomorrow, but I'mma make a few more calls. What's up with the policeman?" Eddie asked curiously.

"Shit, I don't know. I'mma get this money and run. Fuck it. Catch me if they can." Tim said to him.

"Did you do it kid?" Eddie asked.

"Fuck no! MAK, my sister's baby daddy, did that shit." Tim told him.

"Why won't you tell them, man?" Eddie asked.

"I was there. They'll involve me and I'll still go down. Plus, my sister will have a fit. You know she pregnant." Tim said.

"Well, as I said, I'm here for you kid if you need a place to hide out for a while, I got a place out there by Canyon Lake you can stay at." Eddie told him.

"I need that for real, man." Tim said.

"Okay, look, come by the shop about 3:00. I'll give you the key and the directions." Eddie told him.

"Thanks, Eddie, man. I really appreciate it." Tim said breathing a sigh of relief.

Tim turned into the Rigsby, and as the security gate closed, he saw 7 police cars pull to the gate behind him. He turned at the first set of apartments, pulled behind the dumpster, hopped out and ran to the breezeway and hid behind the stairs. He saw the cars pass by going to the back of the apartments.

The officers parked two complexes away from the address for Timothy Jimenez. The marked cars drove around out of sight then parked and met back with the team.

Adams gave instructions. "Solis, you and those two with me," he said pointing at two detectives. "Cantu, you and those 3 go to the back windows and surround the building. The rest of you, spread out throughout the apartments and keep everyone back."

Then Solis spoke up, "This is what the suspect looks like." She had a photo from his mugshots and showed everyone. "This is our man, got it?"

Everyone shook their heads and went their ways.

"You ready?" Adams asked Solis.

"You bet. Let's go get him." She replied.

Tim went to the playground to see if they were going to the apartment. He saw two police men coming across the parking lot, he passed the playground and went to a girl's apartment he knew. She was outside on the steps smoking a cigarette.

"Hey, boy. Where you been?" The girl said, surprised to see him.

"Shit, on my grind. Wanna smoke a blunt?" He said trying to get inside. He knew weed would work.

"Hell yeah! What's up?" She said stubbing out her cigarette.

"Let's go inside though. The laws walking around." She said.

"Come on in. Where's MAK and Vanessa at?" She asked as they turned to go.

"Out at MAK's Aunt's house. Tim said to her.

Just as they walked in the house, the police passed by and they could hear their walkie-talkies as they walked by the window.

Adams positioned himself in front of the door with Solis right behind him. The officer with the warrant stood to the right. The other detective stood back by the front window in case someone tried to run out.

The detective with the warrant knocked and announced, "Police. We have a warrant for Timothy Jimenez. Open the door or we'll kick it in." No one answered so he knocked again.

The neighbor opened her door. Adams told her to go back inside. She told them no one was home. "They all left yesterday and haven't been back."

Solis asked, "Are you sure?"

"Well, it's Vanessa's apartment but her brother Crazy-T stays with her and her baby daddy." She told them.

"What's the baby daddy's name?" Adams asked.

"Everybody calls him MAK." She told them.

"When they come home, can you please call us? Here's my card." Adams said handing her his card with his office number.

"Sure, I'll call... Is anybody in trouble?" She asked.

"No just some unpaid parking tickets. We're doing ticket round-up. Nothing serious." Adams told her not to draw attention.

"Oh, alright. I'll call." She said then closed the door. Adams told Solis to go to the manager's office and tell her to come open the door for them.

Tim sat at the girl's house smoking, nervous cause he didn't know what was going on outside. He thought about calling MAK but decided not to. The girl was talking but Tim was elsewhere in time.

"What's wrong, Crazy? You okay? You look spooked." She asked now aware he wasn't paying attention.

"Naw, I've been getting keyed all night. Ain't had no sleep." He lied to her.

"You got some more?" She asked.

"Yeah. I didn't know you be getting' down like that girl." He said.

"That's causes I don't be puttin' my business out there like that." She said. They started getting keyed while they smoked and got more paranoid than he already was.

Solis came back with the manager, she let them into the apartment. The manager stayed outside while the detectives entered one by one with their weapons drawn.

"Police! Anyone home come out with your hands up." Adams announced their presence. No one was home, so they looked around the apartment. They noticed pictures of Vanessa and MAK all through the apartment.

"Is this who lives here, miss?" Adams asked the manager showing her a picture from the coffee table.

"Yes, that's Mrs. Macias and her boyfriend, John." The manager replied.

"Have you had any problems with them?"

"Her brother is wanted for murder and this is the address we have for him." Adams told her.

"No, I only know the two of them." She said.

Behind them through the door, the neighbor was listening to the conversation. When she heard Tim was wanted for murder, she thought how she could tell Vanessa and Tim not to come home. She Didn't have their number.

Tim heard the walkie-talkie pass the apartment again and looked out the window. The detectives were going back the other direction towards the way they came. He told the girl if she wanted to chill with him later out by Canyon Lake…

"yeah, we can do that," She said.

"Alright, I'll be back in a little bit." Then he left.

Adams told two of the uniformed officers to stay in the apartments and watch for Tim or any sign of someone entering the apartment. The girl next door heard everything.

Tim peaked his head around the corner and saw the people huddled up around the apartment. He could see Adams pointing in all directions- then he saw Becky. He said to himself, "That's her. The fuckin' bitch that tried to set me up." Let's see how she likes this. He pulled out the phone and scrolled through this call log, got to the number and called it. Her phone began buzzing but she ignored it and kept listening to Adams. Tim hung up and ran to his car.

"Okay, everybody got it? Keep us posted on this apartment and if you see any one of those faces call us and don't let them out your sight." Adams addressed the officers.

Then they got in their cars and drove away. Two of the detectives that were to keep watch went to the office with the manager to get another key. The plan was to wait in one of the vacant apartments across the street and watch the door.

As they drove through the gate, Solis checked her phone and screamed, "Holy Shit! Tim just fuckin' called me and I didn't answer."

"Are you fuckin' kidding me?" Adams said. "Fuck, call back."

"What if he doesn't pick up?" She shouted.

"So try anyway." Adams told her.

Tim backed out and drove out the parking spot and saw the detectives cars passing by. He laughed and when the last car passed, he jumped in behind them. His phone rang, it was her.

He answered, "Hey, I'm sorry I missed you last night. But when I got ready to pull in, I saw cops everywhere so I kept going. You mad at me?" Tim said to her.

"No, not at all. Where you at right now? You busy?" She had him on speaker phone so Adams could hear.

"Yeah, I'm kinda busy right now, but look, how bout we meet tonight at my friends apartment?" He said to her.

"Yeah, that's cool. Where is it?" She asked.

Adams phone rang. He was too into Petra's phone conversation with Tim to notice.

"I'll call you back when I finish what I'm doing over here." Tim said to her.

"Where is over here?" She said trying to get him to reveal his location. Adams phone rang again. He was so agitated he took it out his pocket and threw it in the back seat.

"I'm in Austin taking care of some business. I'll be back around 6:00." He lied looking at them through the windshield.

"Okay then, just call me. I really want to meet Tim, baby. Plus, I haven't been with a real man in almost 2 years." She said.

Tim shook his head and thought to himself, "Fuckin' bitch tryna get me with that shit. I'm crazy and I'mma show you why they call me that tonight."

"Well, I'mma take care of that tonight shorty if you let me." He told her.

"Okay, well, tonight then." She responded. Then they hung up.

Detectives turned left and he turned right and they were gone. Adams phone rang again but since it was in the backseat he didn't notice.

It was the phone tech trying to tell them Tim was behind them. Cantu called Adams and asked him what was next because he had something to do.

"Nothing til' tonight. The fucker called Solis and set another date. He's in Austin right now. He'll be back at 6PM. So we're dead til' then. I gotta make a couple calls to the base about those guns." Adams said.

"Okay, well, call me if anything pops up. I'm out." Cantu hung up, then dialed his team leader from narcotics. "Hello, Phil, it's business that needs handling and there's a lot of money on the line." He told him.

"Gotch. Where we gon meet?" The team leader asked.

"My house." Then they hung up.

Westside SA, TX

Blink was the leader of the neighborhood gang, Westside Locos. He got his crew together and told them what Rico said about Timothy Jimenez.

"Hey, brothers, we can be fuckin' rich if we find this guy before the cops! So we can't fuck around and we have to get the box to get the million dollars." He said in his westside accent, pausing in between every 3 words.

The crew was only about 10 to 12, but they were all certified hit men and had no problem killing anyone in their way when they were trying to get money.

"They guy lives in the Rigsby's on the Eastside, so he should be easy to find. It's not a lot of Mexicans out there. Got it?" He shouted to the crew looking at each one eye to eye. Everybody agreed and they hopped in their cars headed to the Eastside with one thing on their minds: one million dollars.

SA, TX Airport

The private G4 jet landed at the airport in San Antonio. Rico, Hector, Lil' Freddy, Jesus and 5 more of Hector's men stepped off the plane. Two trucks were already waiting for them to take them to the hotel. Rico called Mario to let him know he had landed and ask what was the status on the Tim situation.

"Hello, hey, Rico. What's up man? I'm still working on that for you. The address we had, nobody was there. We're going to keep an eye on the apartment." Mario told him.

"I'mma get a couple guys to check into it." Rico said to him, wanting this over as soon as possible.

"Rico, I told you to let me handle it. I'll bring him to you." Mario said in a demanding tone rubbing his thick mustache.

"Okay, I brought some help just in case." Rico informed him ignoring his request to handle it alone.

The drivers of both trucks were friends of Rico and Hector's. Hector told the driver, "Take us to the Rigsby Apartments. You have those guns I told you to bring?"

"Yes, sir. Look in the box in the back." The drivers told him pointing to the back.

Hector told Lil' Freddy to open the box. There were pistols and fully automatic assault rifles plus ammo. "Good." Hector said with excitement in his face. They headed towards the 410 Expressway to the Eastside.

MAK tried Tim again, still no answer. He and Vanessa were at the Walmart on I-35 and Walzem shopping for baby stuff. "Hey, let's go to the movies tonight after we go eat." MAK told Nessa.

"Okay! It's been a while since we went on a date together, just the two of us. I miss that and I know once I have this baby we ain't gon get no alone time." Vanessa said rubbing her stomach.

"Yes, we will. Your mama can watch the baby for us and besides, I wanna move out of Texas." MAK told her looking serious through his dark brown eyes.

"Oh, for real, baby? I've always wanted to move away from here." Vanessa said smiling and touching his cheek.

"Well, look, give me 6 good months and we out of here. I promise." MAK assured her. They got to the checkout line, paid and left.

On the way to the apartments, they stopped at the corner store. On the way in, they bumped into Sara, their next door neighbor. "Oh MAK, where is Nessa? Hurry, get back into the car, boy, before somebody see you." Sara said pushing and rushing him back to the car.

"Girl, what the fuck is wrong with you?" MAK said looking confused.

"Get in the fuckin' car." She said. She pushed him to the car then they both got in. "Drive and don't go home. Listen ya'll, the fuckin' police looking for Tim. They say he wanted for murder." She said in her usual overly excited tone.

Vanessa looked at MAK with a surprised look and said, "What?"

MAK backed out and went the opposite direction of the apartments.

"Yes girl, murder. The manager let them in. They searched the apartment. Before the manager came, they knocked and I heard them yelling. So I opened the door to see what was up. They lied and told me Tim just had parking tickets, but when the manager came they told her he was wanted for murder. They got a picture

Of all three of ya'll. They also got two police in the vacant apartment across the street watching for any of ya'll." She explained all in one breath, eyes wide, nostrils flared and veins pertruding in her neck.

MAK looked nervous.

"Babe, what we gon do? We can't even go home cause of Tim's stupid ass." Vanessa told him with tears in her big hazel eyes.

"Chill. We don't even know if he did it. Just cause them hoes got a warrant, don't mean he guilty." MAK told them both knowing Tim was innocent.

Rico called Blink.

"Hola, Rico. What's going on, man?" Blink told him.

"Not much. We just landed in San Antonio. Where you at?"

"I'm searching for that fucker who jacked you, dawg. I need a million dollars. I know you brought Torro with you, huh?" Blink said.

"Yeah, he's right here." Rico said looking in Hector's direction.

"Tell him I bet the Westside Locos get Tim before he does." Blink said as serious as possible.

Rico laughed and relayed the message to Hector. "Tell him he's on. That's a bet." Hector said holding up a black pistol.

Rico said, "Dude, be careful. There's two detectives watching the apartment from across the street." Rico told Blink referring to the officers watching from across the street.

"Oh yeah? What apartment?" Blink asked looking agitated.

"2120." Rico said.

"Down here, anyone in the way gets it too." Blink told Rico.

"Okay, just be careful and remember my box." Rico told him and slammed his phone in his lap. "Change of plans." Rico told the driver. "Go to the hotel first."

"Sara, we need to go back to my Aunt's house. You want me to drop you off somewhere?" MAK said to her.

"Drop me off at the trail that leads back to the apartments, but give me a number so I can keep ya'll up on everything." She said not wanting anyone to get in trouble.

MAK gave her the cell number and dropped her off at the trail in the back of the apartments. Sara exited the car cautiously. She was only 5'2" with long brown hair, big brown eyes and a few freckles on her yellow skin. She nervously scrambled through the trail.

MAK drove off and Vanessa looked at him and said, "Do you know what she talkin' bout?" In her most upset face, not fully opening her mouth.

"No, babe. For real. I don't know shit." MAK said but knowing in his head they could only be talking about one murder, the one he did. He had to find Tim and let him know.

Tim went to Eddie's to pick up the key to place out on Canyon Lake.

"Kid, I told you 3 o'clock. It's damn near 5:30. Where you been?" Eddie forcibly told him.

"I had some shit to handle." Tim said with a devious look on his almost pink face. Tim had set up a place for him to meet with Becky and those police. He went to Paulette's and got two of the new guns that he and MAK hit for and loaded up on bullets. His plan was to try and kill them all before they knew what hit them.

He got the key and called the girl from the apartment he was with earlier.

"Hey, what's up Tim?" Tiffany said excited he called.

"We still on? I'm on my way." Tim told her.

"Yeah! Come get me." She said already getting ready.

"I'll be there at 8 o'clock." He told her and hung up.

Rico got to the hotel and pulled out the GPS device. He told Hector that the device can tell everywhere the truck had been and by the coordinates it went from the truck stop to a place not far from there. He read out Paulette's address to Hector and told him to take the guys and go check it out to see if any clues turn up.

MAK told Vanessa that he was going to drop her off at Paulette's and he's going to find Tim and let him know the deal.

"Baby, be careful. I don't want to get in no trouble behind Tim, okay?" Said Nessa pleading with MAK through tear-filled eyes.

"I hear you babe, just chill. When we get out here, I'll tell Paulette to tell her friends that me and Tim gone, so don't come by alright." He assured her.

"John, I love you. Please be careful." Vanessa said looking at him in the eyes. Her long eye lashes soaked and stuck together.

They pulled up to Paulette's and Nessa went in. MAK went to Debra's house to tell Paulette that Nessa was going to be there so no one can come over.

"What's wrong nephew?" Paulette asked looking concerned.

"Tim got in some trouble. I need to go find him…" MAK told her sounding disturbed.

"Shit, he just left a couple minutes ago." Paulette told him.

"What? When?" MAK told her wide eyed.

"Shit, bout 20-30 minutes ago. He took something with him. I was looking out the window." Paulette told him.

"Something like what?" MAK said.

"I don't know. Something black. He got it out the house." Paulette told him.

"Alright." MAK went to the house and to the stash spot and noticed two of the guns were gone. "What he finna do with that shit?" MAK thought feeling confused. MAK hopped in the car and left. He dialed Tim.

"Hello?"

"Tim, this is MAK. Where the fuck you at dawg. The fuckin' law looking for you." MAK said sitting up in the car.

"Yeah, I know 'cause your stupid ass nigga. You killed that old man, but them hoes looking for me." Tim said angrily, yelling through the phone.

"I'm sorry man, but why they looking for you?" MAK asked confused.

"I don't fuckin' know but it's yo fault. I'mma handle them hoes tonight." Tim growled rubbing one of the AKSU's.

"What you mean handle them?" MAK asked seriously concerned.

"They want me for murder already, so I'mma commit a couple of them." Tim said looking at his reflection in the rearview.

"Don't do no stupid shit, dawg. It ain't worth it." MAK pleaded with him.

"Oh yeah, it's worth it this time. Tell my sister I love her." Tim said then he hung up.

MAK yelled "Fuck!" He didn't know where Tim was or what he planned on doing. He felt so guilty on what was going on but what could he do? He had to find Tim before the police did but what good would that do? He couldn't turn himself in? How could he help, he thought to himself.

Tim knew a guy who loved getting into it with the laws. Tim paid him 2 grand and half a brick of cocaine to help him with the police. The plan was to call Becky to the house across the street. When they arrive, Tim and Dragon would be laying in the back of a stolen pickup. Before they could react, unload on them and speed away. Have Tim's car parked a couple blocks away, switch cars, go get this girl and go to Canyon Lake.

Tim and Dragon loaded the weapons and Tim made the call. Dragon was a local dope fiend older white guy with mental issues and a hatred for cops.

Hector and his gang pulled up to Paulette's house. Paulette and Debra were sitting across the street.

"Hey, they not there. What you want?" Paulette yelled.

"I'm looking for a guy named Tim." Hector said in his strong accent.

Vanessa heard voices and came to the door and looked out.

"He's not there." Paulette said again but more aggressive.

"Well, do you know where I can find him? It's really important." Hector said trying to sound friendly.

"No, I'll tell him you came by. What's your name?" She said to Hector.

"My names not important. Who are you?" He said back to her with more force.

"I'm his Aunt." She told him.

"Oh yeah!" Hector said surprised, then looked at Lil' Freddy and they rushed her. She ran for Debra's front door. Debra ran too. Lil' Freddy kicked Debra's leg and she fell. Paulette made it inside. When she turned and saw they had Debra and the other guys were still coming after her, she slammed the door and locked it.

They kicked it and she put her back to the door and yelled: "What do ya'll want?"

One guy said, "Tim."

They had Debra by the hair and Hector pulled out his gun. "Open the door or I'll kill her right here."

Vanessa was so scared because she was alone in the house. She closed the door quietly and locked it. She grabbed the phone and dialed the police.

"911 what's you emergency?" The operator said.

"Hello, please send the police. Some guys pulled guns on my Aunt and her friend. They're after my brother. Please hurry. I'm at 11689 Delta Point." Vanessa said crying but trying not to panic.

"Where are you, ma'am?" The operator said.

"I'm across the street in the house but I'm scared they going to come over here. I'm pregnant and alone." She told the lady as she began to shake.

"Stay in hiding, miss. Help is on the way." The operator said.

"Thank you, please hurry." Vanessa begged.

Paulette looked out the peephole. "Please don't kill her." She pleaded through tears from behind the door.

"Well, open the door." Hector yelled.

"Tim's not here." She screamed to them.

"Just open the fuckin' door." He yelled louder and hit Debra with the pistol in the mouth.

"Okay, okay. Please stop." Paulette hesitated with the lock. She knew it would be both of them if she opened the door, but she loved Debra.

Vanessa hung up the phone and called MAK. MAK looked at his phone and saw Paulette's number and said, "Baby, I can't talk right now. You gotta wait." Vanessa let it ring and ring. MAK never picked up.

"All units, there's been a call about some guys pulling weapons out, threatening to kill someone. The lady who called is a pregnant female, alone, across the street from where it's happening. Approach with caution. Men are armed." The call went out over the police CB. Adams heard it over his car radio.

"Bravo1, I'm going out that direction, send back up." Adams looked at his watch and knew he had to meet with Solis at 6 PM for the Tim issue, but this had to be taken care of and he was in the area.

"Hello?"

"What's up, Becky? We still on for tonight?" Tim asked in his smoothest tone.

"Yeah! Of course, What time and where? I'm there." Solis said to him feeling like this time they may bag Tim.

Tim gave her directions and hung up. He and Dragon were snorting lines of coke getting ready.

Solis called Adams, "Hey, where the fuck you at? Tim just called." Solis yelled.

"I was coming from talking to people about the guns when a call came in with someone threatening to kill a pregnant lady. I'm in the area so I'm responding." Adams told her.

"We got a fuckin' murder suspect we're after. Dave, let someone else look into that." Solis yelled at him shaking her head in disgust.

"I'll just stop and see if it's serious and I'll meet ya'll there. Call Cantu and you're in charge til' I get there. Don't go in. Just secure the area." Adams told her.

"Fuck, Dave. Hurry up." Then Solis hung up and called Cantu. "Hey, Cantu, it's Solis." She said in a rushed tone.

"What's up, Solis?" Cantu responded.

"I just talked to Tim. He wants to meet and he's ready." She informed him.

"Stall him for about an hour or so." Cantu told her. Cantu was at home with his team getting them up to speed on the Tim situation and the million hours.

"What do you mean stall him? Adams said to meet him and secure the area." Solis shouted to him anxious to solve this murder and take Tim

"No, listen to me Solis. I got word he's going to his apartment first to pick up clothes. Give me the address. He wants to meet. I'll meet you in an hour." Cantu told her trying to stall for time.

Solis gave him the address but an hour was not on her mind. She was getting a team and heading out there to get Tim.

Cantu wrote the address down and told his team, "Let's go get 'em boys. This should be like taking candy from a baby." Cantu told his team with a sinister smile." He was hoping Solid took the info he told her and went to the apartment.

Vanessa went to the back room, opened the window and crawled out. She kept the cordless phone with her, she tried MAK again-no answer. She looked around the corner and she could see Hector hitting Debra with the gun. She cried and dialed the police again.

"911, what's your emergency?"

"Yes, I just called for help at 11689 Delta Point. Please hurry. They're beating her with a gun." Vanessa whispered through her tear-filled eyes and shaky voice.

"Miss, there's help on the way. Let me put you through to an office." This dispatcher connected to Adams.

"Yes, this is detective Adams."

"Yes, Bravo 1, this is the dispatcher, I have a young lady on the line. She says their beating a person with a gun." The dispatcher said with urgency.

"Let me talk to her." Adam told Dispatch.

"Just a minute." She patched Vanessa through.

"Hello?" Vanessa whispered barely audible.

"Yes, Miss. This is detective Adams of S.A.P.D. and I'm on my way to you. What's going on? Adams asked zig-zagging through traffic.

"Some guys are beating my boyfriend's Aunt's friend with a gun. They chased his Aunt back into the house." She cried trying not to be heard.

"Where are you, Miss?" Adams asked concerned.

"I'm hiding outside in the backyard. They were looking for my brother, so I think they're gone. Please hurry, I'm pregnant." Vanessa cried to Adams pleading for his assistance.

"I'm on my way. What's your name?" Adams asked her.

"Vanessa Macias." She mumbled.

The name hit him the instant he heard it. "What's your brother's name?" Adams asked.

"Timothy." She said. Before she finished, she remembered the police were after Tim and she changed his name. "His name is Marcos." She lied not to get him in any trouble.

Paulette opened the door, soon as she did, the beating started. Once Hector and his gang were inside Debra's, Vanessa ran a few houses down to get away from them.

Solis got a team of 6 men together and headed to meet Tim. She planned on taking him today no matter what, even if Becky had to hug and kiss to do it. She told her team to park down the block. She'd

GREED

go in alone first so he won't be spooked. Once she was in, they'll surround the house and she'll handle him on the inside.

Cantu and his team headed to the address Solis gave him. Cantu had one plan: snatch the kid and find the box. He'd snatch Tim, but tell Solis and Adams it was another no-show on Tim's part.

Blink and his team of bandits entered the Rigby's. Everybody had AK's and bandanas over their faces.

Tim and Dragon lay in the bed of the truck waiting for go time.

MAK rode around trying to find Tim.

CHAPTER 7

Hector and his goons beat Paulette until she told them she didn't know where Tim was, but his sister was across the street. Lil' Freddy shot Debra once in the back of the head. They took Paulette out of the house and across the street to find Vanessa. The door was locked. Jesus kicked it in. They went through the trailer. No sign of Vanessa, so they shot Paulette and left her body in the living room. Hector took his finger and used her blood to write Tim on the coffee table and left.

Vanessa saw them come out of the house and ducked out of sight. She cried for Paulette. She knew something bad happened. Hector then pulled off. As they passed heading to the corner, cop cars came speeding around the corner with Adams in the lead. Vanessa came out of her hiding spot, flagging her arms and pointing at the truck turning the corner but the cops sped past her and down to Paulette's house. Hector saw her but they kept going. It was too many cops.

"Next time, bitch. I know what you look like now." Hector mumbled to himself as the truck turned.

The police quickly exited their cars, drew their weapons and surrounded the house.

"This is the police. We have the place surrounded. Come out with your hands up." Adams yelled over the bull horn.

"Hey! Hey!" Vanessa cut him off yelling. "Hey! You missed them. They drove off in the black Suburban." Vanessa yelled at them running and pointing, tears poured down her swollen face.

"Miss, are you the one who called the cops?" Adams asked

"Yes, they just passed y'all in that black Suburban." She told him again jumping and pointing.

Adams sent 3 units after the Suburban. He put Vanessa in his car then they went inside.

"Hello, Police." He announced as they entered the trailer home. They saw Paulette's feet. They got closer and could see she was dead, one bullet hole in her neck. Adams saw Tim's name on the table and said: "Looks like I'm not the only one looking for Timothy." He told the officers to call EMS.

He started for his car when he heard Vanessa say, "What about Debra over there? That's who they were beating with the gun." She shouted out the window pointing towards Debra's house.

"Stay there." He said to her. He went to Debra's house and looked in. There was Debra dead on the floor. He shook his head and got on the Police Radio and called another 187...

Vanessa asked, "Are you okay?" She asked looking alarmed.

"Miss, they're both dead." Adams sadly informed her.

"Dead? No, no, no." Vanessa yelled and started throwing up bad. Adams ran to the car to help her out. She fell to the ground. She was hysterical.

Blink and 6 of the Westside Locos went to Vanessa's house and kicked in the door. At the same time, the other 6 kicked in the door where the officers were watching at. The officers turned around just in time to catch bullets in the face and body. They fell dead before they could reach for their guns.

Blink and the others were ransacking Vanessa's apartment. Sara, the neighbor, heard it and looked out the peephole. She saw the Locos with guns in the apartment and called the number MAK gave her.

"Hello." MAK answered.

"Say, boy, some Mexicans just kicked in ya'll door. They got guns, too." She told him with a sense of urgency in her squeaky voice.

"What the fuck?" MAK said confused and agitated.

"Where ya'll at?" Sara asked MAK as she paced back and forth, her tiny feet moving fast on over the other.

"We good, but call the police for me. I'mma call Nessa."

Sara hung up and called 911 and told them what was going on.

Solis was 3 blocks away from where Tim wanted to meet. She called him.

"Hello." Tim answered soon as he saw her number.

"Hey, what's up? I'm right around the corner from you." She said ready to take him.

"Okay, you'll see a white mailbox. Just park and come on up. The door is open." Tim told her smiling to himself because he felt his plan was fail-proof.

She said okay and hung up. She told her team to get in position and let her know where they were.

Tim and Dragon were ready, locked and loaded. "No prisoner," Dragon told Tim then smiled.

The team let Solis know they were in position, so she pulled onto the block. When Tim and Dragon saw the light, they got ready. Solis pulled up, when they heard the car stop. Tim told Dragon, "It only sounds like one car."

Solis pushed redial on her phone and Tim's phone rang and she heard it coming from the bed of the pickup. She tried to restart the car. She knew it was a setup.

When they heard the car starting, they jumped up and started firing into Solis' car. One officer yelled "All units move in!"

Solis opened the door and rolled out on the ground but she had been hit multiple times. The armor piercing bullets ripped through her vest like it wasn't even there. The other units came at full speed.

Tim and Dragon opened fire on them so they had to take cover behind other cars on the street. Tim and Dragon jumped in the truck and sped off firing at the cops.

One officer got on the CB radio and called it in. "We got an officer down and shots fired… Suspects fled in a white pickup, older model. Officers in pursuit, request backup."

Cantu heard the call. "Shit! That's the fuckin' place. We need to hurry!" He yelled pissed Solis got there first.

Officers attended to Solis, while the rest went after Tim and Dragon.

"Solis breathe…come on breathe…you gotta breathe." The officer was giving Solis CPR. Solis was hit twice in the stomach, once in the shoulder and another bullet ripped through her rib cage. She was in bad shape. "Officer down, hurry. We got a fuckin' officer down!" The officer yelled into his radio as loud as he could.

Adams got to his car and helped Vanessa up. He wasn't paying attention to the radio calls, until he heard his name. "Adams, Adams where you at? Solis has been shot. Adams, do you copy?" The voice blared over the radio.

Adams grabbed the radio. "Repeat?" He said.

"Adams, Solis was set up. It was an ambush. They shot her. They fuckin' shot her man!" The voice screamed in panic.

"Where are ya'll at?" Adams asked. The Officer gave the address. Adams commanded the officers there to handle that and detain Vanessa. "Don't let her go." He yelled as he switched her to another car and ran back to his. He almost ran into EMS as he sped away. He raced the engine to 115 miles per house, the whole time thinking it was his fault Solis got shot. She told him to come and assist her.

"Please don't die, Petra, please. I'm sorry." Cried Adams as he banged his palm against the steering wheel.

Tim and Dragon raced down the alleys, barely missing people walking, slamming into potholes, sliding around corners. And at the last corner, they saw Cantu and his team coming down the street speeding.

Cantu saw the truck and said, "That's them. Hurry! Gun it! We got 'em." He yelled at the driver slapping his shoulder, jumping up and down like a mad man.

Dragon saw them coming. He backed up and told Tim to get out.

"Fuck you! What you mean get out?" Tim told him looking confused.

"Hey, kid, get out, and I'll get then to chase me. Once we're gone, you run to your car." Dragon said pushing Tim out the passenger side.

"What about you?" Tim asked.

"Don't worry 'bout me, just go." Dragon told him.

Tim hopped out and Dragon gunned it, and just like he thought Cantu was right behind him. Tim hid in a bush. Once they were gone, he came out running to his car. It was parked one more block down.

Cantu and his team were in pursuit of Dragon. The old pickup was doing 90 down the street. Cantu's truck had no sirens on it, so people thought it was trucks speeding through town.

Dragon was having fun looking in the rearview mirror talking to the cops. "Come on, lil' piggy. Can't you go any faster? I'm running, I'm running." He said in a sing-song tone over and over. He saw the highway on-ramp but decided the highway would be too easy. He'd rather stay on the busy street, make the chase last longer.

Blink and his gang took pictures of MAK, Vanessa and Tim from the house after they trashed it, then left.

MAK called Paulette but got no answer. He tried Tim's phone and he answered, "Hey, where you at man? Sara just told me some Mexicans just trashed the fuckin' apartment looking for something." MAK told him over speaker phone.

"Shit, I'm on my way to the hood. I'll check on it." Tim said.

"No, nigga, Sara said they got somebody watching the apartment in case me, you or Nessa try to go back so they can arrest us." MAK told him.

"I ain't going to the apartment. I'm going to pick up Tiffany." Tim told him smiling to himself.

"Tiffany? Nigga you wanted for murder and you worried 'bout some pussy?" MAK yelled at him not understanding his thinking.

"A murder YOU committed." Tim corrected him.

"Still, man, you trippin'. Fuck that girl man. Don't go out there. It ain't safe." MAK pleaded with him.

"Man, look, I'mma do me, you do you. Shit, you got me in enough trouble." He yelled the hung up/

MAK slammed on the gas. He tried to hurry to the apartments to stop Tim from getting jammed.

"Hello, 911, What's your emergency?" The operator said over the downstairs neighbors phone.

"Yes, I just heard a lot of gunshots in the upstairs apartment and it's supposed to be vacant." The old lady said. The shots woke her up.

"Where are you, ma'am? We'll send a unit." The operator asked her.

"I'm in the Rigsby Apartment # 2119 but the shots came from # 2120." The old lady informed her looking at her roof.

The dispatcher put out a call to a unit. The unit came back, "We already have a unit out there on a stakeout. Call them and let them check it out." The officer said.

"Okay, Unit 6." The dispatcher said. "Ma'am, we have a unit in the apartments. I'll call them and have them check it out for you." The dispatcher told the old lady.

"Okay, thank you." The old lady said.

The dispatcher called several times with no answer from the officers. Both officers were dead. Blink's soldiers made sure of that. The dispatcher called other units to go check out the shooting. "Unit

6, this is dispatch. I tried the stakeout. There's no answer. Please assist." The dispatcher told Unit 6.

"What the hell's going on tonight? Calls are coming in like crazy." Unit 6 said frustrated.

MAK turned the corner and next to the trail he saw Tim's car. "He must have walked through here to go get Tiffany," MAK said to himself. MAK got out and walked through the trail to the apartments. At the gate in the apartment, he could see Tim jumping over the security fence.

"Tim!" He yelled.

Tim turned around and saw MAK coming. "Shhh. If the police looking for me, you gon give me up, stupid." Tim said to MAK in a sarcastic but true tone.

"We need to talk, asshole." MAK told him.

"Well, walk with me." Tim told him.

"Where are you going?" MAK asked.

"To meet Tiffany." Tim said not looking back at MAK.

They walked through the apartments talking about what's going on.

MAK got his phone out and called Sara, "Hello. Boy, where you at?" Sara said looking out her living room blinds.

"We in the apartments. Meet us at Tiffany's house." MAK told her.

"Alright. I'm on my way." She said closing the blinds and grabbing her things.

They got to Tiffany's door and heard a loud scream.

Adams raced through traffic with his siren on full blast. A tear rolled down his cheek for his fallen partner. He got on his car radio, "What's her status. I repeat, what's her status? This is Adams." Adams yelled trying to hold back tears.

An officer came back over the police radio, "She's being worked on right now. They're trying to get a pulse. She's in bad shape, Dave."

The officer said with sympathy in his tone as he looked at Solis lying there helpless.

"No, don't tell me that. She's strong. She'll make it." Adams said, now crying uncontrollably.

"I hope so, buddy. We all hope so." The officer said his voice fading off.

EMS was on the scene trying to revive Solis. She flatlined twice. EMS was trying everything. They called the emergency helicopter to come take her to BAMC hospital ASAP.

"We got a pulse!" One of the medics yelled waving his arms trying to get their attention.

The officer on the police radio with Adams relayed the message to him.

Dragon raced down the busy one-way street laughing and shooting out the back window of the pickup. Cantu and his team had closed the distance. They were driving just as reckless as Dragon. Cantu knew he had to hurry and end this before other cars joined the chase.

"Stop those motherfuckers now!" Cantu yelled to the driver now buckling his seatbelt.

One officer used the pit maneuver on Dragon. Soon as the officer bumped the tailgate, Dragon went spinning out of control, slammed into a car at the stoplight and began to flip.

"Fuck, we need to get that fuckin' kid outta there." Cantu yelled as he watched the truck begin flipping.

The truck slammed onto the curb and threw Dragon about 30 yards. He landed on his neck and blood splattered like stepping on a ketchup packet. Cantu's men jumped out and ran to the truck, guns drawn. They looked in and there was nobody in the truck.

"Boss, no one's in there... No one." The confused officer told him looking around.

"That can't be. Where the fuck is he?" Cantu yelled feeling just as confused. "Go check that body and hurry the fuck up."

The officer checked Dragon's body. "It's an old man, boss." The officer yelled.

"Fuck, let's go. What the fuck did they do?" Cantu said, pissed. "Let's get back to where Solis is." He told them looking around.

Adams came around the corner and slammed on the brakes. He jumped out and ran to the EMS truck. They were leaving. "Where is she? Where is Solis?" He yelled as he ran over.

"They flew her to BAMC." One officer said.

"What the fuck went wrong here? I told her not to go in, just secure the house. And where the fuck is Cantu?" Adams was yelling and had no idea he was shedding tears as he stormed around.

"Sir, Cantu told Solis to give him an hour and he'll assist, but Solis insisted on going in alone and that we back her up from down the block." The officer pleaded with him.

Cantu and his team turned the corner as the EMS truck pulled away from the scene.

Chief Garz pulled to the scene and went berserk on everyone. "What the fuck happened here? Where in the fuck were you two? Got dammit Adams, you were in charge and you're off doing what?" Chief Garza yelled as spit flew from his mouth.

Adams dropped his head in shame.

"That was a fuckin' question, Adams. What were you doing while that poor girl was getting shot to death?" He shouted at Adams now getting in his face yelling.

"Sir, I was coming from the base checking on the guns when a call came in for a pregnant girl whose friend was being beaten with a pistol. I went to assist and found two dead women and I also found Tim's sister." Adams told him through saddened eyes.

"Tim as in the murder case you're working on Tim?" Chief Garz asked needing clarification.

"Yes sir." Adams told him.

"Where is she?" Chief Garza asked him.

"I told officers to detain her when I heard the call about Solis." Adams told him.

"Tim's sister made the call?" Chief Garza asked.

"Yes, sir. Her boyfriend's aunt was killed along with her friend, but whoever did it is looking for her brother, too." Adams told Chief.

"How do you know that?" Chief asked curious.

"Because they wrote 'Tim' on the table with her blood." Adams said looking awkward.

When Cantu heard that, he knew it was Rico's guys.

Chief told Adams, "You guys need to get a handle on this shit and find that fuckin' Tim before he hurts somebody else," He said it pointing back and forth at both of them.

"Sir, we need to go check on Solis, please." Adams said with concern about his partner.

"Go get the sister. Lock her ass up in a holding cell for questioning, then go see Solis." Chief shouted pulling off his wire-rim glasses.

Cantu cut in, "Look, sir, I'll go take care of the sister. Let Adams go see his partner in the hospital. She needs him." Cantu said seeing his moment to get some leverage on the diamonds.

"You sure, Cantu?" Chief said.

"Yeah, Chief. I got this one." Cantu yelled walking away.

MAK and Tim knew that scream. It was Sara. Tiffany opened the door but MAK and Tim took off running towards the scream. Tiffany came right behind them.

Sara was kicking and screaming as Blink's crew tussled with her.

"Bitch, where they at?" Blink said trying to contain her feisty little body.

"Fuck you, motherfucker! I don't know what ya'll talking about!" She yelled fighting back.

They slapped her around until Tim and MAK hit the corner. Tiffany hit the corner and stopped in her tracks. She saw 12 Mexicans around Sara and didn't know what to think.

"Wait here." Tim said, running off.

"Where are you going? She needs help." MAK said.

"Yeah, I got two of those straps we stole." Tim ran to his car to get the AKSU-74's. He got back and started shooting. The laser scope made it easy to hit his targets.

MAK and Tiffany were behind the building. They saw the bodies falling. Blink and his crew let go of Sara and started shooting back. Blink ran behind a truck in the parking lot. When he looked, he noticed it was Tim.

"Hey, it's that fucker, Tim. Don't kill him. We need the box." Blink yelled over the bass of the AKSU eruption.

"What the fuck, Blink? He's tryna kill us, man." One of the crew yelled while ducking for cover.

"Shoot the fucker but don't kill him, dude." Blink yelled from his own hiding spot.

Tim had more powerful and efficient weapons. So he kept the Locos ducking for cover. Plus, the AKSU-47 comes with a drum instead of clips like Blink's crew had. Sara was hiding behind the car scared to death with all the gunfire going on around her.

"Sara, run over here. Hurry up." Tim told her while shooting at any moving target.

"I can't. I'm scared, Tim." Sara yelled to him with her hands over her head.

"Get the fuck up or them Mexicans gon kill you ass." Tim shouted to her. Sara jumped up and ran to where Tim was.

"Don't let them get away." Blink said. His men focused their fire at her but Tim and the high-powered AKSU-74 was too much. The bullets ripped through cars like paper. Those same bullets ripped through Solis' vest and had her on life support.

Sara made it to where Tim was. MAK and Tiffany could see them, so they ran around the back side to meet with them. MAK pulled out his pistol just in case he ran into anybody around the corner.

Two police units pulled into the apartments to check on the shooting call in Unit 2120 and heard gunfire.

"This is Unit 6 to request back up in the Rigsby Court Apartments. Shots fired. I repeat, shots fired." The officers pulled to the side, got out of their cars and ran around the side of the wall. "This is the police. Put down your weapons." The officer yelled hoping they'd listen.

No one stopped shooting, so the officers opened fire with 12 gauge shotguns. The blast from the shotgun got everyone's attention. Blink's gang ducked for cover. They were in the middle of the crossfire, the police on one side and Tim on the other. While the Locos were hiding Tim, MAK, Sara and Tiffany ran for the trail in the back where the cars were parked.

Police were on the scene at Paulette's house taking the bodies away. Vanessa felt so bad. She tried MAK's phone again. He picked up.

"Oh, baby, she's dead. She's dead. They fuckin' killed her." She shouted excited to hear his voice.

"Vanessa, hold on. Who's dead and who killed her?" MAK yelled trying to comprehend what she was saying.

"Paulette and Debra. They're both dead. Some men came looking for Tim. They killed her and wrote Tim's name in blood on the table. Baby, what's going on?" She asked crying again.

"I'm on my way. I'm with Tim right now." MAK hung up in her face.

Cantu and his team pulled up to the scene. They got out and looked around.

"Hey Cantu, we got two bodies, both shot to death. What are you doing here? This isn't about drugs." One detective said.

"Yeah! I know. I'm here on other business. Where's the witness?" He said raising his aviator shades over his head looking around.

"She's over there in the car. Adams told us to detain her for questioning." The officer said pointing to the car she was in.

"I'll take her. We need to talk with her about these murders and a murder that happened two days ago." Cantu said with a grin. Cantu went over to where Vanessa was and got her out of the car. "Ma'am, come with me. We need to question you." Cantu told her holding the door open.

Vanessa had cried so much her eyes were puffy and she was weak in the knees. "Where is you boyfriend?"

"I got to call him to see. He said he was on his way out here." She said slightly hunched over.

"Is your brother with him?" Cantu asked.

"I... I... I don't know. Let me call them, please." Vanessa said looking nervously up and down then called MAK. "Hello, baby. Where are you?" Vanessa quietly asked MAK. "The police are taking me in for questioning. Can you hurry?" She told him looking in Cantu's direction.

"We are right around the corner, baby." MAK told her reassuring her.

"Who are you with, baby?" She whispered to him.

"I'm with Sara, Tiffany and Tim. Why?" MAK asked sensing something was wrong.

"Don't bring them. Come alone, please. Okay?" She whispered into the phone.

"Miss, is that your boyfriend?" Cantu asked anxiously.

"Yes, he's on the way alone." She kept trying to hint MAK not to bring Tim to the house. MAK knew his girl well because when they hung up MAK told Tim, "Say you can't come. The police are over here man. Wait down the street 'til I see what's up." MAK explained to him.

"Man, Paulette was like family to me. Man I'm fucking' sorry man. I didn't mean for nothing to happen to her." Tim said sincerely.

"Just stay down the street." MAK said with a hand gesture.

Cantu put Vanessa in the truck and cuffed her.

"What's this for? I didn't hurt nobody." Vanessa said angrily.

Cantu and the others got out the truck, Cantu told them to take her to the station, put her in a holding cell until he got there.

"Okay, boss." The officer said then he drove off.

"No. Where are we going? My boyfriend is on the way." Vanessa pleaded with them her eyes filling with tears again.

"Shut up. You're going downtown." One officer told her. On the way downtown, the officer thought about the million dollars and keeping it for himself. Make Vanessa call Tim and use her as a ransom for the box, but how would he get in touch with Rico, he thought to himself.

Tim parked down the street with Tiffany. MAK and Sara went down to Paulette's house. MAK saw the officers bringing the bodies out of the houses and he felt tears ball up in his eyes. He couldn't believe she was dead. Who could do this and why were they after Tim, he thought. He hopped out of the car and saw her, he fell apart. All the memories came back to him. She's been all the parent he ever had. Sara came to tears along with him. She didn't know Paulette but to see MAK all broke up, broke her up as well.

"Who are you?" An officer asked.

"My name is John Gaurdinier. This is my Aunt. What happened?" MAK was barely able to get the words out clearly.

"Well, according to your girlfriend, some guys pulled up in a black Suburban asking for her brother, then pulled out guns. Beat the lady over there until your Aunt opened the door. They killed the other lady first, then brought your Aunt over here and killed her. They really want your girl's brother. They even wrote his name in blood on the coffee table." The officer explained not showing any emotion or sympathy in his explanation.

"Are you serious? Where is my girl?" MAK asked looking around for Vanessa.

"Ask him." The officer pointed at Cantu who was across the street on his phone.

"Look, Rico, the sister is on her way to the station. I'll hold her til' the brother gets me the box. I think this is the boyfriend coming over to me right now." Cantu said to Rico in a hushed tone.

"Excuse me... Excuse me. That officer over there told me you could tell me what's up with my girlfriend, Vanessa Macias." MAK asked Cantu in an arrogant tone of voice.

"Let me talk to him." Rico told Cantu.

"No, I'll handle it." Cantu hung up. "Come over here, kid. Let me talk to you." Cantu said pointing to MAK to the side. Cantu took MAK over to where the rest of his team was in the other trucks. "Get in." Cantu said shoving MAK forward.

"What?" MAK said in a surprised tone. Sara was still talking with the other officers across the street, so she didn't see anything.

Cantu pulled out his gun, stuck it in MAK's stomach and repeated, "Get in." He said with aggression looking around, making sure no one saw. MAK got in the truck and saw the other officer's weapons pointer at him too.

"Man, what's going on?" He said nervously and confused.

"Shut the fuck up and listen." Cantu said now pointing the gun at MAK's face. "Your girlfriend's brother pissed off some pretty bad people. That trucker he killed worked for somebody who wants something he stole. A black box was in that truck. I can help him out but I need that box and I need it now. You go tell him I want that box tonight at midnight or you nor him will ever see that pretty lil pregnant Vanessa again." He told him with a smile of seriousness.

"What the fuck, mother fucker. Where's my-" MAK began to say before being cut short.

Cantu hit MAK in the mouth. "Watch you fuckin' mouth kid. Listen, tonight, bring the box to the old Butter Crust Factory off Commerce and New Braunfels or Vanessa's ass is dead, you hear me? Oh yeah, and you say a word to anybody, she dies. Now get the fuck out the truck and wipe you face, pussy." Cantu told him then slapped his cheek.

MAK got out, wiped his face and walked over to Sara. "Let's go." MAK told Sara with his head down looking disturbed.

"No, I need to speak with you. It'll only take a minute then you can go." The officer said.

Cantu blew the horn, rolled down the window and told the officer, "We'll be in touch. Oh, and John, take care. Sorry again for your loss." Then they drove off.

The officer questioned MAK for about 15 minutes and left. The only officers there were there to secure and investigate the crime scene. MAK knew the coke and guns were in there but it was under the floor in the back bedroom. He called Tim and told him what was going on.

Tim thought about the diamonds and said, "I don't know what they talking about."

MAK said, "Dawg, they got Nessa and killed my fuckin' Aunt, man. They think you got their box. I gotta get Nessa back, man." He told Tim in a stressed out tone.

"Chill, man. We'll think of something!" Tim told him trying to calm down.

MAK asked one officer was it alright if he got some clothes before he left. The officer said, "Sure, go ahead. We'll give you a few minutes alone."

MAK told Sara to come help him. They went to the back room. MAK grabbed a suitcase and opened the window. He told Sara to close the door. She closed it and he told her to help him move the floorboards. He got a couple packages of coke and four guns with plenty of ammo.

Sara asked, "Where all this shit come from? Is this why they came to ya'll house? Oh my God and killed your Aunt." She said nervous and upset.

"No, Sara. They say Tim stole some fuckin' black box. I don't know what's in the box but even the fuckin' police want it. Sara, they fuckin' got Nessa and said they gon' kill her if they don't get the box, and Tim say he don't know what they talking about." MAK explained to her as tears flowed down his cheeks.

"Oh my God, MAK. What you gon do? You need my help?" Sara told him saddened by the news.

"I don't know what I'mma do but I'd appreciate it if you'd stick around." He told her then grabbed her hand to let her know he was serious.

"You know I'm down. Just don't get me killed. Nessa is my friend. I'll do whatever, okay?" She assured him.

"Thanks, Sara. Right now, I need you to jump out this window and carry this suitcase to the back fence. Don't let the police see you." MAK told her as he struck the suitcase out the window.

Sara climbed out the window. MAK gave her the suitcase. She looked around. All the officers were by their cars talking. She ran the suitcase to the back gate.

"Put it over the fence." MAK whispered to her. She put it over the fence then came back. He helped her in the window. He grabbed some clothes and they left.

MAK called Tim and told him they were on their way.

"Say, that truck you got in is parked two spots away from us right now." Tim told him about the truck Cantu and the officers were in.

"What... What you mean?" MAK said looking around nervous.

"I mean the truck you got in a few minutes ago is not gone. They parked here by us." Tim explained while ducked down in the driver seat of his car looking at them.

"They want me to lead them to you. Fuck! Okay, look, stay where you at. I'll try and lose them in the neighborhood. Once we leave, go on the street behind the house, look in the backyard and get that suitcase and the guns." MAK told Tim.

MAK and Sara passed by Cantu and his crew, got to the corner and turned but Cantu didn't pull out.

"Why they not following us?" Sara asked curiously.

"I don't know. Call Tim and let him know." Sara called Tim and told him Cantu didn't follow them so don't move.

Cantu and his crew were waiting for the scene to clear so they could check the house for the black box. Cantu said he's not leaving one stone unturned. If MAK fell for the Vanessa thing, he'll get in touch with him and if he's got the box, he'll show tonight, but just in case, this house had to be checked.

At B.A.M.C Hospital, Solis was fighting for her life. The doctors were trying everything to save her. In the waiting room, Adams was in another world trying to put everything together.

Tim set up Petra and tried to kill her. Someone killed Tim's sister's boyfriend's aunt and neighbor, but for what? Then there was the call minutes ago about the shooting in the Rigsby Apartments and the stakeout unit getting killed. How did they know about the stakeout?

Nothing was making sense to Adams. He thought about Tim. He needed to make sense of the situation. What could Tim have done to get 2 people killed? Did the killings have something to do with the load he stole or the drugs or guns? Who wants these drugs and guns? California was his only thought. That's where he'd have to get his info.

He cracked his phone and noticed the phone tracker tech had called him over 10 times. He called back. The phone rang 4 times and the tech picked up.

"Hello, Adams. Where have you been, man? I've been trying to reach you all dam day. That fuckin' kid is playing games with you guys. I've been keeping track of all the places he's been getting calls and he was right behind you guys earlier." The tracker told him in his squeaky voice.

"Yeah? It's been a crazy day. Solis got shot by the fuckin' kid. I'm at the hospital now." Adams said sadly.

"I heard that over the radio and news. The kid used his phone about an hour ago at 11686 Delta Point. I've set the tracker to whenever he answers that phone I'll pick him up." The tech told Adams.

"I'm going to need your help. I gotta put this shit together. Call the number and once you pick him up, let me know where he's at." Adams instructed him.

The tech called the number. Tim answered, "Hello... Hello... Say something..." He said in the receiver. He hung up.

"He's still there, Adams, 11686 Delta Point." The tech told Adams

"What's he doing? That's the same area where his sister's boyfriend's family member got killed. What the fuck is he doing. I hate to leave Petra but I need to get a hold of this shit before any more people die." Adams said to the tech then grabbed his things and left.

Cantu's team leader was at the station with Vanessa.

"What happened to my fuckin' phone call. I ain't done shit. Why am I here?!" Vanessa yelled crying and banging the door.

"For such a pretty lady, you got a loud mouth you know that?" The guy said. "So you feel like talking, huh? Well, tell me, why did your brother do it?" The officer told her.

"Do what?" She asked curiously looking at the ground.

"Ah, come on. You know it's all over the news. He killed the truck driver and stole the load. So where'd he stash the stuff?" The officer told her.

"My brother ain't do shit and if he did, I wouldn't tell you." Vanessa shouted at him.

"That's okay, 'cause when we get that black box, we get a million dollars...and your brother is going to get his fuckin' head chopped off." The officer laughed and walked off.

Vanessa sat back and thought about what she just heard, then remembered all the new stuff, MAK coming home with that stack of money, then the old man on the news. "Oh my God, that's what this is all about. MAK fuckin' lied to me. Was he involved in the murder, too?" She thought to herself.

"Ahh! Help, help! I think I'm going into labor! Please help!" Vanessa yelled for help. She had to get out of that cell and to a phone. She had to warn Tim and MAK.

The officer and a female officer came to the cell. "What's wrong, ma'am?" The female officer asked.

"I think I'm going into labor. Please help me." Then Vanessa fell to the floor causing a scene. "Oh my God. Go get help."

"It's okay, ma'am, come on. Let me help you. What's she in here for?" She asked the team leader.

"Questioning-" The officer mumbled but was cut off.

"So she's not under arrest?" The nurse said.

"Uh-uh. No, not at the moment but-"

"But nothing. If she's not under arrest, we need to get her to a hospital. Move." She said. She pushed past the team leader and got to the front desk and called for an ambulance. The team leader didn't know what to do. He went to the back and called Cantu.

Vanessa told the nurse, "I need to call my boyfriend, please." She said through tears.

"Sure. Use this phone right here." The officer told her handing her the phone.

She called MAK's number. No answer. "Come on babe, please don't ignore me right now." The answering machine picked up; she left a message. "Babe, it's me I'm at the police station, but I'm on my way to the hospital. An officer told me Tim killed a truck driver, stole his load and he has a black box worth a million dollars, but once they get it they're going to kill him. You got-" Beep. The answering machine hung up. "Damn!" Vanessa hung up.

"Did you get in touch with him, ma'am?" The female officer said.

"No." Vanessa said very frustrated.

"Well, you can call from the hospital. EMS is going to take too long. I'm going to run you to the University Hospital. Is that okay?" The female officer said.

"Yeah! Please, I just need to hurry." Vanessa said moaning as if she were in severe pain.

"Okay, let's go. Can you walk?" The officer asked her.

"Yeah. I think so." Vanessa said. They got in the officer's car and left.

Cantu looked at his phone but didn't answer it. He was focused on the house. "That million dollars is in the house. We just got to be patient." He said to the other guys in the truck.

"Come on, Cantu fucker." The team leader said as he waited on the ringing phone. "Fuck!" He said then hung up. He went back to the front and sat in one of the chairs.

"Can I help you?" One of the nurses said.

"No. I'm with the pregnant girl?" he responded.

"The one that was just up here 5 seconds ago." He said now sitting up straight.

"Well, I just got here and nobody was here." The nurse said.

"The fuckin' lady was calling an ambulance for her. She was going into labor." He said now getting aggivated.

"Sgt. Little?" The nurse asked.

"I don't fuckin' remember her name. She was short and blonde, her hair was in a ponytail." He said to her.

"Yeah, that was Sgt. Little. I don't know where she is." The nurse told him while straightening up her desk.

"Well, can you find her, please?" He said then he got his phone out and tried Cantu again.

Rico was at the Hotel looking at the news. He saw the Rigsby incident. All the Westside Locos were killed by S.W.A.T., but officers were killed in the shootout as well. Hector had already called with news of what happened at Paulette's. Rico told him not to come back without Vanessa or the box.

Rico called Cantu. The phone rang twice. "Hello, Rico. What is it?" Cantu yelled into the phone.

"Have you seen all the news? You guys aren't doing too well. How did a kid manage to kill one of your officers and come away clean?" Rico growled with sarcasm and disgust as he paced back and forth.

"Did you call me to complain or do you want something?" Cantu growled back at Rico.

"I want my box tonight at midnight, Cantu." Rico shouted in the phone.

Hector and the crew wanted to go to the Rigsby, but police were everywhere, so they switched cars to go back out to Paulette's house to see what may pop up.

MAK and Sara were on the access road waiting for Tim to call back to see if he was okay.

"We need to go back and pick up that stuff you threw over the fence. It looks like Tim and Tiff are stuck for a while." MAK told Sara.

"You sure you want to go back now? They might think something if they see us come through again." Sara told MAK in a scared voice thinking cautious.

"I know. That's why they not gon see us. We gon park and walk over there." MAK explained to her as he drove.

Tim and Tiffany were getting restless sitting and waiting, then all the police started packing up and leaving. Once all the cars left, Cantu and his team went down to the house. Tim and Tiffany pulled away slowly after everything was clear. They pulled up to the house where MAK left the guns. Tiffany jumped out and ran to the back fence and grabbed it.

As they were pulling away, they saw Sara and MAK. Tim said, "Get in."

"We parked over there. We thought ya'll was going to be stuck for a while." MAK told them looking around nervously.

"What's the plan?" Tim asked.

"Man, we gotta get that box to that dude by midnight or he gon kill Vanessa." MAK told all of them with pain in his voice.

"I don't know what they're talking 'bout. All I saw was dope and guns man. I swear" Tim said, knowing he was telling a lie. Greed motivated him.

Cantu and his team were in the house going through everything trying to find the box.

"I want everything turned inside out, you here me?" Cantu yelled as he flipped couches, chairs, drawers and closets.

It was already 9:30 PM and MAK had no idea how he was going to get his Nessa back. Then Sara said, "Hey, I got an idea. Let's call the police, tell them everything about the box and them kidnapping Nessa. Tell them where to meet us and then they can catch dirty cop and we get Nessa back."

"It sounds good, but what if they alert the officer who has her and he kills her anyway? He said don't say shit to nobody." MAK said remembering his conversation with Cantu.

"Well, we just can't sit around, time is running short." She said.

Tim's phone rang. He looked at it and it was Eddie. He mumbled so no one could hear him talk.

"Hey, what's up Eddie? Please have good news for me?" He said under his breath.

"Yeah, kid, my guy in Houston said if we can come to Houston he can unload the whole thing for us." Eddie told him.

"Are you serious, man?" Tim said excitedly.

"Yeah, kid. He said he made some calls and there's a couple guys looking to buy big end shit." Eddie told him.

"Where you at?" He told Eddie, not whispering.

"Look kid, meet me at the Canyon Lake house."

"Alright, we're on our way." He told Eddie.

Only one thing on Tim's mind was money; Greed had overtaken him. He didn't care about his sister or MAK's feelings for her. He was wanted for murder and he was trying to get money and run for it.

"Come on guys. I got somebody who gon try and help us. Follow me." Tim said to them as he started the car. Sara and MAK got out of Tim's car and followed them to Eddie's place out by the lake.

The phone tech called Adams. Adams answered right away, "Yeah, what is it?" Adams said hoping for good news.

"He's moving. He's not out there no more. He's moving down 35, headed south." The tech informed him.

"Hey, call Cantu and tell him to load his team and direct them to me." Adams told the tech rushing to solve the case.

Vanessa was thinking of her next move. She had to get in touch with Tim and MAK. "Can I trust this lady?" She thought to herself. She wanted to tell her what the officer told her about the black box and the money but was scared she wouldn't believe her.

On the way to the Canyon Lake house, Eddie stopped and picked up his gun from the shop. Then he headed to the house. The guys he got in contact with were ready to pay a lot for the diamonds. He told them he was thinking about selling the shop and retiring for good off this deal. He pulled up to the house. It was a mile away from the lake. It was big cabin style house, a lot of trees, very dark without lights. He got out and turned the truck off. He went inside and cut the lights on and looked around. He hadn't been out here for a while. He grabbed a beer and waited.

The tech called Cantu and told him Adams needed his back up with Tim. Cantu told his team to move out. They were going after Tim again. Just as they were leaving, Hector and his crew passed by the house. Hector recognized Cantu and decided to follow them. They looked like they were in a hurry.

Cantu called Adams on the radio, "Adams, this is Cantu, do you copy?" Cantu yelled over the radio.

"Copy, what's your 20?" Adams asked.

"I'm headed south on 35 like the tech said." Cantu told him.

"Okay, good. We don't know where he's at, but the tech is tracking him now so keep coming until he gives the word." Adams told him.

"Roger that." Cantu said.

Vanessa and Sgt. Little pulled up to the University Hospital and Sgt. Little asked Vanessa if she could walk.

"Yeah, I think so, but can I try my boyfriend again?" Vanessa pleaded with the Sgt.

"Sure, use my phone." Little told her handing her the old cell phone.

Vanessa dialed and Sara picked up. "Hello…Hello." Sara yelled, but the reception out by the lake was no good.

"Hello? Who is this? I can't hear you." Vanessa said on the other end beginning to cry.

"Who was that?"

"I don't know, it hung up." Vanessa told the Sgt.

"Well, try again." The Sgt. told her.

She tried but the call was dropped again. She started to cry and the Sgt. helped her up, they walked toward the hospital doors.

"Who was that?" MAK asked.

"I don't know. It hung up before I could hear anything." Sara said looking back at the callerID. "210-664-1938 sound familiar?" Sara said shouting out the number.

"No. Call back whenever we get where ever the fuck we going." MAK told her.

Tim's phone rang, it was Vanessa calling from the Sgt.'s phone, but the call had a lot of static. Tim couldn't hear her.

The tech picked him up and called Adams. "He just exited 181 out by Canyon Lake, buddy." The tech told Adams.

"Alright, I'm on it. Keep calling every few seconds to keep me in view." Adams told him stepping on the gas trying to close the gap.

Tim pulled up to the cabin and saw Eddie's truck outside. They got out and he came to the door.

"Hey, kid. What's all this?" Eddie said looking confused.

"These are my friends and you remember MAK, my sister's boyfriend, right?" Tim said to him.

"Hey, Eddie." MAK said.

"Come on in." Eddie told them. They all came in and sat down. MAK got the stuff out the car and brought it inside.

"Hey Eddie, is it okay if we get high right quick?" Tim asked Eddie needing to shake off some problems.

"Sure kid, whatever." Eddie told him.

"How can you get high at a time like this?" Sara said to Tim.

"Look girl, my nerves are bad. I need to mellow out. Besides, mind ya own, alright?" Tim told her with a hint of aggression.

"Your fuckin' sister needs help and you wanna get high? That's sad." Sara said snapping at him.

"Ya'll chill." MAK said trying to calm the situation.

The tech called Tim's phone and he answered, "Hello…Hello… Who is this?" Tim said yelling into the phone.

"Uh, it's Frank. How do I get to your store?" The tech said, making up something so he could zero in on Tim's exact spot. He noticed the dot stopped moving on the GPS.

"What do you mean?" Tim said confused.

"Nevermind. I must got the wrong number." The tech said then hung up. "Gotcha, kid." He called Adams. "He stopped at 409 Lake View Run. I'll call the local authorities and have them on alert in the area." The tech said.

Adams entered the address in his GPS and headed for the house. He called Cantu and gave him the address and told him make sure they don't let the kid get away.

Tim, MAK, Sara and Tiffany were in the living room. Eddie was in the back garage. He called Tim out back. The room was set up for carpentry work but it had an office.

Tim left his phone on the couch and it started ringing. Tiff handed it to MAK and he answered it. It was Hector. "Hello." MAK said trying to hear through the static.

"Well, well, well. Where have you been hiding all day?" Hector said with his accent sounding happy to hear this voice.

"Who is this?" MAK said.

"This is your worst nightmare. I need that box kid. I've been looking for you all day. Look, you killed my worker and that's cool. I know sometimes people get into a jam and robbery is the only option."

MAK got up and walked to the kitchen. "How do you know it was me?" MAK asked as if he was Tim.

"Because, stupid, you're using Jose's phone. How do you think I found you?" Hector told him laughing now.

"Holy shit." MAK said to himself. "What do you want?" He asked.

"The box. That's all. You can keep the dope and the guns. I just need that box. The police are on their way right now. They've been tracking you through this phone. Give me back the box and I can promise this will all go away." Hector told him in a sinister whisper.

"But we don't got the box, man. It was no box in there." MAK assured him.

"Sure it was, but since you don't have it. I can't help." Hector told him now raising his voice.

"What if we find it can you get my girl back from the cop?" MAK asked him.

"You find the box, call this number and we'll swap but you better hurry. The police are on their way." Then Hector hung up.

MAK went back to the front and told the girls what Hector said. He went back to tell Tim but when he walked into the carpentry room, the office door was closed. He walked in without knocking and on the table was the black box full of diamonds. Tim and Eddie were counting them out.

"Hey, get the fuck outta here." Tim told MAK. Then he pushed him out the office and closed the door behind them.

"What the fuck, nigga? Is that what the fuck everybody talking 'bout, that fuckin' box?" MAK yelled trying to get past Tim to get to the office.

"Chill, nigga, chill… You trippin', let me explain." Tim said pushing MAK in the chest.

"Let you explain? Motherfucker, they got yo sister and you lying saying you ain't got it! What the fuck ya'll fina do with the shit?" MAK shouted pointing to the office.

While MAK and Tim were arguing outside the door, Eddie grabbed all the diamonds, put them in a plastic bag, stuffed it in his pocket, closed the black box and grabbed his gun.

Outside the cabin, Adams and Cantu's team surrounded the cabin, ready to take whoever was in there down.

"Remember, we need the kid alive." Cantu said.

Sara looked at MAK's phone and dialed the number back that had called.

"Hello, Sgt. Little. Who is this?" Sgt. Little answered in her Alabama accent.

"Hello, did you just called this number?" Sara asked.

"Who is this?" Little asked.

"I'm a friend of MAK's. I have his phone right now and earlier, well, a few minutes ago someone called but the call was dropped." Sara told her.

"Oh yeah! The pregnant girl used the phone. She was trying to call her boyfriend." Little told her smiling as she talked her ocean blue eyes wandering as they always do.

"You mean Vanessa?" Sara said excited.

"Yeah, I think so." Little said playing with her blonde ponytail.

"Where is she?" Sara asked in panic.

"We're at the University Hospital. She thinks she's going into labor." Little explained to Sara.

"Please, Miss, you have to help her. They said they were going to kill her at midnight if they don't get some black box." Sara started explaining.

"Who said that?" Little said now paying attention. She began biting her bottom lip.

"Some police officer. It has something to do with an 18-wheeler being jacked." Then Sara heard fighting in the background.

MAK hit Tim in the face. Tim fell over a bucket in the floor… He grabbed MAK's leg and tripped him. They were exchanging blows until Eddie came out the office with the gun.

"Stop that shit. Get the fuck up!" Eddie yelled. And as they did, he hit MAK in the head with the gun. MAK fell to the floor but crawled to the other side of the carpentry table.

"Eddie, look, man, I need those diamonds. They have my girl and they gon kill her if they don't get them at midnight man, please." MAK pleaded with Eddie as blood leaked from his head.

"What's he talking about, Tim?" Eddie asked Tim pointing the shotgun his direction.

"He's a fuckin' liar. He wants them for himself. Shoot 'em, Eddie and let's go." Tim said pointing at MAK.

"What the fuck you mean shoot me? I'm your friend, man. What's wrong with you?" MAK said not believing what he was hearing.

"Fuck you. I told you don't shoot that guy and you did. Now I'm wanted for murder. I'm through with your ass." Tim yelled over the table to MAK.

"What about your sister?" MAK asked.

There was another sawed-off shotgun in the office behind the door. MAK could see it from where he stood.

Eddie said, "I don't give a fuck about none of this shit. There's a lot of money for these diamonds and they're getting cashed in one way or another."

Outside the cabin, Cantu's two men went to the backside of the house. Cantu was in front with Adams and two more officers. Cantu looked through the window and saw Tiffany on the couch snorting lines, but he didn't see Tim.

"I don't see him." Cantu told Adams in a whisper.

"Nobody move til' we see Tim's face." Adams said over the police radio.

Tiffany heard the police radio and looked out the window. She saw one of the officer's shadow behind MAK's car. She told Sara, "Hey, somebody out there. I see a shadow behind the car."

"Wait, girl. I gotta tell MAK that Vanessa is at the hospital." Sara ignored her comment and ran to tell MAK.

"I'm for real. I saw somebody." Tiffany said feeling paranoid.

As Sara came around the corner to give MAK the news about Vanessa, she saw the confusion.

While Eddie talked and pointed the gun Tim said, "Shoot him and let's go get this money."

Sara saw the black box in Eddie's hand. The look on MAK's face told her something was wrong. As she stepped back, she got back on the phone with Sgt. Little and told her somebody had a gun on Vanessa's boyfriend and he had the black box everybody was after.

Sgt. Little saw Vanessa come from the back changing and told her what Sara told her. Vanessa started to cry and let Sgt. Little know what was going on. She told her about Paulette's house, the killings and the officer telling her a million dollars was on the line for the box. Sgt. Little was in shock and told Vanessa she won't let anything happen to her, her baby, or her baby's father.

They got back on the phone. "Where are you all now?" She asked Sara.

"We're out at Canyon Lake at some guy's house." Sara said to her in a hushed tone. "Tim said it was a friend of his, but the guy has a gun on MAK." Just then, Sara heard two gunshots and ducked into one of the rooms. "Someone just shot." She told Sgt. Little as she scurried for cover.

"What the fuck man… What are you doing?" MAK yelled at Eddie as he scrabbled around the room. Eddie shot Tim then tried to shoot MAK but missed. MAK hid behind the tool boxes and tried to talk to Eddie.

"Come out or I'll kill him." Eddie told MAK. Tim was hit in the shoulder but was on the ground with the gun aimed at his head.

"Eddie, chill man please. I'm comin' out." MAK could see the shotgun, but wasn't sure if it was even loaded. But he had to try. If he came out he was dead for sure.

He grabbed a monkey wrench and threw it around the tool box. When Eddie ducked, MAK dived in the office, grabbed the shotgun and pulled the trigger. One loud blast erupted from the barrel and knocked splinters out of the wood table in the carpentry room. Eddie ducked over for cover and ran out the room.

He stood at the doorway and yelled around the door. "You only got 5 more shots, kid. Better make 'em count cause I'ma kill yo ass and saw you and your little homeboy over there on the floor tried to rob me like you did the 18-wheeler guy." Then he laughed.

Sara hid in the other room in the closet, she still had Sgt. Little on the phone. Tiffany was hiding in the front closet after she heard the shots.

The officers were being cautious but they needed to hurry before the girls got hurt or whoever owned this house. They had no idea the homeowner was the aggressor.

At the back doors, the officers could hear the shots inside so they kicked in the door and rushed in. "Police!" They yelled as they filled in. they saw Eddie.

"Officers! They're in here. They tried to rob me. I shot one of them but that one is armed. Please help!" Eddie yelled to the officers from the carpentry room.

MAK peeked around the corner and saw that Tim was crawling towards him and was bleeding bad. Eddie was not in the room but MAK could see his shadow at the door. There was a window in the office. MAK shot the light out in the room so it was dark except for outside light bleeding in.

Cantu kicked in the front door gun drawn. Adams and the other two followed behind him. Tiffany was in the closet where MAK put the guns and dope. It wasn't closed all the way. When she saw the police badges, she was about to come out until Cantu told his two tea, members, "Handle him. I'll get the box."

Adams looked confused. Then the two officers opened fire at close range. The bullets knocked Adams off his feet and to the floor. His gun flew out his hand. It slid by the closet door. Tiffany could see it. She put her hand to her mouth to hold back her scream.

Eddie heard the shots and turned to the direction of the shots. "Who's there?" He yelled through the house.

"Police. Sir, put your weapon down. It's okay." Cantu told him.

"They're in there."

"Who's there sir?" Cantu asked looking around.

"The guy Tim that the cops are looking for tried to rob me." Eddie told him pointing down the hall.

MAK crawled to the window, jumped out, but kept the shotgun.

"Put your weapon down, sir." Cantu told Eddie. Eddie put the gun down and before he could react, Cantu shot him between the eyes. "Get the kid and let's go, hurry." Cantu told the two who came through the back, but before they grabbed Tim, the officer saw the box under Eddie's body.

"Cantu, the box. There it is." They guy said. He handed the box to Cantu. Just then they heard police sirens outside.

"Fuck, let's hurry. Get out of here." Cantu ordered. They went out the back door. Cantu fired a shot that hit Tim in the chest. "That's for Solis." He told Tim as he exitted the house.

"Freeze!" The local Canyon Lake police yelled as Cantu and the team ran out. Cantu turned and showed his badge. "We're in pursuit of another suspect. He went that way." Cantu said pointing north of the lake.

Canyon Lake police were not trained to handle these type of situations, so they were dumbfounded. "What do you want is to do?" He asked Cantu.

"Go back to your vehicles and let us handle this." Cantu said now patting the officer on the back.

"Are you sure?" The officer said looking into Cantu's big face.

"Yeah, we can handle this, but you know what, check the house cause there was a female. She might be upstairs." Cantu told him. The officer ran upstairs with his partner. Cantu and his team jumped in the trucks and drove away.

Adams crawled for his weapon. His vest caught all the bullets. They knocked the wind out of him. When he saw Tiffany, she was crying.

"Are you okay, sir?" She mumbled from the closet.

"Yeah! Help me up." He asked trying to catch his breath. She came out and started helping him up when the other officers came back down stairs.

"Freeze, on the ground, ma'am!" The Canyon Lake officers yelled pointing their weapons.

"It's okay. She's cool." Adams said slowly getting up with Tiffany's help. "Where did those other officers go? They're dirty. They shot me." Adams told him.

"Oh my God. Are you okay?" The officers said in surprise.

"Yeah, but we're going to need help." Adams said reaching for his phone.

MAK snuck in the back door to check on Tim. He was dead. Tears came to MAK's eyes. He saw the bag in Eddie's pocket so he grabbed it and ran to his car, jumped in and left.

Sara peeked out the closet when she heard Tiffany yelling.

"It's okay. Come out." Tiffany said as she walked down the hall. Adams and Tiffany came around the corner and saw Eddie's head cocked to the side and blood all over the wall behind him. Then they saw Tim.

Tiffany fell to the floor yelling and screaming, "No, Tim, no!" Tiffany yelled getting weak in the knees. Sara heard her so she came out. When she walked out she scared everybody.

"Where were you?" Adams asked her.

"In the closet. They started shooting, so I hid." She said with her hands up. She saw Tim and started to cry. She told Sgt. Little, who was still on the phone, "They killed him. The fuckin' police killed him." She yelled to Little.

"Killed who, ma'am?" Sgt. Little asked curiously.

"Tim. He's dead." Sara managed to say.

"Oh my God!" Sgt. Little said now concerned. She looked at Vanessa and Vanessa saw the look of sadness in her eyes.

"What happened? Please tell me they're okay." Vanessa said.

"Tim's dead." Little told her.

Vanessa let out a scream that scared all the people in the hospital rooms. "NO, NO, NO! Where's John? Where's John? Is he okay?" She yelled as she grabbed her stomach.

"Sara, where's John?" Sgt. Little asked.

"I don't know. He was here, but he's not. They told him they had Vanessa. He might be gone after them." Sara told her looking around the house.

"Who is that?" Adams said looking in Sara's direction.

"Sgt. Little, she with Vanessa."

Adams got on the phone and told Sgt. Little to protect Vanessa with her life and don't let her out of sight.

"She's in good hands, Adams." Sgt. Little told him. "What are you going to do?" She asked Adams.

"I gotta go help her boyfriend. They'll kill him if he tries to get in their way. He shot me."

"Who? John?" Sgt. Little asked.

"No, Cantu." Adams said.

"You're going to need help, Adams." She told him.

"Yeah, I know. We'll call it in, but not over the police radio cause he'll pick it up. Use cell phones." He told her. He asked Sara did she know where they were going.

"Yes! They're supposed to meet at the old Butter Crust factory on Commerce tonight at midnight." She said biting on her already shredded nails.

Cantu called Rico. "Hello, Mario. Do you have good news for me?" Rico said as soon as he picked up.

"Yeah. Do you got a million dollars for me?" Cantu said in a cocky voice, looking at the box.

"Let's talk. Meet me at the motel." Rico told him feeling satisfied. Rico was ready to get this over with and get back home to his good life.

MAK got on the freeway and called Hector. The phone rang 4 times then he picked up, "Hola, Tim do you have something for me?" Hector said with a smile.

"Yeah, I got the fuckin' diamonds and Tim's dead. That fuckin' cop killed him. I'm his brother and before you get these diamonds, I wanna see my girl." MAK demanded shaking his head looking in the passenger seat at the diamonds.

"Sure, kid. Where you wanna meet?" Hector told him rubbing his huge hands across the dashboard.

"The same place. The Butter Crust factory." MAK told him.

"Got it. Bring those diamonds." Hector said.

Adams told the Canyon Lake police to get S.A.P.D out there and secure the house. "Call EMS and if anybody asks what happened have them call this number." Adams said to the Canyon Lake police. Adams left to try and help MAK before he got himself killed.

Sara told Tiffany, "We gotta go help MAK." Sara said feeling helpless.

"What can we do?" Tiffany asked curiously.

"Where did MAK put those guns?" Sara asked looking around.

"In that closet over there." Tiffany said remembering seeing them.

Tim's keys were on the table so they grabbed the bags, the keys and left before the officers started questioning them.

Sara called Tim's phone. "What?" MAK answered in an angry tone.

"Where are you? This is Sara. Me and Tiff are on the way. We got the guns you had." Sara said trying to ensure MAK was not alone.

"Where's the police?" MAK began to ask. Then the call was dropped. MAK's battery was going dead.

"Fuck." Sara said.

"What happened?" Tiffany asked her as she swerved in and out of traffic.

"The damn battery died." Sara said frustrated.

"Plug it in the lighter, hurry." Tiffany said looking from the road to Sara. "Why didn't you tell him Vanessa's okay?"

"The fuckin' battery died. Didn't you hear me? Do you know where the Butter Crust factory is?" Sara yelled.

"Yeah. Do you know how to use a gun?" Tiffany shot back.

"I've seen it in movies. I'll figure it out. If I have to." Sara said looking back at the gun.

"Well, we gon have to." Tiffany said.

Hector called Rico. "Hola, Hector. The job is done. The box is on the way." Rico said with joy in his voice.

"Yeah, I know. I just talked to the kid. He wants to meet but he says without his girl, we don't get the diamonds." Hector told Rico, putting a pin in his balloon.

"What kid?" Rico said now looking sick in the face. "Mario said he killed the kid and he had the box. He's on his way now." Rico told Hector.

"Well, Tim's brother said Mario killed Tim, but he has the diamonds and how would he know it's diamonds we're after if he hasn't seen them?" Hector reassured Rico about the content.

"Look, Hector. I don't know what's going on, but we need those diamonds. Meet that kid and don't let him leave." Rico hung up and called Cantu.

"Hey, I'm down the street Rico. Give me a minute." Cantu said confidently.

"Do you have the box?" Rico said agitated with his hand on his hip.

"Yeah, why?" Cantu said curiously.

"My guy just got a call and some kid told him he has the contents of the box in his possession and they are going to meet but he wants his girlfriend. Do you know anything about that?" Rico asked him in a drill sergeant tone.

"Wait. What do you mean he has the content of the box?" Cantu asked looking at the box.

"Evidently you're holding a useless box, asshole. Shake it and tell me what you hear.

Cantu shook the box and heard nothing. "I don't hear shit." Cantu said.

"That's because ain't shit in it. The kid's got the shit." Rico told him slapping a shot glass off the table.

CHAPTER 8

Adams got on his phone and called the chief. The phone rang 6 times.

"Hello. Ok" Chief answered.

"Chief, it's Adams." Adams said sounding in panic.

"Adams, you do know it's 11:30 at night. This better be an emergency." Chief told him reaching for his glasses.

"It is. Cantu's dirty. He set me up and had me shot. Lucky I had on my vest. He's after some black box that was in the truck that came from California with the dope and guns. There's some guy paying a million for that box and kid, Tim, but Tim is dead. Cantu killed him but Tim's brother-in-law was told that they kidnapped his girlfriend and they were going to kill her if they don't get the box. The bad thing is Cantu lied. The girl is safe. She is with Sgt. Little at the University Hospital, but the boy doesn't know that yet. He thinks they have her." Adams told the Chief dodging cars as he drove up to 100 miles per hour.

"When did all this happen, Adams?" The Chief asked now sitting up on the side of his bed and clicking on the night lamp.

"Tonight, but we need to hurry. They're meeting at midnight at the old Butter Crust factory. The kid's going to get himself killed if we don't help." Adams said breathing fast, trying to get every detail out clear.

"Okay, I'll get S.W.A.T. together and we'll meet you there." Chief told him as he started getting dressed.

"Meet me at the carwash around the corner." Adams told him.

"Okay." Chief said.

"Chief, bring the helicopters. We might need them", Adams said.

"Roger that and Adams don't get shot again." Then they hung up.

Sgt. Little and Vanessa were in the parking lot. Vanessa was broken up about Tim and everything going on. I got some place you'll be safe until we hear from your boyfriend or the other girls, Little told her, *"No I gotta get to John. Please. We gotta help him or they'll kill him."*

"No, they don't. Adams is on the way to help him"

"Help him? The police are the one's killing everybody", "Calm down I trust Adams and you can trust me okay? Now come on. Calm down and let's get away from here somewhere safe." Vanessa went back in to get her stuff together while Sgt. Little waited by her car.

Cantu went crazy when Rico told him the other kid had the contents of the box. He called the leader to bring him Vanessa, "Hello, bring that bitch to me now! I'll be at the YMCA on Commerce"

"Boss, she's gone"

"Gone? Gone? What the fuck do you mean gone? I told you to keep her locked up."

"Yeah she was but then she started having labor pains and some Sgt. Lady came and pulled her out of the cell. When I stepped to the side to call you, I turned around and they were gone"

"Gone where, stupid?"

"I don't know."

"I don't know. I asked around, but no one seen them."

"Tell them to page her, call her or whatever they have to do to find her. Tell them the girl's a suspect in a murder and we need her"

"Yes, sir!" He said. They hung up. Cantu dropped his head in his hands. *"This shit is falling apart. I can't believe this shit"* he said to no one in general.

At the station, the team leader went to the desk and asked the receptionist, "What did you say that lady's name was again?", "Sgt. Little"

"I just talked to my boss and we need that girl now! She's our suspect in a murder and we need to question her"

"Let me check the in and out logs. Maybe Sgt. Little went on break".

The lady check the log and it read University Hospital transport, *"sir, she's out on a transport to University Hospital"* before she could finish he was out the door in full sprint. He called Cantu back, the phone was answered on the first ring

"What? University Hospital. Get there."

"The Sgt. Bitch took her to the hospital." the officer said.

Cantu hung up and told his driver *"Go to the University Hospital now!"*

Sgt. Little's phone rang *"Hello, this is Little"* she said. *"Hey, Sgt. this is Lucy from the station. An officer is on his way to you right now. He says that girl you're with is wanted for a murder. She's the suspect"*

"Fuck, he's lying Lucy. They're trying to kill her. Thanks for calling." Little hung up and ran into the hospital.

Rico called Hector, *"Hola, Rico"* he said. *"Come get me. I'm going with you to make sure we get these diamonds and make sure nothing else goes wrong"*

"I'm on my way" Hector said. They hung up. Rico grabbed his gun and went downstairs in the lobby to wait.

MAK pulled up to the Butter Crust factory, no sign of anyone so he parked and got out. He broke out the window and climbed in. There were many offices, stairs, curves, hiding spots and possible weapons. He still had the shotgun with him but only a few shots.

He went upstairs to an office where he could see down to the parking lot and it was high enough so he could see down both streets, Commerce and New Braunfels Avenue. He hid half the diamonds. Then he put the other half in his pocket. He'd use the other half for insurance to make sure they'd give him Vanessa.

Tim's phone rang. MAK answered it but then remembered Hector told him the police were tracking him so he hung up fast, but it was too late. The tech had him already.

"He's at the factory, Adams." The tech told Adams.

"Damn it. He thinks they have his girl. He's going to get killed. Try and call him back and tell him his girl is safe. They lied. They don't have her." He told the tech.

"Yes, sir. But what if he don't answer?"

"Text him."

"Okay, I'm on it." The tech said.

Adams other line clicked. "Call me back," he told the tech. "Hello?" He answered on the other line.

"They're on the way. They found out she's here." Little said to Adams with heavy breathing.

"How do you know that?" Adams said.

"The receptionist at the station just called me and told me an officer told her the girl was wanted for murder and they need to question her. When she told them where we were, he ran to the door." Sgt. Little explained breathing heavy.

"Both of you get out there fast as you can. Cantu will kill. Don't trust nobody at this point. Just get out of the hospital." Adams instructed her.

"Okay, bye." Little said.

"Hey, Little." Adams said.

"Yeah?"

"Be careful, please." Adams told her.

Sara and Tiffany decided to go to the hospital to get Vanessa. They were down the street from the exit to the University.

"Is that damn phone charged yet?" Tiffany asked Sara.

"I got like two bars." Sara said staring at the phone. Sara called the number back and Sgt. Little answered.

"Hello, is this Sgt. Little? Where is Vanessa?"

"I'm going to get her right now. Those police are on their way up here." Sgt. Little said nervously with shaking in her voice.

"She said they on their way to get him." Sara said to Tiffany looking scared.

"Who?" Tiffany said.

"The crooked police." Sara told her sounding disturbed.

"Tell her we'll pick them up by the tracks. We're down the street." Tiffany told her, trying to give Little and Vanessa a getaway. Little agreed and they hung up.

"Get one of those fuckin' guns out that bag." Tiffany told Sara. Sara got one of the AKSU's out the bag and looked at it.

"Girl, what the fuck is this?" Sara said looking confused at the military weapon.

"Those are the guns they use in Iraq and don't point it at me." Tiffany told her.

"Okay, I know this is the trigger. This is the clip. That's all I know, girl." Sara said touching things on the weapon.

"Point it out the window and pull the trigger." Tiffany told her pushing the auto on the window, letting it down.

"You for real?" Sara asked curiously.

"Yes, I'm for real. We need to know how it shoots." Tiffany told her barely missing a pickup truck on the road.

Sara stuck the barrel out the window and pulled the trigger and closed her eyes. Nothing happened. "What's wrong?" She asked.

"Shit, I don't know. Push some buttons or something." Tiffany told her.

She clicked the gun from semi to fully automatic and pulled the trigger again, still found nothing. She saw the safety switch and clicked it. Soon as she touched the trigger, the gun spit 4 instant shots. The car next to them was almost hit. It scared Tiffany. She swerved a bit then they both laughed.

"Come on. Let's go help me friend." Sara yelled out the window.

Sgt. Little got off the elevator on the fourth floor and saw Vanessa coming out the restroom and told her, "Hurry, we got to go. They're coming."

Vanessa was scared, she was caught off guard. "Who's on the way?" Vanessa said nervously looking around.

"The police who killed your brother." Sgt. Little whispered trying not to start a panic.

"Oh my God! Are you sure?" Vanessa said trying to hide her face.

"Yeah. Let's go. Hurry and stay close." Sgt. Little told her.

"Okay." Vanessa said. They ran for the stairs. "Why not the elevator?" Vanessa asked Little.

"Because they might be on there, or waiting at the bottom." Little told her pulling her arm. They ran down the stairs. When they got to the second floor they were met by the team leader.

"Stop. We need that girl, Sgt. She's a suspect in a murder." He told Sgt. Little pointing at Vanessa.

"No she's not. I already know what's going on. Please don't make this difficult. Just let us by. You don't have to be involved in this mess." Little told him stepping in front of Vanessa.

The team leader reached for his gun but Sgt. Little was faster to her side piece and popped off two shots. The team leader was fast. He ducked out the way and ran back down the stairs, but he fired a few shots in their direction, as he fled the shots all hit the wall.

Vanessa screamed and ran through the emergency exit as Little followed her. They ran down the hall to the elevator. "No, what if they're waiting for us, Miss?" Vanessa screamed.

"We just gotta take the chance. Sara and Tiffany are waiting for us by the track." Little informed her hoping the girls would be there.

"How do you know?" Vanessa said in a shaky voice.

"I just talked to them before I ran into you." Little told her. They hopped on the crowded elevator and moved to the back. Sgt. Little told them don't panic. She's the police.

On the elevator, Vanessa told Little, "I'm scared."

"I know, but we'll be okay. Just keep your head low." Little told her wiping her tears and trying to calm her.

When the doors opened, everybody got off the elevator except Little and Vanessa. The team leader yelled, "Is there anybody else on there?" The people said no and the door closed.

"What are we going to do? He's waiting for us." Vanessa mumbled.

"Okay, we'll go back up to the second floor, then come back down. He'll think we got off. Then he'll head for the second floor, but we'll be back down." Little told her now feeling the nervousness Vanessa felt.

The team leader called Cantu, "Hey, what's up?" Cantu answered. "Where the hell are ya'll? Hurry the fuck up." The team leader yelled through the phone.

"We're pulling in now." Cantu told him.

On the second floor, three people got on the elevator. "Did you see the police out there anywhere?" Little asked them.

"No. Are you okay?" A man in a jean jacket and hat asked them.

"I need your help. Take my jacket and give me yours and that hat." Little told him trying to change outfits. She put the hat on Vanessa and she put the jacket on. "When we get to one, let us get off with them. You stay on okay. I need to get her safe." Little said. Then she gave him a hundred dollar bill.

Cantu and his team came through the door. "Over here." The team leader yelled. "They were on the elevator, but I think they went back up."

"We'll go up. You stay here and don't let her pass." Cantu said gun drawn and breathing heavily.

The elevator came back down to the first floor. The team leader stuck his head through the door and yelled to Cantu, "The elevator's back."

Two of the passengers, Vanessa plus Sgt. Little exited together and went the opposite direction of the team leader.

"Is there anybody else on there?" He said.

"No." One lady turned and said nervously looking at the officer's weapon.

As they turned, the team leader recognized Little's work boots. "Stop or I'll shoot!" He yelled, but they took off. He yelled for Cantu and the others. "They're running. I got 'em. Hurry up." He yelled into the radio. But they were already up the stairs, they couldn't hear him. The team leader ran by and the guy in the elevator jumped out on him. They fell to the floor and tussled for a while. Then the team leader yelled, "I'm a fuckin' cop!" He told him as they tussled.

Little and Vanessa were out the back and on the way to the track to meet Sara and Tiffany.

"There they go." Sara told Tiffany.

"Go. Go." Sara yelled pointing in they're direction.

The team leader came bursting out the door at full stride, radio in one hand and gun in the other.

"He's coming. Oh shit, he's coming!" Vanessa yelled speeding up, praying they make it to the car.

"They're running. Cantu, I need help. We're out by the track, hurry man!" The team leader yelled into the radio.

Cantu came back, "We're on the way, stay with them." Cantu said in an agitated voice.

Hector and his team pulled up to the hotel where Rico was waiting outside.

"Come on. Hurry. Let's get this kid." Rico said sounding excited.

Hector told him, "Look what I got." In the other truck there, was a Mexican girl tied up.

"What the fuck is that?" Rico asked in a confused tone.

"Our trade. We leave her in the truck, get the diamonds and he thinks it's his girlfriend." Hector told him with a grin.

"But she's not pregnant, Hector." Rico said looking at the shaking female sitting there.

"So he's not getting out man. She's just for show." Hector told him in a reassuring tone of voice.

"Okay, whatever man. Let's just go." Rico said ready to get this all over with.

Adams pulled up to the carwash, hit his lights and called the Chief. "I'm on it already. We're on our way buddy." Chief said on the phone.

"I'm already here Chief. I'll wait for you guys, but I'mma go look around first." Adams told him.

"Be careful, Adams. I can't lose you too." Chief said. They hung up and Adams got out the car looking around. He went to his trunk and got out his AR-15 assault rifle and his other vest. He put the other vest over the one he wore already for extra protection.

With Tim dead, the only person to pay for what happened to Solis was Cantu and whoever put this million out for the box, Adams thought to himself. Adams walked over to the side of the Butter Crust factory. That's when he saw MAK's car. He ducked behind the building.

"That must be Vanessa's boyfriend, but where is he?" Adams looked around and yelled out, "John! John Gaurdiner!" He waited then yelled again. "John Gaurdiner, this is Detective David Adams. I'm here to help you!"

MAK heard his name and ducked down and peaked out the window. He saw nobody so he went to the other window and he saw Adams kneeling down behind the wall.

He came down the stairs and went to a window right over Adams head. He saw Adams yelling around the corner. He stuck the barrow to the window and busted the glass out. It scared Adams so bad he fell.

MAK pointed the shotgun at him and said, "You move, I squeeze."

Adams knew the shotgun would take his face off if MAK squeezed the trigger so he laid his AR-15 down and started talking. "Look, John, I'm here to help." Adams told him with both hands in the air.

"Shut the fuck up. Where is Vanessa motherfucker?" MAK yelled at him aiming the shotgun directly between his eyes.

"She's okay. They lied to you. They don't have her. She's with one of the Sgts. at the hospital." Adams said to MAK.

"You fuckin' liar. Your homeboy told me ya'll got her and that motherfucker said he gon kill her if I don't give ya'll these diamonds." MAK said then pulled the half bag out his pocket and showed Adams.

"Look, kid. I don't give a fuck about no diamonds. I'm here to warn you and stop my dirty partner. That's it." Adams told MAK not amazed by the sight of the diamonds.

"You think I'mma fall for that shit? I should blow your fuckin head off for your partner killing my brother-in-law. Get up." MAK ordered him. Adams got up. "Let me see your hands," he told Adams. "Now move back away from the window."

Adams took a few steps back then started talking again, "Kid, listen, listen to me. You don't have to do this. Vanessa is okay. Let us handle Cantu." Adams tried telling him.

"Cantu, yeah that's his name. He's the one who killed Eddie and Tim and got my girl." MAK said recalling Cantu's name.

"No, he don't." Adams yelled trying to get MAK to believe him.

"Shut up." MAK yelled then they heard cars pulling up in the parking lot. "Shit, there they go." MAK said.

"Don't go out there, kid. It's a set-up. Look, I'll call and let you talk to Vanessa. I'm on your side." Adams assured him.

"No, you're not. You want these diamonds so you can get the money. Walk to that door, get on your knees and put your hands behind your head." MAK told him.

Adams walked to the door and did what was told. MAK came down, opened the door and walked over to Adams. "Where 's your other weapon?" MAK asked.

"In my holster. Look, just let me call so you know I'm not playing games." Adams said to MAK. MAK walked over and grabbed the AR-15 off the ground and told Adams to stand up.

Sgt. Little looked back and could see the team leader on their tail with Cantu and the others behind them. She pulled her weapon and fired a couple shots but the team leader never broke his stride. The team leader popped off a couple shots. One hit the back of Little's vest and knocked her down.

Vanessa stopped. "Get up, Sgt.!" she yelled in a panic.

"Run. You gotta get away Vanessa." The Sgt. told her, but Vanessa came back to help her up.

"Are you okay?" Vanessa asked her looking for signs of blood.

"Yeah. I got on a vest, but you don't. Let's go." Little got up but stumbled. The team leader was too close so she just aimed and started shooting. The team leader zig-zagged. All the shots missed then Little's gun jammed. The team leader took aim and fired.

Sara and Tiffany slid to a stop right in front of Vanessa and Sgt. Little. The bullets hit the front end of Tim's Impala.

"Get in, get in! Hurry!" Sara told Little and Vanessa. Sara aimed the AKSU out the window and squeezed. Bullets raced out the barrel and with an eruption so loud it scared Little and Vanessa and made both of them scream.

One bullet hit the team leader in the arm. Another hit him in the chest so hard it went through both sides of the vest and threw him in a backflip landing on his neck.

Sara and Tiffany started yelling, "We got 'em! We got 'em!"

"There's more coming." Little told Sara.

"Go, go, girl!" They told Tiffany. She stepped on the gas and the Impala burned rubber. Cantu and his team let off shots that hit the rear of the car. The only thing stopping the bullets from entering through the backseat were Tim's speakers and amplifiers hooked to the backseat.

Cantu yelled in his radio, "They're coming around by the track. Cut them off!" The drivers of the suburbans rushed out the parking lot to try and cut them off.

"Hurry! Hurry!" Sara told Tiffany.

"Okay, okay. Let me drive." Tiffany said. They drove through the university's huge property. The other cars were making it difficult to get out.

"Move, move!" Sara yelled to the slow driver.

"Oh, shit! Watch out!" Sgt. Little yelled.

The Suburban came speeding over a speed bump. Tiffany smashed the gas and ran into the back of the car in front of them, pushing it into the grass. That freed them from behind the driver so Tiffany drove through the grass. The other Suburban was coming in the other direction.

"What do I do? What do I do?" Tiffany asked.

Sara told her to stop.

"Stop? What do you mean stop?" Tiffany yelled.

"I'mma shoot they ass. Get the other gun, Miss." Sara told Sgt. Little. Little looked in the bag and got the other AKSU and Tiffany stopped.

Sara and Sgt. Little got out and opened fire. Bullets ripped through the Suburban like swiss cheese. The driver lost control but the truck was still coming at the car.

"Get in. Hurry!" Tiffany told them. Then she hit the gas. Neither Sara nor Little had time to get in, but they both dove to the side and was barely missed. Tiffany and Vanessa looked back to see if Little and Sara were alright. They both got up and run back to the car and hopped in. The truck slammed into a tree and exploded.

Cantu and the team fired at them with no success. Cantu and the team hopped in the other Suburban and started after the girls.

The girls hit the main street out of the University parking lot and started cheering.

"Yeah, did you see that shit, girl?" Tiffany said.

"Is everybody okay?" Sgt. Little asked.

"Yeah, we good up here." Sara and Tiffany said.

"Yeah, I'm okay." Vanessa said… She felt a wetness between her legs. She was bleeding. She thought she was having another miscarriage.

"Where the hell did you girls get guns like this?" Little asked them.

"We found them." Sara said.

"Where's MAK?" Vanessa asked them.

"We're going to help him right now. He thinks those guys kidnapped you but I think somebody is setting him up." Sara told her.

Just then, the rear window shattered and they all screamed. Cantu and his team were behind them and coming fast shooting.

"Shoot back!" Vanessa yelled.

Sgt. Little pointer her gun backwards and let loose. Hot bullet shells jumped out and landed in Vanessa's shirt. She panicked and started swinging and yelling, trying to get the shells out her shirt and hit Sgt. Little, which caused her to drop the gun out the back window. It fell to the back but the strap was hooked on the spoiler on the truck of the car.

"The gun, I dropped it! I dropped it!" She yelled, but Tiffany didn't pay attention. She was trying to concentrate on the road.

More shots from Cantu hit the car. Little tried to climb out the back window to get the gun. "Grab my feet!" She told Vanessa. She climbed out and Vanessa got hold of her feet. The Suburban was coming. "I can't reach it." She told Vanessa.

Sara looked back. "What the fuck ya'll doing?" Sara said in surprise to see Little out the window.

"She dropped it out the back." Vanessa told her.

"It's another one in the bag, stupid." Tiffany said.

Vanessa and Sara pulled Little back in. "Forget the gun. It's another one in there." They told her. Sgt. Little told her to get off on the next exit. She had a plan.

Adams stood up and MAK made him walk into the abandoned building. With both hands holding guns, MAK slipped and let Adams turn too fast. Adams turned and was face to face with MAK before he could react.

Adams grabbed him, slammed him to the wall then grabbed both arms, head-butted him and kneed him in the stomach. He snatched the gun from his right hand, but the bad thing was it was the shotgun.

They took aim at each other. "Look, kid. I'm here to help you. Just cool out man, please, I don't wanna hurt you."

MAK aimed the AR-15 at Adams head. "Fuck you. How you gon help me head butting me in my damn face… You buss my shit, motherfucker." MAK told him feeling blood drip from his nose.

"You made me, man." Adams phone rang. They both stood looking at each other. "Look, kid. That could be my Sgt. with your girl right now. Let me answer. I'm going to put the gun down and answer it, okay?" Adams said putting the gun down. Then MAK's phone rang.

Adams put the shotgun down. "Kick it." MAK told him. He kicked it a few feet. "Don't move." MAK said still holding the AR-15 at him. He looked at his phone. It was Hector.

He answered it, "Hello?" MAK said.

"Hola, Little man. I see your car, but I don't see you." Hector told him.

"Where's my girl?" MAK asked staring at Adams.

"She's right here." Hector slapped the girl. She yelled. "Did you hear that?" Hector asked.

MAK looked at Adams with an evil gaze. "You fuckin' liar!" He said to Adams.

"Who you talking to, kid?" Hector asked confused.

"Your fuckin' homeboy. This dirty ass cop." MAK said shaking his head in disgust.

"He's got the cop, Rico." Hector said.

"Oh, yeah? Let me talk to him." Rico said. Hector gave Rico the phone.

"Hola, is this Tim?" Rico said in his smooth voice.

"No, Tim's dead. Who the fuck is this?" MAK asked.

"This is the owner of those diamonds you're holding. I want them back and you want your bitch back, am I right?" Rico said.

"Yeah." MAK told him.

"You kill Cantu, give me my diamonds back and I'll give you your girl. I'll drop 50,000 dollars in this nice little car of yours and we'll go our separate ways." Rico told MAK thinking he had Cantu.

"I'll kill this pig for free. I just want my girl." MAK said wanting to pull the trigger.

While MAK was talking to Rico, Hector had his men walking around the building. MAK took the phone away from his mouth and sked Adams, "What's your name?"

"Detective David Adams." Adams said.

"He called you Cantu," MAK said.

"Hang up. He'll call back." Adams said. MAK hung up. "Look, Cantu was my partner, but he's after money. Those guys think Cantu has your girl. This is a set up." Adams told him.

"I just heard my girl, man." MAK said.

"Trust me kid, please. Here, answer my phone." Adams told him. He threw MAK the phone.

GREED

MAK picked it up and answered and Little screamed through the receiver, "Adams, we need help. They're right behind us and closing in."

"Who is this?" MAK asked.

"Who is this?" Little asked him hysterically. "Where is Adams?"

"Ask her about Vanessa." Adams told him.

"Where's Vanessa? This is John." MAK said.

"Oh my God, she's right here. Are ya'll okay? Where is Adams?" Little asked.

A tear came to MAK's eye.

"Vanessa, it's your boyfriend." Little said. Little gave Vanessa the phone.

"Hello, John. Where are you? Are you okay?" Vanessa said now crying.

"Yes." MAK told her experiencing the same emotions.

"Look out!" Adams yelled. One of Hector's men shot through the window. It grazed MAK's ear and shattered Adam's phone. MAK dropped to the floor and crawled to a corner out of sight of the shooters. Adams did the same thing then he got his glock out his holster.

MAK went up the stairs to get an angle on the men outside. Adams popped two shots at the window. The shooter ran away. Adams ran and grabbed the shotgun. MAK let off shots with the AR-15 that hit one of the gunmen, the other ran to the side.

Hector heard the gunshots and told Rico to get back in the truck and to stay out of harms way. He'll take care of this, Hector and the rest of the men pulled the girl out and yelled, "Hey kid, come out or I'll kill her!"

The girl was on the side of the truck. Hector made her get on her knees. MAK came to the window and saw the girl, Hector and his men. "What the fuck is going on?" He said to himself. "I got you diamonds mother fucker. Let her go." MAK said yelling with his head down.

"No, you come out like a man and get her." Hector yelled back. There was a shooter waiting for an open shot with his rifle sitting in the truck with Rico.

"Take the shot soon as you get it." Rico told him.

"Yes, sir. It's a glare from the lights." The shooter said looking through the scope of his rifle.

"Don't trust him, kid. That's not Vanessa." Adams told him as he came around the corner. MAK pointed the gun at him.

"Shut up. I don't trust you." MAK said.

"Kid, you just talked to your girl." Adams said.

"Well, who is that?" MAK said.

"I don't know, but it's not Vanessa." Adams said. MAK looked back out the window at the girl then back at Adams.

The shooter fired. The bullet hit MAK in the shoulder and knocked him over the rail. He fell to the floor. He tried to brace for the fall by putting his hand out and broke his wrist.

"Ah, my fuckin' hand!" He yelled in excruciating pain. He dropped the AR-15. Adams went to his side.

"Shit, kid. Come on." Adams said. He grabbed the AR-15 and MAK and they ran for the other side of the factory.

Hector and his men rushed the door where they thought MAK fell. The door flew open and Adams let off a hail of bullets with the Glock. Hector and his men ducked away from the door.

"Get him!" Rico yelled. They charged in again but Adams rained bullets at the door.

"We can't get in, Rico."

"Find another way, asshole!" Rico yelled out the window.

Adams and MAK hid in an office that used to hold old paperwork. Adams gave MAK the Glock. "Use your other hand, and if anybody comes through the door, kill them. You hear me?" Adams told him.

"Yeah. Where you going?" MAK asked him.

"To try and buy us some time." Adams told him.

The Chief pulled up to the carwash and noticed Adams car. "Oh, shit, he went in alone." Chief said. "All units hit the factory now. Adams is alone." They raced toward the factory. The helicopter flew overhead and lit the whole factory in artificial sunlight and announced, "This is S.A.P.D., put your weapons down.

Hectors men opened fire on the chopper. "Go, Rico!" Hector yelled.

"Not without you." Rico told him.

"Go, man. Get outta here." Hector demanded.

Rico and the sniper grabbed the girl and sped off in one of the trucks just in time. The police squad hit the corner full blast by the dozen.

Hector was inside the factory armed with a MAC-90 submachine gun with an infrared beam. He crept around one corner and almost got his head knocked off. Adams fired three shots from the AR-15 right at him but missed. Hector ducked and let off a few shots in Adams' direction.

MAK could hear the shooting all around him and didn't know what to do. He was hurt from the bullet in his shoulder and his broken hand. All he could think of was Vanessa.

He stood up, crept around the office and came to a corner of the wall. He could see Adams peeking around the corner. Then he saw Hector's infared beam shine on the back of Adams' shirt.

He yelled, "Look out!" Adams turned and jumped to the side. Hector's bullets rarely missed Adams, but left Hector wide open. MAK squeezed two shots and Adams let go a hail of bullets at the same time. All the bullets found their mark, ripping Hector's chest open.

"Good shot, kid." Adams said.

"Thanks." MAK said.

Outside it was gunfire everywhere. The police surrounded Lil' Freeddy and the rest of the crew so they gave up. They were all arrested. Then the police stormed the factory.

"We're okay." Adams said, flashing his badge.

"Anyone else in the building?" The Chief asked.

"No, just the dead gun." Adams said. They went outside.

"Hey, where's my girl?" MAK asked Adams and the Chief.

"She's with Sgt. Little." Adams said. "Let me use your phone, Chief."

Adams dialed Little's phone. Little answered, "Hello?" She said breathing hard.

"What's wrong?" Adams asked.

"Is this Adams?" Little yelled.

"Who is this?" Adams said.

"Help us, this is Little. Cantu is after us. We're on I-10 right now. He's coming Adams. We can't shake him." She said looking back at the trucks in pursuit.

"Okay, we're on our way." Adams told her. "Chief, get that helicopter over here. We gotta get those girls. Cantu is chasing them down I-10 right now. We gotta get them." Adams told them in a hushed tone.

The Chief radioed the chopper to land and pick them up.

"There are too many power lines, Chief. Sorry, no can do." The pilot said.

"Fuck! They can't. It's too many power lines." Chief said looking around at the lines.

The pilot came back and told the Chief, "Go down to the corner of Commerce. I can land in the intersection." They jumped in the car and raced to the intersection.

"What kind of fuckin' plan is this lady?" Sara told Sgt. Little.

"We got off one freeway to get on another one and this one's more crowded than the other one was. Are you on our side of theirs?" Sara yelled to the backseat.

"I'm on your side. Be quiet. I can't hear." Sgt. Little said to her. "Adams, we need your help. You got to hurry. Yes, Vanessa's fine, but I don't know for how long. Cantu is on us." Little said to Adams in an urgent tone.

Tiffany ducked in and out of traffic, but it was getting a lot heavier and Cantu was getting closer by the second. Two shots rang out and both hit the passenger tire. It blew out.

The girl screamed, the car swerved but Tiffany kept control. They were 6 to 7 cars ahead of Cantu from Tiffany switching lanes. Up ahead, traffic was at a standstill.

GREED

"Let's get out and run." Vanessa told them feeling panic sitting in traffic.

"No, we can get further." Tiffany said.

"No, she's right. We got a flat and traffic is dead still. Let's make a run for it. Adams is on his way." Sgt. Little said.

Once traffic was at a standstill, the girls hopped out, got low and ran through traffic.

"There's the car, Cantu. About 6 cars up. The traffic stopped. They ain't going nowhere now." The driver of Cantu's truck told him.

"Let's go. You stay here in the truck." Cantu told the driver.

Cantu and 4 guards got out the Suburban and started for the car with their weapons drawn. Once they were close, Cantu popped two shots through the driver window.

"Get out with your hands up!" He yelled. People in other cars were scared and ducking when they heard the shots being fired.

The girls were down the street, climbing to the access road when they heard the shots.

"Nobody's in here, boss." One guard said. Cantu opened the door and everyone was gone.

"Fuck. Find them." He said. Cantu saw the bags on the floor and checked it. He found one of the guns and some drugs.

"There they go, boss. Up there, on the access road." The officer told Cantu pointing to the access road.

Cantu looked up and the girls were already on the top of the freeway on the access road. "Come on!" He yelled at him and his team burst into full stride.

"They're coming, hurry up let's go." Tiffany said when she saw them running. They ran across the access road to the nearby apartment complex. Sgt. Little used the phone to call Adams. The phone answered on the first ring.

"Yes, Sgt. We're on our way. Where exactly on I-10 are you?" Adams asked over the loud helicopter blades.

"We exited I-10 and got on 410 but the traffic was stopped so we got out and made a run for it. Cantu shot out the tire on the car. We are in the apartments of Starcrest Drive."

"Which ones?" Adams asked knowing the area.

"The first ones behind the Circle K." Little told him.

"Okay, we're on our way. I'm sending help." Adams told her.

"Please hurry." She said in a shaky tone.

Cantu and the team ran through traffic and climbed the wall after the girls. The girls climbed through a hole in the security fence to get into the apartments. They ran through and saw a couple people standing outside. When people saw the guns, they panicked and ran.

"No, no. I'm a cop. We need your help." Sgt. Little said.

One older lady was in her doorway. They asked her for help.

"Can we please hide here. Please?" Sara said. "My friend's pregnant and someone's after her. Please?" The lady let them in.

Neighbors were looking scared, didn't know what was going on. One lady even called 911.

Cantu and his team came running through the apartments at full speed. They ran into some of the people that Sgt. Little and the girls just scared and they saw Cantu's badge and pointed, "They went that way, officers. Inside the old lady's house."

The girls went to the backroom to calm down. "Oh my God, Vanessa you're bleeding. Are you shot?" Sara asked her.

"No, I'm okay." Vanessa said breathing heavily.

"No, you're not. You're bleeding girl. We need to get you some help." Sara told her staring at the blood-stained clothes.

"No, I need MAK. Please. I just need my baby, please." Then she broke, tears flowed and fell to the floor. "I can't take this shit." She said.

"It's going to be okay, Vanessa. MAK is on his way." Tiffany said.

Sgt. Little was looking out the blinds when she saw Cantu and the team hit the corner. "Oh, shit. It's them." She said.

The girls got scared and started to scramble. "Vanessa, you stay here in the closet."

"Yeah, girl. It might get ugly and I promised MAK I wouldn't let nothing happen to you." Sara said.

The helicopter raced across the city. Adams had all units headed to Starcrest Drive. "No one leaves that area. Do I make myself clear?" He yelled into the radio. As they flew overhead, they could see the traffic jam. It was because further down 410, a Ford F-150 ran into a Dodge Neon and totaled it out. The further down you got, the worse traffic was.

Cantu and his team spread out in the area. The lady that called the police was looking out her window. She saw Cantu, hit the corner and got his attention.

He looked up when he heard the tapping on the window. The old lady pointed at the apartment the girls went in. Cantu signaled his team and pointed out the apartment.

Sgt. Little, Sara and Tiffany were in the front looking out the blinds. "That old bitch told on us." Tiffany said.

Sara went back to the room with Vanessa. "Nessa, they know where we are. They're coming, okay. Please trust me. I won't let nothing happen to you." Sara told her in her most gentle voice and she meant the words.

"I'm scared, Sara. I don't want to die. MAK needs me." Vanessa said crying uncontrollably.

"You're not going to die." Sara said, unsure if she believed it herself.

Cantu sent one officer to each window and told them shoot whoever comes out. He went to the front door and knocked. He had two officers with him.

"Police, ma'am. Please open the door. The people you're hiding are wanted for murder. Unless you want to be arrested for obstruction of justice, open the door and come out with your hands up."

"I don't want to go to jail." The lady told Sgt. Little. She then reached for the door.

Tiffany pointed her gun at the lady and told her, "If you touch that door, lady, I'mma shoot you. I swear to God."

"Tiffany, stop." Sgt. Little said.

"She's going to get us killed, Sgt." Tiffany said not lowering her weapon.

"Stop!" Little continued. "Ma'am, please don't do it. Those people aren't really police. They're after the girl in the back." Little explained to the old lady.

Sara came to the front and told them the guard was at the window trying to see in.

"Miss, go hide somewhere." Sgt. Little told the old lady. The old lady ran to the back. "Help me put the couch to the door." Little told them. They moved the couch to the door and waited.

"Call the guy with MAK again. See where they at." Tiffany said.

"This is your last chance to open the door or we're coming in!" Cantu yelled. Cantu ordered one of his guys to kick the door in. He kicked the door and three bullets landed in his chest.

Cantu and the other guy ran for the side of the building out of firing angle.

"You bitches gon pay for that!" Cantu yelled around the corner.

"What the fuck was that shit, Tiffany?" Sgt. Little yelled to her.

"I'm not gon sit here while they come kill us off. We're stuck in this apartment. They have us surrounded. You got any better ideas? Let me know, but right now, I'm in self-preservation mode. I wanna live, I don't know about ya'll." Tiffany shouted back at her.

"Okay, look. I got an idea." Sgt. Little said.

"Hell, no. Your last plan got us stuck in this damn apartment." Sara said.

"Just listen, Thelma and Louise." Little said to both of the girls. "Sara you go with Vanessa. We'll hold cover fire so ya'll can get away. If we're going to die, it's going to be fighting. Tiffany, you stay up here and every few seconds shoot two or three times just keep them back. I'll get this guy from the window so Sara and Vanessa can go out the window and make a run for it."

Just then, gun shots blast through the window, followed by two of the officers.

Sara ran to the back room, Tiffany ran to the kitchen, Sgt. Little ducked into the hallway. One officer stayed on the floor behind the ladies entertainment system, and the other hid behind the couch. He popped two shots towards Little in the hallway.

From the outside, Cantu could see into the house through the window. He fired at the wall leading up to the hallway. The bullets ripped through the cheap sheetrock wall.

Sgt. Little was in a bad spot. Tiffany sat behind the kitchen counter praying. She peeked around the corner to see the officer on the floor crawling towards her. She got up and slowly got on top of the counter. When the officer stuck his weapon around the corner, he fired a couple of shots that hit nothing.

He looked and saw Tiffany wasn't there. But she said, "Hey you." He looked up and she fired one shot to his face. At the close range the bullet made a perfect dot in the center of his head, but it blew a patch of hair and brain matter all over the back.

"Tiffany, are you okay?" Sgt. Little yelled.

"Yeah, I'm good." She shouted back.

Cantu fired a few more shots then jumped through the window and hid behind the entertainment system. The officer behind the couch fired at Tiffany. She ducked down and the officer rushed to the kitchen.

He tried to fire but the gun jammed. Tiffany tried to fire, but he grabbed her by the hair, pulled her head back and hit her in the face twice and busted her mouth.

Tiffany's knees buckled and she almost fell. "Oh no, bitch. That's not it. Get up." He said. He stood her up to the wall and kicked her in the stomach. She yelled.

"Tiffany, what's wrong?" Little yelled around the corner.

Tiffany yelled again. The officer had her in a choked hold.

"Shit," Little said to herself then she saw Cantu's shadow coming around the corner. She aimed and backed down the hallway.

Sara and Vanessa were at the window waiting on the word from Sgt. Little that it was okay to go. When Sara saw Sgt. Little back into the room, first thing she thought was, "Tiffany... Where's Tiffany?" They both asked, fearing the worst.

"She was in the kitchen." Little said as she aimed her weapon.

"What do you mean 'was?'" Sara said.

Cantu fired down the hall. Sgt. Little jumped out the way. Cantu ran into the next room and ducked in. "I'm coming, Vanessa." He taunted them his voice was close. "I'm coming. Can you feel me? I can hear your baby's heartbeat." He said in a spooky sing song voice.

Tiffany was slowly losing air. She put her feet on the counter and thrust backward, slamming the officer's back into the oven. His grip let loose, but he regained ground fast. He kicked her, but she grabbed the drawer to stop from being pulled back but it opened and they both fell backwards and made the contents spill all over the floor.

Tiffany kicked backwards like a bucking hose and landed in the officer's stomach. He grabbed her leg and kicked the other one from under her.

On her way to the floor, her face slammed into the counter and busted her right above the eyebrow. When she hit the floor, the officer sat on her back and pulled her hair so her head pulled up.

She yelled in pain. The officer laughed at her them slammed her head to the floor. She just laid there. The officer got up and started to walk off. Tiffany grabbed one of the knives off the floor and stabbed him in the calf muscle. He fell to one knee. Then, with the same knife, she stabbed him in the back twice.

He fell to the floor, rolled sideways and kicked her backwards. She flew back, but scrambled to get back at him. He back peddled to get away from her but she was relentless in her pursuit. He kicked and she stabbed at his feet. He backed to the wall in the corner. He was bleeding excessively from his back.

Tiffany peeked around the corner and didn't see Sgt. Little. So she yelled, "Hey, ya'll okay?" Nobody said anything, so she figured they were hiding.

The officer was inching to the gun his partner dropped when Tiffany shot him. Tiffany turned and saw him and she threw the knife. It missed but if gave her time to run. She ran out the kitchen through the living room and jumped out the window. She got up and ran to the room window where Sara, Vanessa and Sgt. Little were.

She knocked on the window and Little aimed at the shadow, "Ahh! It's me. Wait, it's me.!" Tiffany yelled. "Come on. There's nobody out here." She told them.

The girls starting climbing out and Cantu fired into the room. Sara got out but Vanessa and Sgt. Little had to jump out the way. Little fired at the wall to get Cantu to back up, so she and Vanessa could go for the window.

CHAPTER 9

"This is as far as I can go. You will have to get out here. There's nowhere to land over there." The pilot of the helicopter told Adams and the Chief, plus two officers they brought along for extra help. "I'll stay overhead for support."

Adams, Chief Garza, Franklin and Reyes got off the chopper and hurried to the apartments.

"Look, when we find them, you two secure the girls. We'll handle Cantu." Adams told Franklin and the Chief.

"Gotcha, kid." Chief said.

As they entered the apartments, the Suburban turned the corner speeding to the apartments.

"Fuck, that's one of Cantu's guys. Come one men, double time." The Chief said.

Before Sgt. Little could fire at Cantu's position, he fired into the room. Vanessa screamed and ran for the closet again.

"No, Vanessa. The window. Get out there." Little told her.

Cantu fired again and rushed in. Little was taking cover when he charged in. He hit her with a tackle that knocked the wind out of her.

Sgt. Little was well trained in hand to hand combat and three forms of martial arts, but Cantu had no idea. With Little on the ground out of air, Cantu started for the closet, gun in hand. Sgt. Little jumped up. Cantu spun around to shoot. Little side-stepped him and kicked his leg from under him. Cantu fell to one knee. Little kicked out but he grabbed her leg and threw her to the wall. She slammed to the wall harder than she had expected.

She was shaken up a little and Cantu bent to get his gun but she came back with two jabs to the face. He reached for her. She ducked, grabbed his arm and side kicked him in the ribs. He slammed into the wall but shot back at her in a fury. He landed a couple punches to her face that dazed her. She fell against the wall and Cantu got his grip on her. He picked her up and slammed her to the floor as hard as he could. Cantu did it again then threw Little out the window.

Sara and Tiffany ran to her. "Oh my God. Are you okay, Little?" Tiffany asked.

"Come here, sweetie." Cantu said to Vanessa. He picked up his gun and fired out the window at Sara, Tiffany and Sgt. Little. They scrambled for cover.

Vanessa was in the closet in the fetal position when Cantu grabbed her by the head and dragged her out. She was screaming for help and kicking.

Cantu told her, "Stand up, bitch, or I'll kill you right here."

"Okay. Please don't shoot me." Vanessa whimpered with both hands up.

Over the radio he heard, "Cantu, where are you? I'm in front of the apartment." It was the driver of the Suburban.

"Stay there. I'm coming to you." Cantu said. He heard shots up front. "What the fuck?"

Reyes let off two shots that hit the mark. "Cantu, it's over. We got you." Adams yelled down the hall.

"Fuck you, redneck. You don't got nobody." Cantu yelled back then shot down the hall. "Come on, bitch. We're making an exit." He told Vanessa dragging her by the head. He grabbed her by the neck and went for the window he threw Sgt. Little out of. When they got to the window, he saw the Chief and Franklin running with Sara, Tiffany and Sgt. Little.

He climbed out the window and pulled Vanessa out behind him. They ran towards the front of the apartments. On the way, he told the driver of the Suburban to take out the Chief and the other.

Soon as the Chief and the others hit the corner, the driver opened fire on them. Franklin took a bullet in the thigh, Sara took one to the stomach, but it didn't hit any major organs. Just a flesh wound. The Chief and Tiffany ran for the hole in the security fence. Sgt. Little went back to help Vanessa…and Adams. The Chief told Tiffany to run for help. He had to go help Sara and Franklin.

Adams and Reyes raced down the hallway to find the hole in the window where Cantu and Vanessa just left out. "Damn it, he's out." Adams said.

Sgt. Little could see Cantu and Vanessa running in her direction, but they didn't see her. As they hit the corner, Sgt. Little jumped out with all her force into both of them.

All three of them fell, Cantu dropped the gun. Him and Little were again in a tussle.

"Run, Vanessa." Sgt. Little said as she posted up for combat.

Vanessa got up and ran as fast as she could. Sgt. Little hit Cantu in the nose then swept his feet. He stumbled, but didn't fall. She charged him full blast. He didn't move. When she slammed into him, they crashed into some bushes on the side of the buildings.

Cantu grabbed her around the throat and started choking her with all he had. He heard the shots around the corner from the driver of the Suburban. He punched Little in the face and dazed her.

He got up and grabbed the gun but just then he saw Adams and Reyes. "Saved by the white man, bitch…" He said to Little with a grin and wink.

Then he ran towards the truck. He saw the Chief, Franklin and Sara. Vanessa was helping Sara up until she saw him hit the corner and she panicked. She took off for the hole in the fence at a stride.

Cantu ran to the Suburban with his driver and they raced out the apartment after Vanessa. Adams helped Sgt. Little up and they ran after Cantu and Vanessa. When they saw Vanessa exit through the hole, they tried to catch her but she was gone, panic driving her.

From the sky, the helicopter pilot could see everybody running through the street. He got on the radio, "You guys better hurry! That Suburban just exited the apartments and I got two girls running down Starcrest." He told the Chief over the radio.

Adams and Reyes came running through the fence followed by Sgt. Little. "Vanessa!" They screamed, but she didn't hear.

"Tiffany! Tiffany!" Vanessa yelled. She could see Tiffany on the other side of the street running toward the access road.

Tiffany turned and saw Vanessa coming. "Vanessa!" She screamed then saw the Suburban come speeding to a stop right in front of Vanessa.

Vanessa tried to run in the other direction, but the driver got out and chased her down. He grabbed her and pulled her toward the Suburban.

"No! No!" Yelled Tiffany from down the street tears filling her eyes. Adams and Sgt. Little yelled also. Then they opened fire at full blast.

"Stop! Stop! You'll hit he girl." Reyes told them. They paid him no attention. They were trying to kill Cantu and the driver.

Cantu jumped out and fired a few shots that made Little and Reyes duck but Adams was full speed ahead with rage in his eyes.

They dragged a kicking and screaming Vanessa in the truck and sped off. Adams got on the radio and told the helicopter pilot, "Don't let that truck out of your sight."

"Roger that. I got him." The pilot told him.

At the police station, Lil' Freddy and the rest of the crew were in holding cells.

"Fuck, I wonder what happened to Rico." Lil' Freddy said to Jesus.

"Man, call Rico and tell him to send somebody to get us out before they fuck us." Jesus said to Lil' Freddy sounding like he was about to crack.

In the holding cell, Lil' Freddy used the phone to call Rico's phone. The line rang, "Please say your name." Lil' Freddy said "Hector". He knew Rico wouldn't accept for anybody else.

"Your call was accepted."

"Hola, Toro." Rico said.

"No, this is Freddy." Lil' Freddy told him.

"Where is Toro?" Rico asked in a surprised tone.

"They killed him, Rico. Those fuckin' pigs got him at the factory, but me, Jesus and the rest of the crew are in jail. We need help before they try and hit us with all these fuckin' charges." Lil' Freddy told him holding his head down looking at the floor hoping Rico agreed.

"Jesus?... Jesus?... I heard that's why all this shit is going on. That motherfucker picked this fuckin' Jose guy and he decided to stop in this fuckin' city. You wanna take Toro's spot as my number one?" Rico said grinding his teeth.

"Are you serious?" Lil Freddy said now lifting his head in excitement.

"Yeah. it's what Toro would've wanted." Rico told him.

"Hell yeah!" Lil Freddy shouted to let Rico know he was serious.

"Well, your first job is to take out that piece of shit. I'll have you out in the next few hours." Rico told him then hung up.

Freddy looked at Jesus and told the crew, "Rico said he'll get us out, but we gotta take out Jesus for this mess he started."

"What... What mess?" Jesus asked curious and nervous at the same time. "And you gon listen to him? I'm your friend." Jesus said trying to shake Freddy's hand.

"Hey, our lives are on the line." Freddy said, pulling his hand away. Then the assault started, but the cops came and broke them up.

On the way out Jesus yelled to all of them, "I got ya'll motherfuckers. I'mma hit where it hurts, especially you and Rico. Freddy, we were better than that. "He told them with blood dripping from his nose and mouth. The officers took him to a separate cell and he asked can he speak to somebody he had info on murders and drug dealing from Florida to California.

Rico and the driver sped down the freeway headed to the small city of San Marcos to hide out for a minute before flying back to San Diego. They still had the girl with them in the backseat.

Rico called his friend Arron. Arron lived on one of Rico's properties in San Marcos. The property was a small farm like...

couple horses, cows and chickens, but the house is very upscale. Arron lives there with his mother, wife and 5 children.

Arron's wife answered the phone when Rico called.

"Hola, this is Rico, where is Arron?" Rico asked.

She was happy to hear from Rico. He made a way for them to get out of Mexico. She took the phone, "Honey, it's Rico." The wife said.

"Hola, Rico. Long time. How's it going?" Arron said exhaling smoke from his cigar.

"Fine, brother, fine. I need to crash for a couple of days." Rico told him.

"No problem. I'll clean the guest house out for you." Arron said like the president was coming to town.

"Thanks, I'll be there in thirty minutes." Rico told him.

"Oh, you're in town? Good, I'll tell the family and we'll cook something." Arron said cheerfully.

"Okay, fine. I have company with me." Rico said, then they hung up.

At the hospital, MAK was giving them trouble. He was trying to leave but they wanted to keep him. He was hit pretty badly in the shoulder. He was worried about Vanessa, Sara and Tiffany.

"Let me use the fuckin' phone. I need to use the phone. My girl is in trouble!" MAK yelled at the hospital doctors.

The guard that was with him told him to calm down and he'll get his phone out his property in a minute.

"Sir, just please check with your people and see what's up with my girl and my friends. Please man." MAK said fighting through the pain in his shoulder for his love of Vanessa.

The officer pulled out his radio and tried to get a word from Adams or the Chief, but he got no reply from either. "I'll check later, kid. Nobody's answering right now, but I'm sure everything is okay." The officer told him, not knowing thing weren't okay.

MAK put his head down in disappointment. The worst crossed his mind.

Vanessa yelled and kicked at Cantu and the other officer. Cantu grabbed her by the hair and started punching her over and over and over. His frustration and anger had taken over him.

The first punch knocked Vanessa out, so didn't feel the rest of the assault. He banged her head to the door. He punched her in the stomach as he yelled, "Bitch, where is that fuckin' boyfriend of yours?! Do you hear me? Do you hear me?"

"Boss, Boss, she can't hear you, man. She's out cold. Forget her. How are we going to shake the chopper? They're on us like a hawk." The driver told him grabbing his arm to stop the assault.

Cantu leaned out the window and fired at the chopper. The pilot got clear and got on the radio and told the Chief he was being fired upon.

"Turn right, here." Cantu told the driver. "Once we get to a good spot, we'll get out on foot." He told the driver.

"What about the girl?" The driver asked.

"We'll have to carry her." Cantu told him.

The helicopter pilot was on them and sending directions back to the Chief who was riding along with Adams and Sgt. Little. They were being followed by Reyes and a team of other officers.

"Chief, they turned off Starcrest and headed right on Butler." The pilot told the Chief over the police radio.

"Roger that. We're coming across 410 and Starcrest. Now, keep us posted and if you lose sight of that truck start looking for a new job. Do I make myself clear?" The Chief shouted through the radio.

Adams sat in the back of the car while Sgt. Little drove. He hadn't said much since they jumped in the car. As the car raced through traffic, his mind drifted back to Kerrville Country 3 years ago…

"Please, sir, help my brother. My stepdad is going to kill him." He remembered the 14-year-old saying to him. Then the kid ran around the corner. "Hurry, sir, hurry!"

"Look, kid, stay back. I won't let nothing happen to your brother." Adams assured the kid. When he entered the apartment, the mother was on the floor bleeding from the mouth and the step-father had the brother in the corner with a knife at his throat. "Freeze, police. Put the knife down or I'll shoot." Adams yelled at the step-father with his weapon drawn.

"Fuck you, cop. Mind yo own business and get out my house." The man shouted back screaming hysterically.

"Sir, this is the last time or I'mma shoot." Adams warned him. Without hesitation, the step-father stabbed the brother in the neck and threw the knife at Adams' head. Adams ducked the knife but was tackled by the step-father. The step-father was high in PCP and never felt the shot Adams managed to get off in his arm. He hit Adams, they fell into the kitchen table and the gun slid out Adams' hand.

The step-father jumped up and ran towards the front door. Adams got the gun and fired three shots. The step-father managed to get out the door. One bullet hit him in the back. He fell after a couple steps, but when Adams got up and went outside to see if he hit the step-father, he saw the 14-year-old kid laying there in front of the door with one bullet in his chest.

The slamming of the breaks brought him back to the present time. Sgt. Little slid around the corner in the direction the pilot gave them.

Cantu came over the Chief's radio and told the Chief if they don't back off he's going to kill Vanessa.

"Sorry, Cantu. No can do. We're not making any deals. You've gone too far." Chief growled at him.

"You got rules you have to follow, Chief, remember that. I can see the headlines now. Hostage killed because of cocky Chief refused to back off and follow protocol. Now back off or she gets one in the head and thrown out the truck for everyone to see." Cantu shouted into the radio with everyone listening.

"You won't get away with this, you son of a bitch. Do you hear me?" The Chief yelled knowing Cantu was right. If the hostage is killed, Chief can lose his job. "Back off, Little." Chief instructed Sgt. Little.

"What do you mean back off? We need to get the girl. In case you didn't notice, he still has her." Sgt. Little shouted at him still driving.

"Yeah, I noticed, but he says he'll kill her if we don't back off." Chief said.

"No… Fuck no." Sgt. Little refused to give in to the Chief's instruction.

"Keep going, Little." Adams told her as he scooted to the edge of his seat, leaning forward.

"No, got damn it. Stop this car, and that's an order, Little." Chief shouted in her face.

"Chief, please." Sgt. Little pleaded.

"No, we have rules we must follow and we're going to follow them. Now, stop. We'll have the chopper keep us posted." Chief told them.

Sgt. Little brought the car to a stop. The rest of the units came to a stop behind them. Reyes jumped out the car, stormed past the other officers. "What's going on here? We need to catch Cantu." Reyes said pointing down the street.

"He threatened to kill the girl if we don't back off so Chief called off the chase." Little said sarcastically.

The Chief just sat in the car with his head down while Adams built his courage up to go with his gut. He jumped out the car, stormed past the other officers and hopped in one of the other cars.

Reyes and Little got in front of the car. "What the hell are you doing?" They both asked with their hands on the hood.

The Chief said, "No! Do you want to lose your damn job?"

"I promised that kid I'd save his girlfriend and I promised myself I wouldn't let another innocent person lose their life on my watch, and I'm not. Even if it costs my job." Adams told them with his head out the window.

"We'll, I'm going with you." Sgt. Little said and got in the car and they sped off.

"What the fuck? Where are they going?" The Chief yelled.

Reyes looked at the Chief and said, "To do their job." Then he hopped in his car and sped off.

Chief got one of the radios and yelled into it, "All three of you, get back here, now! Do you hear me?" They couldn't hear him and he knew it, but he made it look good in front of the rest of the officers.

Rico and the others pulled up to the property and were met at the gate by barking dogs. Rico punched in his wife's birthdate and the security panel turned green. The gate slid open.

Arron came outside to see Rico coming up the long trail that led to the house. Arron whistled for the dogs to move for Rico to pass. They pulled up and into the garage and got out.

"Hola, Rico. How's it been going buddy?" Arron greeted with a big hug for Rico.

"Everything's been good but I've got some trouble right now down in San Antonio. My friend and I need a few days to lay low. How's the family? Where are they?" Rico asked Arron with a half-smile and pat on the shoulder.

"They're inside. Come in. They're waiting on you. Mom cooked for you and your company." Arron told Rico with a huge smile.

Rico told the driver to get the girl out and bring her inside.

Inside the house, Arron's wife and mother had set food out on the table. When they saw Rico, they all came over to hug him.

"Who's this, Rico?" Arron's wife asked with an attitude because she knew Rico's wife and this wasn't her.

"This is a friend of a friend. I'll explain later. Can you take her upstairs for me while I talk with Arron, please?" Rico asked Arron's wife.

"Sure." They took the girl upstairs. Arron's wife led the way followed by the girl, the driver, and Arron's mother. "Ya'll can use this room." Arron's wife said.

The girl was so confused, tired and hurt. Hector's men picked her up on a corner on the eastside of San Antonio and promised her money for sex. The next thing she knew, she was in the midst of a gun fight with police, being pistol whipped and now here in San Marcos at this house being held hostage.

"What do you want from me?" The girl asked the driver in a weak tone.

"We don't want anything. You have served your purpose. I'm just waiting on the word from my boss that we don't need you anymore." The worker said to her.

"Then what?" She asked.

The driver just laughed and turned on the small TV in the room.

Rico and Arron walked to the living room and sat on the couch. "Rico, are you okay?" Arron asked sensing the disturbance in Rico's demeanor.

"Yeah, Arron. I'm okay. It's just one my deals have gone bad on me and Nora's dad is going to be fuckin' pissed." Rico told Arron with his head down.

"Oh, Rico. You know Carlos' attitude is bad. Is there anyway I can do to help?" Arron asked.

"Not unless you got 50 million dollars worth of diamonds laying around here anywhere." Rico said.

"No, sorry brother. I don't got nothing even close to that, but you're welcome to whatever I have." Arron reassured him.

"No, it's okay. Thank you brother. I just need a few days to let the heat in San Antonio die down, then I'll fly back to San Diego and see what I can do." Rico said looking unsure.

"What about Carlos?" You know when Carlos gets pissed, he doesn't think straight and if he thinks you're trying to hide from him, he'll send Death after you." Arron said putting his hand on Rico's back.

'Death' is Carlos' Cuban hit squad. They are known throughout the world for their murder and mayhem. No one is safe from 'Death'. Entire bloodlines have been murdered by the hands of 'Death' and they take orders from Carlos. Carlos told Rico once, "Please don't ever give me a reason to dislike you, Rico, because I won't hesitate to turn you into a memory."

"Well, I don't care about him sending 'Death' after me. I'm more concerned about the money I'm losing on the damn thing." Rico told Arron.

At the police station in San Antonio, Jesus sat in the hallway waiting on word from Chief.

"I'm only talking to somebody who can help me. My life is in danger and a lot more people might get killed if ya'll don't listen to what I got to say." Jesus said out loud, ready to snitch on everybody.

"Look, kid, the Chief is on his way. He said you can put everything in writing and we'll do what we can for you." An officer guarding him asked.

"I want it in writing before I do anything." Jesus told him not trusting him.

"Look, do you want to go back in there with you lil homies or you want us to help you?" The officer threatened.

"Okay, I'll help. Give me some paper." Jesus reconsidered.

"No, look, we'll just record it all, and you can write it later. We need this info now." The officer said. The officer took Jesus to the interrogation room and turned on the camera. He called in a detective to do the interview. He and two others watched from behind the two-way mirror.

"State your name for the record." The interrogating officer asked.

"Jesus Martin." Jesus said into a mic.

"Where are you from?" The officer asked.

"San Diego, California." Jesus said.

"Okay, please begin…" The officer told him.

"Okay. First, I want to say I'm sorry for any trouble I've caused, but I was forced to by my boss, Rudolfo De Luna or 'Rico' as we call him. He's this rich guy from San Diego, but is deep into the drug trafficking business. The reason we came to San Antonio is because he was shipping 50 million dollars worth of diamonds to his father-in-law, Carlos Jiminez, across the water. The shipment got jacked here in San Antonio and some crooked cop named Mario

Cantu told us who jacked the load, but he said he'd get it back for us. Rico still wanted us to come down and help. Feddy Cruz is Rico's number one man. He controls all the street work. He's killed over 50 people and his most recent kill was in San Diego a couple days ago. The driver of the load that got jacked, Jose Vasquez's sons were killed by Freddy."

Jesus kept going until he had the police full of info they could use against him and the rest of Rico's squad. He even gave them Rico's home address.

The officer got on his phone and called the Chief. "Chief Garza." The officer said proudly.

"Who is this?" The Chief asked.

"Chief, this is Rob at the station." The officer said.

"What's going on Rob?" Chief said.

"We just interviewed one of those guys from the factory shoot out and this thing is pretty big and funded by some pretty big people, plus Cantu is right in the mix." The officer told the Chief.

"Well, fill me in cause Adams, Reyes and Sgt. Little are on their way after him right now." Chief said as he drove.

Rob filled the Chief in on everything. Chief told him to organize a meeting and get with San Diego P.D. to put watch on all Rico's businesses, locate all his properties and hit him ASAP. "Lock down the airport. Nothing goes out of San Antonio without them knowing. Set a perimeter of 10 miles." He told the officers with him. "Find Rudolfo De Luna." The Chief shouted.

The helicopter was overhead, but the trees in the neighborhood made it difficult to keep visual on the truck. Adams, Little and Reyes were at least half a block back trying to keep up.

"I lost visual. I lost visual." The pilot came over the radio.

"Stay up there and find them!" Adams yelled.

Cantu and the driver pulled up to an old man on the side of the street who was getting out of his car and rushed him. They flashed their badges and demanded his car. The old man didn't put up any fight. All he said was, "Here, officers," and handed over his keys. He was just coming from the H.E.B. down the street.

Cantu threw the bags on the ground. They got Vanessa out the truck and sped away in the old man's car. The car was an old Delta 88 Oldsmobile. Not as fast as the Suburban, but a different look. They left the truck in front of the old man's house.

"Get me a fuckin' visual!" Adams yelled into the radio.

"I got nothing, Adams. They must've gotten out or stopped somewhere. I'll stay hovered here to see if they pass by." The pilot told him.

"Fuck! Fuck!" Adams said as he slammed down the radio.

"Oh, shit. Cantu, the helicopter is still up there." The driver said.

"Just fuckin' drive." They came off the street, made a right and were off. They both laughed.

"Ha, ha. They're not moving. We fuckin' made it." The driver said. Cantu got on his phone and dialed Rico's number.

Adams, Little and Reyes came down the street and they saw the Suburban parked in front of the old man's house.

"Here we go." Little said getting ready for action. They slid to a stop and hopped out their cars, guns drawn.

"Cantu, we will fire!" Adams yelled. Reyes circled around the drivers side.

"Nobody." Reyes told Adams and Little. Their instincts told them to take the house. The old man was putting the bags on the table when he heard the door come open.

"Police!" Reyes yelled in.

"I'm in here." The old man said.

"Where is who, sir?" The old man asked nervously at the sight of their weapons.

"The people in that fuckin' truck in the front." Adams yelled.

"There not here sir. I'm sorry." The old man said.

"Clear... Clear..." Little and Reyes came back and said, "Sir, listen to me. Where are the people who were in that truck?" Adams tried to speak clearer.

"I don't know." The old man said looking confused.

"The fuckin' truck is in your front yard and you don't know where they went?" Reyes said to him getting agitated with his answers.

"No, I don't know where they went. The nice police man asked for my car, so I give it to him." The old man said.

"Fuck man! Why didn't you say it at first?" Reyes said.

"Cause you asked me where were they and I don't know that, officer." The old man said slowly.

"Okay, nevermind. What kind of car do you have?" Adams asked the old man.

"I have a blue Cadillac or an Oldsmobile I really don't know models that good. I got it from a friend a couple-" Before he could finish, Little cut him off.

"Do you have a picture of it?"

Adams got on his radio and told the pilot to look for a blue car in the area, a Cadillac or Oldsmobile model. "Got it, Adams." The pilot said.

"Let's go," Little said as they ran out the door.

Rico's phone rang twice and he picked up. "Hello, Mario. You owe me big. So what do you want?" Rico said very angrily.

"I got that bitch from them like I promised. Where are you man? They're all over me." Cantu told him.

"What good is she now that the police are everywhere?" Rico asked him.

"Her boyfriend will still give you your box for her." Cantu told him.

"And where is he now?" Rico asked curiously.

"I don't know. We'll call him and make him talk." Cantu said.

"Okay. I'm at a friend's house. Do you remember where Arron lives?" Rico asked him.

"You mean Arron from San Marcos?" Cantu said.

"Yes. Come here and we'll sit for a few days, call the boyfriend and you'll get yours." Rico said with every intention on killing them all once he got the diamonds. They hung up.

Cantu told the driver, Let's switch cars one more time then head to San Marcos."

CHAPTER 10

Over at BAMC Hospital, Solis had come out of her coma, but remembered nothing. Her injuries were serious. One bullet hit her spine. She felt nothing from the waist down. An officer was in the room keeping guard when she awoke. He called for a nurse to come in.

"Hey, excuse me. She woke up, miss." The officer told the nurse at the desk.

The nurse rushed in the room to check her vitals. Everything seemed fine besides the obvious wounds. Solis couldn't talk because a tube was down her throat and had her gagging. The nurse removed the tube and Solis threw up.

"Where am I?" Solis asked the nurse confused.

"You're at BAMC Trauma Center. You were shot several times by a high caliber bullet days ago. You've been in a mild coma since. Your partner asked us to call as soon as we get any movement out of you. The doctors thought you might not wake up. We need to run a few tests then we'll call your partner." The nurse told her.

Solis laid there confused and then closed her eyes and drifted out from the medication in her I.V.

Adams, Little and Reyes searched for an hour for the old man's car with no luck. "How the fuck did we lose them?" Adams said frustrated and disappointed.

"What are we going to do now?" Little asked Adams and Reyes.

GREED

"Call chief and let him know and be prepared for his mouth. We all may be suspended." Reyes said.

"We can't give up. Not yet." Adams said.

Reyes got on the radio and called the Chief. "Chief, this is Reyes, come back."

"Reyes, where is Adams and Little?" the Chief asked in a not so pissed voice.

"They're right here. We lost Cantu. He switched vehicles on us. He's in a blue Oldsmobile." Reyes informed him.

"Do you have a plate number?" Chief asked hoping for a yes.

"Yeah." Reyes read the number out to the Chief then the Chief instructed them to get back to the station. On the way, he told them what he knew from what Jesus told Rob.

Cantu and the other team leader were on their way to San Marcos in a different car they hijacked using their badges.

When they switched cars, he put Vanessa in the trunk of the car. He got his phone out and scrolled his call log, and dialed Tim.

It rang but there was no answer, so he hung up.

"This fuckin' kid has caused too much fuckin' trouble for me." Cantu said to the driver staring at Tim's number. He called Rico and let him know that they were 20 minutes away and they'd be there shortly.

When the driver saw a roadblock up ahead he panicked. "What do I do?" He asked Cantu.

"Flash your fuckin' badge. You're a police officer stupid." Cantu told him.

"But what if they are already looking for us?" The officer asked.

"I doubt that very seriously." Cantu said matter-of-factly.

They pulled to the officers and Cantu asked what was going on. The officer said, "We were told to stand guard and to be on the lookout for a hostage situation. Something about a guy named Rudolfo De Luna. I really wasn't listening. I'm kinda under the weather right now." The guard at the roadblock told them.

"Well, if we see anything we'll radio in. Take it easy." Cantu smiled and they drove on.

At the hospital, MAK had been all patched up and placed in a room. While the nurse walked out, the guard was down the hall. He decided to use the phone to make a few calls. First number he dialed was his cell phone. The phone rang a couple times and Tiffany picked up.

"Hello." Tiffany said.

"Hey, who is this?" MAK said.

"MAK, is that you?" Tiffany asked him.

"Yeah, who is this? Tiffany or Sara?" MAK asked still confused.

"It's me, Tiffany. Where are you?" Tiffany asked him.

"I'm at the hospital. I got shot, but I'll be okay. Where is Vanessa and Sara? Are they okay?" MAK asked her worried about Vanessa.

"MAK, they got Vanessa and they shot Sara. Sara is fine. It only put a deep gash in her stomach, but that fuckin' cop got her." Tiffany told him.

"Which cop?" MAK asked.

"Some crazy motherfucker, but some white cop helped us, or at least tried to." Tiffany said.

"Tiff, I need yo help. I know what they want. I got it. We need to get Nessa back. I need you to come get me. I'm at Southeast Baptist, please." MAK told her.

"How am I supposed to come get you? The cop shot the tires out of your car and we had to leave it. I'm at Northeast Baptist with Sara. They got cops everywhere, so nobody can get close to us and we can't leave till Sara's done. Then we're being taken into protective custody till this is settled. Sorry, there's nothing I can do." Tiffany told him feeling helpless.

"Okay, well. I need to make some more calls. I need to get my girl back." MAK told her thinking of his next move.

"Good luck. I wish I could help. Keep me posted. I'll hold your phone. Do you still got Tim's phone?" Tiffany asked him.

"Yeah, but it's in my property. The nurse went to get it for me. I'll call you back later." MAK told her, then he hung up.

Back at the station, the meeting was under way. Chief was giving out instructions on the plans they were to follow. He had a list of all the businesses, homes and all other properties belonging to Rudolfo De Luna. They were to hit all the local and surrounding areas simultaneously.

Chief sent the word out about 5 minutes earlier that Cantu was wanted and got a call back from two guards saying they saw him and another officer headed towards the Austin-San Marcos area. Chief put together two special units to raid the two properties in that area. Rico had a business in Austin and a house in San Marcos.

The units in San Diego were on standby ready to take all Rico's properties too.

Chief was going over things with Adams. "Hey, you okay, kiddo?" Chief asked him sensing distress in his face.

"Yeah, Chief, I'm good." Adams said not so convincing.

"Look, we're going to get this all wrapped up soon. Then we can all go home happy. You just hang in here and don't let your emotions get the best of you. I've also got good news for you." The Chief told him holding both hands together as if he just clapped.

"What could possibly be good at this time?" Adams asked looking Chief in the eyes.

"Solis woke up." Chief told him smiling.

Adams thought he heard wrong. "Are you serious Chief?" Adams said with joy in his voice.

"I wouldn't kid around with you like that. She woke up 2 hours ago asking for Super Dave." Chief told him. Adams smiled with confidence Chief hadn't seen all day. "So, listen kid, when we get outta here, remember we do this the right way and do it for our fallen officers." Chief reminded him.

"Let's move!" Chief yelled out and everyone shook hands and headed out.

Cantu and the team leader pulled up to the house and were surprised by the weapons and dogs. The car was surrounded and they ordered Cantu and the driver to get out.

"What's going on?" Cantu said with an attitude pushing one weapon out of his face. No one said a word. One guy fired a shot into the chest of the driver and told Cantu again to get out.

Cantu got out of the car. They searched him and found a Glock. They took the pistol and asked for the girl.

"She's in the fuckin' trunk." He told them looking around for an emergency exit. Instantly the others began beating Cantu to the ground.

Rico and Arron stepped out onto the porch and looked at Cantu trying to fight back with no progress.

Once Cantu was unconscious, they dragged him out to the guest house. They brought Vanessa inside and laid her in one of the guest rooms. They used Cantu's cuffs to cuff her to the bed. Then Rico and the others went out back where Cantu was being held.

"Rico, what the fuck is going on, man? We had a fuckin' deal, man." Cantu said after they woke him up with a slap to the face.

"Shh, I don't like a lot of noise, officer." Rico said sarcastically.

"Look, Rico, man. I brought you the girl, man. Just give me my money and we can go our ways." Cantu told him, hoping his bluff would work.

"Go our ways? Go our ways? How do we go our ways when every fuckin' cop in San Antonio is probably looking for us now?" Rico asked him raising his usually smooth voice.

"We just passed some fuckin' police. Nobody is looking for me, Rico." Cantu assured him.

"Okay, well, what about me?" Rico asked him.

"You think anyone is looking for Mario? I can get you outta Texas man. Remember, I'm the law." Cantu said pleading.

"Then what, Mario? Where do I go from there?" Rico asked. Before Cantu could say anything, Rico pulled out a blade and cut him across the face. The blade sliced Cantu from the left eye to the bottom of the chin. Cantu yelled as blood poured to the ground.

"What the fuck, Rico, man. Are you fuckin' crazy?" I'm a cop and you can't do this to me." Cantu said starting to panic. He knew what came next.

"Oh, I can't? I do what the fuck I like, pig." Rico told him then kicked him in the face.

The men held Cantu tight by the arms. He struggled to get loose but it was no use. They took him to the restroom and threw him in the bathtub. One of the men shot him in the knee and in the foot. Cantu yelled and fought with the men but the pain was too much.

They turned on the water and clogged up the tub. It started to fill fast. The men grabbed him by the head and forced it under water. Cantu fought hard for a while but he was weak from the loss of so much blood. The water entered through the nose and quickly filled his lungs. It burned for only a second.

Then his brain felt as if it was going to explode. His eyes went wide as the life left his body with every bubble. Then he went limp.

Rico laughed and fired up a cigar and sat on the edge of the bathtub talking to Cantu's dead body. "Hey pig, how does that feel? You like that motherfucker…huh? I'm talking to you. What? Rat got your tongue?" Rico got up and told his men to get rid of Cantu's body.

Rico and Arron went inside to where they had Vanessa. When they walked in, Vanessa started kicking and yelling.

"Get the fuck away from me, motherfucker! Where am I?" She screamed.

Rico told her to calm down. "Hey, little lady, such a foul mouth. You're at a safe place. Don't worry." Rico assured her, trying to calm her.

Arron's wife came into the room with towels and new clothes for Vanessa. "Rico, she needs a doctor. She's bleeding. She can't keep those clothes on." Arron's wife told him.

Rico said, "No, No fuckin' doctor. This little lady has something I need and I'm going to kill her if I don't get it."

"What the fuck do I got? I don't have shit. I just wanna go home to my boyfriend." Vanessa said with tears in her eyes and pain in her broken voice.

"Your boyfriend took my diamonds and set me up. He got my best friend killed today. Now, where is he? We have unfinished business." Rico told Vanessa grabbing her by the face.

"I don't know. I haven't talked to him since he was at the factory today." Vanessa tried to explain to him, hoping he believed her.

Arron's wife cut in, Rico, let her clean up first."

Rico got very mad and yelled at Arron's wife, "No, she doesn't get shit til I get what I'm after. This bitch and her boyfriend is the reason why Toro is dead and 50 million worth of diamonds are lost. How the fuck do I explain that to Carlos and his fuckin' death squad?" Rico rounded in her face.

When Arron's wife heard Carlos' name, she got quiet and left the room. The Death Squad murdered her brother and his crew of drug runners 7 years ago. Her brother's crew was of about 20 members who were on the rise in Mexico, until they refused to pay Carlos for the dope he fronted them. Carlos sent Death to their doorstep. All the members were killed within one week. Her brother was dropped off in their front yard without his head or hands. The family had the funeral and two days later the head showed up on the doorstep and the hands were in the mailbox.

The nurse came in the room with MAK's property and asked if he needed anything.

"No, I'm good. Thank you." He said smiling at her. MAK looked at the phone and got Cantu's phone number and dialed it. Cantu's phone was under 3 feet of dirt along with Cantu. They buried his body in the field next to the property.

MAK looked for Rico's number and dialed it. "Please answer," MAK said to himself.

Rico picked up. "Hello." Rico said.

MAK replied, "I still got yo diamonds motherfucker. Where is the police with my girl?" MAK said.

Rico put the phone to Vanessa and let her talk. She said nothing, but MAK heard her whimpering.

"Nessa, is that you baby?" MAK asked her, tears welling up in his eyes.

"Baby, please come get me." Vanessa said sounding like all the life was out of her.

"Where are you, baby?" MAK said.

"I don't know, John. I'm scared. They hurt me bad. I need you. I can't take this anymore." She cried out to him with no energy.

"I love you, Nessa." MAK told her.

Rico took the phone away from her and she cried out for MAK. "Now, listen kid. You only get one more chance. I'm not nice like Mario. I'll kill this bitch. You understand me? I want my fuckin' diamonds or she dies a slow painful death." Rico shouted to him meaning every word.

"Tell me when and where, but I need your word that you'll give me my girl alive." MAK said.

"Why? You don't trust me, kiddo?" Rico said sarcastically.

"Fuck you. I don't even know you, plus ya'll tried to kill me at the damn factory." MAK reminded him.

"I didn't bring no police. He just popped up." MAK said.

"Yeah! Sure. Just don't let it happen again, okay?" Rico told him.

"Okay, please man. I just want my girl. I don't care about these fuckin' diamonds." MAK let him know.

"Come here to San Marcos. We'll be waiting for you and remember to come alone. You have 2 hours." Rico said. Rico gave him the address and hung up.

"How the fuck am I supposed to get to San Marcos?" MAK asked Rico, not knowing he hung up. "Hello…Hello? Fuck man! What the fuck am I going to do? these motherfuckers are going to kill me and Nessa." He said to himself.

The Chief's phone rang twice and he answered it. "Hello. What is it? I'm busy!" He yelled into the receiver.

It was the phone tracker. "Chief, that phone was just used again. The call came from Southeast Baptist Hospital to a number in San Marcos." The tracker told him.

"Where in San Marcos?" Chief asked. When the specialist gave the address, the Chief tapped Adams. "Guess what, kid? That phone we've been tracking was just used and made a call to the same address we are headed to." Chief said with a smile.

"Where did the call come from?" Adams asked curiously.

"Southeast Baptist." Chief said.

"Holy shit, that's John. I hope he doesn't think he can take these motherfuckers on his own. I need to talk to him right away." Adams told them.

Chief told the specialist to patch them through to MAK's line. The specialist patched the call through, it rang 4 times and MAK picked up.

"Hello?" MAK said.

"Hello, John. This is Detective Adams." Adams yelled. MAK hung up.

"What happened?" Adams asked.

"Sir, he hung up. Want me to call again?" The tech said.

"Yes, hurry." Adams told him.

The call was made and MAK answered. "What man? What?" MAK yelled in frustration.

"Listen to me kid, we know you just talked to the people who have Vanessa. Don't play with these people. You will get both of you killed. Do you understand?" Adams tried to explain to him.

"Fuck you. You told me you'd save her and now she's in fuckin' San Marcos and I only got two hours to save her. I'mma give that fucker his diamonds and he's going to give me Nessa." MAK said convincingly.

"No, he's not. He's going to kill both of you and leave no trace of you. You've caused him too much trouble. He won't let you live." Adams pleaded with him.

"We got him. He's at the corner of the Southcross and Pecan Valley at Valero." The tech said over the Chief's radio. He whispered to Adams, "Keep talking." He radioed for a unit to go get MAK ASAP.

They called the unit at the hospital. One officer went and checked the room and radioed his partner, "Yeah, he's gone alright." They both ran out the doors of the hospital and to their cars to find their tires out of air.

"Damn it, that fucker flattened our tires." They radioed Chief and told them what happened. Chief told them to pursue on foot. Then he radioed for another unit to assist with the capture of MAK.

"Kid, just listen to me. We are going to take this bastard down and get your girl back. We know you are just caught in the middle of her brother's mess." Adams said to MAK in genuine voice.

"You don't know what the fuck you're talking about her brother…" MAK said but before he finished that thought, he realized they thought Tim killed the truck driver and he could get away free. He changed his sentence. "Her brother was a good man and didn't deserve to die." MAK said. No need to tell on himself.

"We understand kid, but let us handle this. You can't go in there alone and think you're going to walk out with the girl." Adams assured him.

Just then, MAK saw S.A.P.D. cars everywhere. They surrounded him. He was trapped. "I hate you motherfucker." He said in his phone to Adams.

The arresting officers took his phone and asked, "What do you want us to do with him, sir?" He asked.

"Bring him to San Marcos." Adams gave the officer the meeting address. The rest of the officers cleared the way for them to go through.

"Where are we going, man?" MAK asked the officer.

"We're going to meet Adams and the Chief in San Marcos." He told him.

CHAPTER 11

Back at Bexar County Jail, Jesus sat in a holding cell alone wondering what was going on outside the jail. With the information he gave the police, it should be hell right now for Rico.

Jesus felt the walls closing in on him. His conscience was talking to him, telling him he was a dead man. It's either let the police let him out or he goes to prison. The voice was loud in his ear, literally driving him crazy. He tried to ignore it but couldn't. He took his shirt off and started crying and shaking his head.

An officer walked by and told him to put his shirt back on. He asked the officer to open the door. "Please man, just open it a little bit. I can't breathe in here." Jesus said feeling a panic attack.

"You should've thought of that before you came to our city and started killing people. Now put the fuckin' shirt back on." The officer said.

Jesus jumped up and started banging the windows and door and screamed, "Help me! Help me! I can't take this shit, please!"

The officer looked around and saw no one was around. He opened the cell and Jesus backed up. The officer said, "Is that better?"

"Yes sir, thank you." Jesus said.

The officer walked to Jesus and punched him in the stomach. When Jesus tumbled over, the officer kneed him in the face. The assault went on until the officer was tired and Jesus was battered and bloody. The officer slammed the door and locked it behind him. He went to the restroom to clean himself up.

Jesus took his shirt off and tied it in a knot around his neck. He stood on the toilet then tried it to a slot in the roof where sheet rock tile used to be. He stepped off the toilet, ending it all.

When the officer finished cleaning up, he stepped out the restroom and saw officers running to Jesus cell. "What's going on?" He asked one of them.

"That fuckin' kid in cell 7 just hung himself with his shirt." The officer said.

On the other side Freddy and the rest of his crew were trying to see how Rico was going to get them out of jail. Freddy was on the phone with one of Rico's goons.

"Kid, listen, Rico is busy right now. Call back." The guy told him aggressively.

"Call back? Man, I'm in jail. I need to get out of here. That fool Jesus got away from us and I think he's going to roll over on us all. Now tell Rico that." Freddy yelled at him.

While Freddy was on the phone, one of his crew saw the medics wheeling Jesus out of the other cell with a neck brace on. "Hey Freddy…Freddy… Check this shit out, it's Jesus." The guy said tapping Freddy on the shoulder.

Freddy turned around and saw Jesus who looked pretty bad. His face was all busted up and swollen and he wasn't moving. "See what happened to him." Freddy told the worker.

The other guy knocked on the door and asked the officer about Jesus. The officer told him, "The kid was hanging by his shirt in the cell. Guess it was too much pressure on him." The officer said.

"Holy shit. Freddy, the lawman said Jesus killed himself." The worker said. Freddy told the man on the other end of the phone.

"Tell Rico Jesus is gone. Don't worry about him." Freddy said in a satisfied voice, thinking he could use Jesus suicide as if he killed him.

The Chief, along with Adams and the SWAT team got everything together at the meeting point in San Marcos. As they finished up the plans, the car with MAK arrived. They got MAK out and gave him the plan, while they did, the SWAT went to set up.

The plan was simple. Send MAK in with one SWAT member in the trunk of an unmarked car. MAK will have a gun and bulletproof vest on at all times. No time will be wasted and nobody moves until it's confirmed that Vanessa is there. When word is confirmed, they will assault the house full blast and take no prisoners except for Rico. Everyone else will be shot on sight.

Officers who surrounded the property and the team sent word back, "We are in position. There is activity on the property. We have 3 guards on outside patrol, but we have snipers at the ready point to take them out. We can confirm that the prize is on the second floor of the house and Rudolfo DeLuna is in the lower level of the house with 4 others. Be advised there are women and children in the house…come back command…over." The snipers told Adams and the Chief.

"This is command. Proceed with the snipers. Over." On the Chief's word, the snipers took aim from their covered positions and took the guards out one at a time.

"Command this is SWAT. Phase one complete. Send the kid in, over." The sniper spoke through the radio.

"We copy. Okay, kid. You ready? This is it. We're in. you got it? Remember, you and Little got get Vanessa and shoot anything in your way. Reyes will be leading your way. Look at me kid, she'll be okay." Adams coached him looking at his face. MAK seemed nervous.

Reyes climbed in the trunk of the car and MAK drove up the hill to the house where Rico waited for him. MAK had the diamonds in his pocket, but hadn't told Adams or the Chief that some were missing. The rest of the team set their positions.

When MAK pulled to the gate, two dogs came barking. No guards came to the gate so MAK blew the horn. Rico and Arron expected one of the guards outside to be at the gate. When they weren't, they jumped up and Rico began shouting orders in Spanish.

The outside SWAT were already closing in on the rear of the house. Rico and the others grabbed guns and came out on the porch to see the car sitting at the gate.

"Where are the fuckin' guards who supposed to be out here?" Rico shouted in Spanish. He told one guy to go look around.

"Command, this is the sniper team. We have sight on Rudolfo and the others. Permission to take this shots? Over."

Chief responded, "This is command, take shots but we need Rudolfo alive. Over."

"Roger that, command." The snipers took their shots and killed Rico's whole team and one bullet struck Rico in his knee. The bullet brought him to the ground in mind-numbing pain. He yelled as the team took the house.

MAK smashed through the gate when he saw Rico fall. Once in the house, the sniper team secured Vanessa and everyone else on the 2nd level of the house.

The officers handcuffed Rico and dragged him off the porch. When Chief, Adams, Reyes, Little and MAK walked up they all looked at Rico and MAK spit on him.

"You'll all pay for this. That I promise." Rico mumbled as he tried to ignore the pain.

They went in. When MAK saw Vanessa, he couldn't believe it was her. She had been beaten so bad by Cantu that she was swollen and dried blood was everywhere. Nessa cried upon seeing MAK's face.

"The EMS are on their way. We are going to fly her by chopper back to B.A.M.C." The Chief said. The Chief looked at Adams and said. "It's over, kid. Solis would be proud of you. And to the rest of you, great job. Let's go home." He said as they wrapped it up.

On the flight back to San Antonio, MAK got in touch with Sara and Tiffany and told them the news of the rescue. "The doctors are waiting for us right now at B.A.M.C., so we'll be there in a minute and ready to check her out." MAK told Tiffany. Tiffany was so happy to hear the news. MAK said he'll have the officers bring Sara and Tiffany to the hospital because Vanessa really wanted to see them.

Rico was on his back to San Antonio, but in handcuffs and a bullet in his knee. Upon arrival at the hospital, Rico was taken to the floor where prisoners were held during surgery.

He was taken to a room and undressed. They placed him on an operating table and began to work on his knee. The bullet shattered Rico's knee, but it was repairable. It was only Rico and 4 doctors he was handcuffed to the bed.

He told the 4 doctors, "How would you four like to make 2 million dollars?" He asked them as they prepped him for surgery. The doctors looked at each other and laughed at Rico. They thought the morphine had him talking crazy.

"No, I'm serious," He said. "Who's in charge here?"

The lead doctor spoke up and Rico told him, "Look I'm a very rich man and I can make you just as rich if you get me outta here. I haven't committed any crimes. I'm just an illegal here from Mexico and they want to deport me." Rico said using a bit much on his accent.

"I heard you're a murderer." One of the doctors said.

"I haven't harmed anyone. I swear to you...2 million dollars. Just fix my knee and get me outta here. You can say you had nothing to do with it after the surgery. You left the room and that's it."

The doctors looked at each other and continued working.

Vanessa was being checked out by nurses and doctors. She had serious cuts and bruises on her face and hands. One of her ribs was cracked out and her vagina was bleeding due to too much stress on her insides. The baby was fine and that was her and MAK's main concern.

MAK sat in the waiting room waiting on Sara and Tiffany to arrive. He was exhausted and falling asleep, but everytime he closed his eyes, he saw Tim's face and it woke him back up.

The doctor came out and told him, "Sir, everything is going to be okay. Your girlfriend is pretty banged up, but she and your baby are going to be just fine. We'll keep her here a few days for observation then we'll release her." He told MAK looking at Vanessa's chart.

"Can I go see her now?" MAK asked.

"No, give then a few minutes to clean her up. We gave her some medication for the pain, so she'll be out a few hours." The doctor said to him.

On the other side of the hospital, Adams was visiting Solis.

"Hey, Petra. We got the case closed." He said to her while holding her hand.

"So, it's finally over?" She mumbled to him. The meds were strong, but she was still lucid. "Super Dave, I love you. I wanted to tell you before it was too late." She said.

"What do you mean before it's too late? You're going to be okay. The doctors said you're alright." Adams said to her with a tear in his eye.

"Yeah! I know, but this lets me know tomorrow isn't promised to us." She said squeezing his hand.

"Stop, Petra. Let's not sad talk. This is a happy moment. We solved a case, caught the bad guys and we're all still alive." Adams said starting to get emotional.

"Okay, buddy. But I never got to tell you I've had a crush on you since you came to the force." Solis confessed.

They both smiled and he kissed her lips. "Get some rest and we'll talk about that when you come home." Adams told her.

"You promise, Super Dave?" Solis said smiling.

"Scout's honor, babe." Adams told her raising two fingers.

"Dave, what happened with Cantu?" Solis asked.

When he mentioned Cantu's name, it hit him that Cantu was still missing. "I'll be back, Petra. You get some rest okay?" He said. He ran out the room down the hall. He got his phone and called Chief's number. It rang, but there was no answer.

He got outside to the parking lot and his phone rang. It wasn't the Chief, it was Sgt. Little.

"Hello, Detective Adams." He said.

"Yes, Adams, this is Sgt. Little. I was calling because I wanted to ask what happened to Cantu. I don't remember seeing him at the house in San Marcos. Should we put and A.P.B. out on him?" Little asked.

Adams paused for a minute and said, "Yes, where are you Little?" Adams asked her.

"I'm at the station writing my report and Reyes brought it to my attention that Cantu was still MIA." Little told him.

"Okay, I'm on my way. Put the A.P.B. out." Adams told her.

"Got you. How's Solis?" Little asked.

"She's fine. She was about to go to sleep before I left." Adams told her.

Back in San Diego Nora was being detained at the police headquarters and questioned about Rico and his involvement in the San Antonio murders, drugs and guns.

"Mrs. DeLuna, do you know that you can be held accountable for your husband's crimes?" The detectives told her.

"Fuck you, pig! Let me make a fuckin' phone call because I don't know nothing about Rico's so-called involvement in shit!" Nora fired off.

"Well, if you don't tell, maybe his hot girlfriend in there will." The detective told her referring to his assistant Stephany.

A scared look went over Nora's face. Then she thought, maybe he's trying to play psychological games with her to turn her against Rico.

The Officer left the door open so Nora could see down the hallway. He went into a room and came back down the hallway with a very attractive young blonde.

She didn't know Stephany except that she was a worker in Rico's

Building. The officer took her to a conference room. The room had a long metal table, a two-way mirror and listening devices so the officers can observe suspects during questioning. He left Stephany in the room while he went and got a female officer to do the interrogation. He went to the room where Nora was and told her to come with him to observe this interrogation of Stephany.

"What's going on?" Nora asked confused.

"Well, Mrs. DeLuna, this is your husband's secretary. Let's see what she has to say about your little Rico." The officer said with a grin.

The officer came over the speaker and advised the female officer she could start the questions she had for Stephany.

"Hello, ma'am. I'm Detective Johnson. I'm going to ask you a few questions and I need you to answer as honest as possible." The detective said.

"Yes ma'am. I understand. Am I in any trouble?" Stephany asked looking nervous.

"Not at this moment, but your boss is." The detective told her. "Okay, how long have you worked for Mr. De Luna?" The detective began questioning.

"I've worked for him for seven and a half years now." Stephany responded.

"How did you meet him?" The detective asked her looking directly in her eyes.

"We met at a bar one night." Stephany recalled.

"Is your relationship with him strictly professional or is it more than that?" Detective Johnson asked her which surprised Stephany.

"Are you asking if we're having sex?" Stephany asked her readjusting in her chair.

"Well, are you?" Johnson pried further.

"What the hell does that have to do with anything?" Stephany barked uncrossing her legs and leaning forward.

"Just answer the question, ma'am." Johnson yelled slamming her hand on the table.

"I'm not answering anymore of your perverted questions." Stephany shouted then she got up and tried to leave the room.

"Ma'am, you're not leaving this room until you answer questions, so sit back down." Johnson told her.

"Yes, we have sex. Does that help your case?" Stephany said not looking at Johnson.

When Nora heard that, she clenched her fist in anger.

"What is your relationship with Mr. DeLuna?" Johnson continued.

"He's my boss." Stephany said now sitting back down with her head down.

"The truth, ma'am." Johnson asked.

"Mr. DeLuna is my boyfriend." Stephany mumbled.

"Do you know that Mr. DeLuna is married?" Johnson told her.

"Yes, I know, but things aren't happy at home, so we started seeing each other. There's no crime in that." Stephany said beginning to cry,

"What do you know about his illegal activities with drugs and guns?" Johnson asked.

"I don't know anything about guns and drugs. I only work in the office. That's it…" Stephany assured her both hands in the air in a surrender motion.

"You're his girlfriend, but you don't know about his outside life?" Johnson continued.

"Mr. DeLuna is real good about keeping things to himself." Stephany told her.

As the questioning continued, the officer in the room with Nora took her back in the other room and asked her, "Now, you sure you don't have anything you want to tell me?" he asked Nora hoping she'd crack. Nothing like a woman scorned.

"You think because you put some slut in a room and says she's fucking my husband that I'll tell you anything you want, even if I knew anything? I don't talk to police. I need my phone call." Nora shouted in his face and crossed her arms.

"We'll give you your phone call in a minute." The detective said.

"Please hurry. My father won't be pleased about me being held for no reason." Nora said.

The officer left and brought her a phone back. He plugged it in and left the room. Nora got on the phone and dialed Rico's number but she got no answer. She hung up and dialed Hector's number and still no answer, so she dialed her father.

Over in Puerto Rico, Carlos was at the table having a drink in the back by his pool. Several Puerto Rican females swim in the pool

naked, while bodyguards walked around and secured the fortress with AK-47's.

His phone rang and Carlos' right hand man, Juan, took the phone.

"Hola," Carlos said in a deep latin accent.

"Papa, this is Nora. I need your help. I'm at a police station in San Diego. The police raided the house looking for guns and drugs. They took me in for questioning about Rico. They said he's involved in murder in San Antonio, Texas. Something about stolen diamonds and I found out that he's been cheating on me with his fucking secretary. I can't fucking believe him, papa. Please come get me." Nora said all in one breath, tears flowing like the Nile.

"Where is Rico, Nora?" Carlos asked sitting down his glass.

"I don't know." Nora said.

"I'll send someone to get you right away and see if they know where Rico is." Carlos told her.

They hung up and Carlos slammed his phone on the table. Juan looked at Carlos with a look of concern.

"What's wrong, boss?" Juan asked.

"That fucking son-in-law of mine has got my daughter in jail behind his fuck-ups. She found out he's been with another woman and he may have fucked up my diamond deal with the Cubans." Carlos said to Juan staring at the phone.

Carlos went in the house and got on the phone and called Rachelle Benson, the family lawyer. Mrs. Benson was one of the best if not the best lawyer money could buy. She got many of Carlos' friends and family off murder cases, drug trafficking, kidnapping and the record goes on. The courts hate to see Mrs. Benson enter the room, because she's always a bulldog about her work.

Her phone rang twice and she answered. "My friend, how's the island life going?" She asked in her usual cheerful voice.

"Oh, fine. Thanks for asking. I have a problem. I'm not sure the size of it as of yet, but my daughter is in jail in your area. I need her out at any cost, money's no option. I also need to find out where her husband is. The police said something to her about San Antonio, TX." Carlos told her with urgency in his voice.

"Okay, well, I got a buddy down there. I'll call and check if he's locked up or what. Give me an hour and I'll get back to you, okay?" Rachelle told him writing as they talked.

"Hurry with my daughter, please." Carlos told her.

Back in San Diego, Stephany held her ground. Even with the threats of jail time, she never rolled on Rico.

The officer pulled her out the room and placed her in a small waiting room.

"She's no going to break, sir. Either she doesn't know anything or is too in love to tell." Johnson told the other officer.

"Okay, let her go, but keep a tail on her. If she does know something, it'll come out." The officer said.

"What about the wife?" Johnson asked.

"She's not finished. We have more to talk to her about." The detective said.

MAK had one of the officers escort him to the apartment, so he could gather some things for Vanessa and change clothes.

"Oh, sir, do you think I could jump in the shower right quick?" MAK asked feeling ugly from the events he just went through.

"Yeah, take your time. I know you've been through a lot. I'll wait outside in the car." The officer said.

MAK looked around the place and all the damages. Then he saw the picture of him and Tim. He picked it up and tears fell from his eyes. "All we been through, now you're gone." He thought to himself.

He went to the back to change and get in the shower. As he got undressed, the bag of diamonds fell out his pocket. "Oh shit, I forgot I still had these." He closed the door and poured them on the floor and looked at them sparkle. "Oh and I forgot the rest at the factory. I wonder if the laws found them." He smiled then got in the shower.

As he got out, he heard voices. It was the manager and the officer who was waiting outside. MAK got dressed and came out.

"Hello, John. How is Vanessa? I saw the news. I feel so bad for you both." The manager said.

"Oh, she's going to make it. She's at B.A.M.C. right now. They're going to keep her a few days to make sure the baby is okay." He told her.

"Well, I told the officer I'd get maintenance in here right away to fix your apartment, so don't worry, you won't have to pay for anything." The manager told him.

"Well, we might not want to stay. It's too many memories that I don't think she'll wanna live with here. Plus, my Aunt had a place right outside of town. So, we might go out there." MAK told her.

"If you guys decide to stay, you're more than welcome." The manager assured him.

In Rico's hospital room the doctors were finished with Rico's surgery. He was still out from the meds he was on. Doctor Green and Felix were talking to each other as they went along.

"Hey, you really think this guy has 2 million bucks on hand like that?" Felix said to Green.

"I don't know, but that's a hell of a lot of money. Money I could never make working here." Green said. They exchanged looks and thought hard about it.

Outside in the smoking area, Green asked Felix if he thought they could get in a lot of trouble if they helped an illegal alien.

"Who would know we helped?" Felix asked. "All we have to do is get him out of here and somewhere he can get us money. We can keep him tied up and drugged, get out cash and let him go. By the time the drugs wear off, we'll be long gone and 2 million dollars richer." Felix said as serious as he could.

"You really thought this through, huh?" Green said.

"Yeah, I want that money." Felix told him.

Green hit his cigarette and looked around then told Felix, "I'm in."

CHAPTER 12

Within hours, Rachelle, along with her assistant Michelle Smith, and two federal officers walked into the San Diego Detectives office with papers signed by a judge for the immediate release of Nora. The detectives tried to dispute, but the Feds were not hearing any argument.

Rachelle showed the Chief the papers and told him to escort her to where Nora was being held or he'd added to the lawsuit that she was filling against the arresting officers.

They escorted her to the room Nora was in. When the door opened, and Nora saw Rachelle, she was relieved to see her face. She knew daddy came through for her.

"Nora, are you okay?" Rachelle asked.

"Yes, please just get me out of here." Nora said tired from the wait.

"Come on. We're leaving now. Your father will be pleased to hear from you." Rachelle told her. They gathered her things and left the station.

When they got in the car, Rachelle gave Nora the phone. "Call your father." Rachelle told her handing her the phone.

Nora dialed Carlos' number. "Hola, papa it's me, Nora. Yes, I'm out. Rachelle came to get me… Okay, I love you, papa." Nora said to him.

She handed the phone to Rachelle. "Hello, Carlos. Everything had been taken care of and as for Rico, he was shot in a raid in San Marcos. He's been taken to B.A.M.C. hospital in San Antonio. He's being detained in connection with murder charges, capital murder charges, aggravated kidnapping, and about 8 more charges. Those are just the worst of the bunch. Do you want me to go to San Antonio and see what I can do?" Rachelle asked.

"No, I'll send someone else." Carlos said.

"Who's better than me, Carlos?" Rachelle asked curious.

"Juan." He said. When he said that, Rachelle's facial expression went blank and she looked at Nora with worry.

Carlos told Rachelle to get Nora on a plane to Puerto Rico and he'll transfer some money to Rachelle's offshore account. She agreed and hung up.

Nora looked at her and asked what her father said about her Rico.

"Well, he said to put you on a plane to Puerto Rico, but as for Rico, he said he'll be sending Juan for Rico." Rachelle told her not looking her in the face.

"What! What do you mean he's sending Juan?" She said then she hurried up and redialed her father's phone.

Juan is the captain of "Death", the hit squad. If Carlos sends Juan for Rico, it's only to kill him. She was heartbroken over the news of his cheating, but he was still here husband and she didn't want him dead.

"Hello." Carlos answered the line. "Dad, why are you sending Juan for Rico?" Send Rachelle, she got me out. She can get Rico out too." Nora pleaded with Carlos.

"Rico is no longer your concern, baby girl. Just go to the airport and board the plane. We'll talk when you get here." Carlos told her in a tone like she was a child. And he hung up.

"Papa-papa." Nora yelled to a dial tone.

"Rachelle, I'm not going to Puerto Rico. I'm going to San Antonio to warn Rico." Nora shouted at Rachelle.

"Please, Nora. Your father will have a fit if I don't do what he asked. My job is to get you to Puerto Rico and I take my job seriously." Rachelle told her.

"Rachelle, Rico is my husband and I don't want him dead. I'm not going." Nora shouted at Rachelle with tears strolling down her face.

She tried to get out the car, but one of the Feds grabbed her arm and pulled her back in, then they drove off.

Dr. Green told Dr. Felix they had to work fast before anyone noticed Rico was being moved. Rico was under heavy drugs, administered through an I.V. They went to the front desk to check out for the night. Then they went to another patient's room, who was under heavy sedation and moved him into Rico's room. They bandaged his face and put the oxygen mask on him.

Felix was nervous. "Hey, Green. I don't think this shit is going to work man. I have a bad feeling." Dr. Felix told him.

"What can go wrong, Felix? Give me one good reason we shouldn't get this 2 million? Besides, he's only here illegally. What kind of crime is that, really? These people just try to get away from the madness in Mexico." Green looked him in the eyes and said.

Felix wasn't buying it. "Look, man, the news said he was wanted for murdering cops, man." Felix pleaded.

"Okay, you go I'll do it alone, more money for me." Green said determined to go through with the plan.

Felix looked at him and decided to stay on. "Let's go man, but this is wrong." Felix said.

They switched the men out and headed for the rear exit. Felix went to talk with security, while Green loaded Rico into the brown Dodge Durango. Once he had Rico in and out of sight, he called Felix on his cell and told him to follow him.

"Hey, Adams, nobody has heard anything about Cantu. I already put the A.P.B. out." Sgt. Little told Adams as he walked through the doors of her office.

"Have you asked the old lady or the children from the house?" Adams asked.

"Nope. I was waiting for you." Sgt. Little said looking up at him.

"Okay, well, let's go see what she has to say." Adams said. Adams and a translator went into the room with Arron's wife. She was still very broken up over the situation in San Marcos.

"Hello, ma'am, my name is Detective Adams. I have a few questions for you." The translator translated.

Arron's wife yelled, "I fuckin' speak english!"

"Okay, well that's wonderful. Miss, there was another officer at your house with your husband and Mr. DeLuna, do you remember him?" Adams asked politely.

She spit in Adams face and yelled, "You killed my husband and you expect my help?" She yelled through tears and grief filled eyes.

Adams used every fiber in him to control himself from treating Arron's wife like a man. He got up and walked out. He got a towel and wiped his face, then asked Sgt. Little to go try.

Sgt. Little went in and informed the lady of her Miranda rights and let her know she was under arrest for assault on an officer.

"Assault? I haven't assaulted anyone." The lady said in her deep Mexican accent.

"Oh, yes you did ma'am. In this country, you spit on an officer, that's assault and your ass will do time. Then we'll ship your ass back across the border. Now, do you want to go through with all that? Not to mention we'll take those kids and you won't see them anymore once they get lost in the system." Sgt. Little shouted in her face.

"No, you can't take my children, please." The lady said now more humble.

"Will you help me and I'll help you. I think some helpful information…might persuade my partner to drop the charges." Sgt. Little told the lady.

"Okay, anything you want. I'll help. Please, just don't take my kids from me." The lady pleaded with Sgt. Little.

"Okay, the cop he asked you about, do you remember him?" Sgt. Little asked.

"Yes, I remember. He brought the girl to Rico." The lady recalled.

"What else, ma'am…?" Sgt. Little asked.

"They killed him and his partner." The lady told her.

When Adams, Little and the other officers heard that, they couldn't believe their ears.

"What do you mean, they killed him?" Little asked her in disbelief.

"I mean, they killed him and buried him in the backyard." The lady told her.

Sgt. Little turned and looked at the two-way mirror where she knew Adams was. The light blinked, which was the signal to Little to come out the rooms. When she came out Adams asked her, "Do you believe her?"

"I don't think she'd lie, Adams. We better get somebody out there to check for the body." Sgt. Little told him with urgency.

Adams walked down the hall to notify the Chief of the update on Cantu. Sgt. Little yelled down the hall to Adams, "What do you want me to do about her?"

"See if she had some place to go, because that property in San Marcos is now S.A.P.D. property." Adams yelled back to her.

"So, she's not under arrest?" Sgt. Little asked.

"For what Sgt? We got nothing on her." Adams said.

"Adams, she was there when her husband killed an officer and kidnapped Vanessa and we're going to just let her go?" Sgt. Little said walking in Adams direction.

"We already got who's responsible for all of that. As a matter of fact, that dead officer tried to assist in the murder of my partner, kidnapping Vanessa and almost killed you not too long ago, or did you forget?" Adams told her in a no-regrets tone for Cantu.

"No, I didn't forget, but she's part of it, so she should pay with the rest of them." Sgt. Little continued.

"Sgt. Little, let the woman and her kids go. End of discussion." Adams said.

Sgt. Little looked at Adams with anger in her eyes, but obeyed and walked away.

Dr. Green and Dr. Felix pulled into Green's garage, parked and both got out. They got Rico out of the backseat and carried him into the house and into the spare room.

"Watch him. Let me talk to my son." Green told Felix, then he left out the room.

He went into the room where his son was watching TV with the neighbor.

"Jeff, come in let me talk to you for a second." Green told his little boy.

"Yeah! Dad, what's up?" The boy joyfully responded.

"Dad has a patient in the guest room who's really sick and I'm going to need you to stay out of there for a few days, okay?" Green explained to him with a no-nonsense look on his face.

"Yeah, sure Dad, no problem." The boy said.

Green went back in the room with Felix and told him, "Look, we're going to keep him here until the money is transferred then we'll let him go." Dr. Green said.

"Why here? What if they figure out it was you and come looking?" Felix told him.

"Before they realize he's gone, he'll be out of here and back in Mexico." Green told him. Green went to the garage and got a chain and two pad locks to chain Rico to the bad. He came in and they linked his feet and hands. Then locked him to the bedrails.

"Tomorrow, we'll wake him up and take care of the money issues as soon as possible." Green explained in a very convincing voice.

After talking to Rachelle earlier, Carlos ordered Juan to go to San Antonio and take out Rico. Juan was a professional hitman and always eliminated his targets. Juan gathered his four man team and they boarded Carlos' private plane.

The mission was simple, take out Rico and get information on the whereabouts of the diamonds. Anyone in the way will be taken out too. Keep things as quiet as possible. Juan had done 'Death' work for Carlos since he was younger. He's even done work for Rico, but taking Rico out was all just a part of business to him.

Nora cried the whole way to the airport, yelling and cussing at the officers and Rachelle. Rachelle started to feel bad for Nora as they pulled into the airport's private plane area. She thought about the consequences of her next move if Carlos felt disrespected, but her heart felt sorrow for Nora and Rico.

She informed the feds to cuff Nora and leave her the key, She'll be taking Nora herself to see Carlos. The fed officer looked puzzled, but didn't dispute the request.

When they arrived at the plane, they cuffed Nora and handed the key over to Rachelle and were dismissed. Once they boarded the plane, Rachelle took the handcuffs off Nora and advised the pilot to go to San Antonio, TX instead of Puerto Rico.

When Nora heard the request she jumped up and yelled, "Thank you so much, Rachelle…Thank you."

"We have to hurry. Juan will kill Rico fast. That's his job." Nora shouted and pleaded

"Just calm down, buckle your seatbelt and have a drink. I'll make a few calls to insure nobody gets in or out of Rico's room without police clearance." Rachelle explained to Nora.

They buckled in. The pilot started the plane for San Antonio. "I'm coming, babe." Nora said under her breath.

The next morning, back in San Antonio at Dr. Green's home, they were waking Rico to discuss the money.

Rico looked around and was confused from dosing off the meds. He remembered Dr. Green's face then he looked around. He noticed the chain and padlocks and he smiled, 'Greed' he said to himself.

Dr. Green got straight to the point, "Look, we did this for you only for the 2 million. You make good on your word and we set you free. If not, we fill that I.V. back up with morphine and haul you back to the hospital, where hundreds of police will be looking for you in about a day or two. So I'd advise you not to waste any of our time."

Rico laughed and looked down at his leg. "Look, I need to make a call to the bank and it's done." Rico assured them both.

"We are not responsible for you further at this point. We got you from the hospital and out of custody, that was the deal." Felix told Rico feeling guilty inside.

Rico looked at him and said, "You must be the boss. Are you the brains behind this operation, sir?" The he laughed again.

"Look, you arrogant son of a bitch, we just want out money and no games. It's bad enough we're doing this at all." Felix snapped at him.

"Yes, sir." Rico said still laughing the sarcastic Rico laugh.

"Get me a phone and we'll handle this." Green handed Rico his cell phone to call the bank. Rico asked, "How do I know that once the money is transferred you'll let me go?"

"You have my word." Green told him.

"Your word? I don't know you word is good. I need more than that. Take these chains off and give me a change of clothes." Rico asked him.

"Fuck no." Felix said.

"How can it hurt, man? He is shot in the leg." Green responded as he started to undo the locks and chains. He got them off and Green got him a change of clothes.

"Can I have something to drink?" Rico requested.

"Yeah, right after you transfer that money to our accounts." Green told him.

They both gave Rico their account numbers and Rico made the transfer. Green took the phone, called his bank to see his new account balance and read out one million five thousand and seventy dollars. He jumped through the roof.

"Ha ha, I'm rich!" He yelled. Felix stood by with a smile on his face as well.

"Can I go now?" Rico said.

"Yes, sir. You are a free man now, buddy." Green said in a sing song voice.

At the University Hospital, Vanessa was up and moving around. They let her walk down the hall to see Sara and Tiffany. They saw each other and went hysterical. They called and traded 'I love you's'

"You guys saved my life. Thank you so much." Vanessa told them sincerely.

"That's what friends are for, but don't ever put us through no shit like this again. This is going to be one hell of a story to tell that baby." Tiffany said to her as they all laughed and hugged.

"Sara, are you okay?" I heard you got shot. Is it bad?" Vanessa asked her.

"No, it wasn't bad, but it hurts like hell. The doctor said it was just a flesh wound. I'm okay. I can still walk around…" Sara said showing the patch where the wound was.

They all laughed then hugged some more. "Sorry about your brother." Tiffany told Vanessa.

Vanessa just looked at the floor and grabbed her stomach.

MAK and the other officer came up to the elevator. When the door opened and he saw Vanessa and the girls standing in the hallway, his blood pressure went through the roof. He was so happy to see Nessa up and moving around – being that it was his fault. Tim had told him not to kill the truck driver.

On the plane, Juan made a few phone calls to set things in place for the mission. "Take Rico out, along with MAK, get the diamonds back and make it back to Carlos within two days."

He called one of his head members in Austin for a helping hand. Cola was one of the leading hit men in the south region.

GREED

Ring, ring, ring…on the third ring, Cola picked up the phone with laughter in his voice. "What's up my friend? Where have you been hiding?" Cola asked Juan-which only Juan knew as Darrel.

"Nevermind that. I'm on my way. We have a hit. Get my things ready and pick me up at the airport at midnight." Juan said.

"I'll be there at 11:30 boss." Cola replied. Cola and Juan have worked together on several occasion. So Juan knows Cola's a stand-up guy, so things should go smoothly.

"Hello, yes my name is Rachelle Benson, I'm Rudolfo DeLuna's attorney. He's been recently arrested and is being detained at University Hospital there in San Antonio. There has been a death threat on his life and I would like to request extra police security on his room until we arrive." Rachelle requested.

"Okay, ma'am, we'll transfer your message over to the guards on post at the hospital. When will you be arriving?" The operator asked.

"Within the next few hours or so." Rachelle told her.

"No problem, ma'am." The operator said then they hung up.

The operator replayed the message to the officers on patrol. The officer, who took the call, notified the Chief, then the Chief notified Adams. Adams asked the Chief where the info came from. He responded as he was told.

"From his fuckin' attorney, Adams. You believe that shit? He causes all this bullshit in our city and somebody wants us to protect him?" Chief said shaking his head.

"Well, Chief, I'm not going to do it. I'm going home and get some rest soon as we dig up Cantu's body." Adams told Chief sounding so certain.

"Oh, yes, you are doing it. This is your gotdamn case and it isn't over until it's over." Chief said to him.

"Chief, it's over. We got the bad guy. He's in there. Get somebody to sit in front of the door and we're good. I'm not doing it." Adams hung up the phone and sat back.

MAK, Vanessa, Sara and Tiffany sat in Vanessa's room talking about the next move for all of them. MAK told Sara and Tiffany how much he appreciated all their help and offered them a new place to stay. He told them they could come out to the house with him and Vanessa for a while, so they could clear their heads from all that had just went on. The girls gladly agreed to the idea. The doctor walked in with Vanessa's chart and said he needed to keep her for observation on more night.

"Is there something wrong, doctor?" Vanessa asked.

"No, this is just a special precaution for the baby's sake." The doctor told her.

"Okay, that's fine. We'll all stay until tomorrow." MAK said.

Rico hopped down the street on crutches, thinking of how he'll regroup from this. He was in terrible pain, but he tried to block it out his mind. He had a mission that was incomplete.

He came to a corner store and saw a young female coming out of her car using her cell phone. He got her attention and she came to where he was leaning against the wall.

"Hey, do you mind if I use your phone? I really need some help. I just got robbed for my wallet." He lied to her, the old sympathy trick.

"Yeah! Sure, are you okay?" The ditsy girl asked.

"I'll be okay in a minute. I just need to get to my friend's house." Rico told her wincing in pain.

"Well, I'm getting gas. I can give you a ride, sir." The girl said.

GREED

"Let me make this call and I might need that ride. You know there aren't many people as kind as you around here anymore." Rico stroked her ego.

"Oh, it's not a problem. Go ahead and use the phone while I gas up." She said.

Rico smiled. That smile he does when he's up to no good. He dialed Carlos' number. He knew he was about to get the third degree because things went out of control for the first time since they've been doing business together.

Carlos answered his phone, "Hola, this is Carlos." He said with Spanish music loud in the background.

"Carlos, this is Rico I need help now."

Carlos heard Rico's voice and jumped out of his chair. "Rico, where are you? I was told you were in the hospital with your leg shot up." Carlos said surprised to hear from him.

"We'll part of that is true. My leg is shot, but I paid a couple of greedy doctors to get me out of police custody before anyone noticed." Rico told him.

"I sent help for you already, Rico. Juan is on his way to bring you back with the diamonds. Do you know where they are?" Carlos explained to Rico.

"Not at this moment, but I know who has them, and they're at the same hospital I just left from. So I can't go back there. Juan will have to go in himself." Rico told him.

"That's fine, as long as you're fine and we get those diamonds. Go somewhere and hide out. Juan's plane lands in Austin at midnight he will make the necessary arrangements to get you safe." Carlos told Rico chewing on a Cuban cigar.

"Alright, Carlos. Thanks man. I'll clean all this up. Have you spoken with Nora?" Rico asked him sincerely.

"Yes, she knows about your situation and she's very worried, but I'll notify her. You just get somewhere safe and call me back to let me know where you're at." Carlos told him.

They hung up. As soon as they hung up, Carlos called Juan. "Hola, Juan. This is Carlos."

"I just talked to Rico. The son of a bitch escaped, but he's been shot, so he'll be an easy mark. He's going to find somewhere to hide. Then he'll call me back. I told him you're on your way to help him." Carlos said to Juan.

"And he believed you?" Juan asked curiously.

"He's hurt right now. He's desperate at the moment. By the time he realizes you're going to be there with a gun to his head with my diamonds, it'll be too late." Carlos said to him.

"Well, call me as soon as he calls you. I'll have Cola go to San Antonio to get him and hold him." Juan told Carlos.

"Don't kill him until he shows you this guy who has my diamonds Juan." Carlos said with the upmost urgency.

"Boss, this isn't my first job. Just call me when he calls you." Juan explained then they hung up.

At the store in San Antonio, Rico asked the young lady, "Ma'am, if I transfer some money from my account to yours, could you get me a motel room until my friend gets in town?" Rico said with a sad hurt look on his face.

"A motel? How long is your friend going to be?" The tall goofy brunette asked.

"His plane lands tonight at midnight, so I need to rest my leg until he arrives." Rico told her.

"Well, I just live right down the street and you seem pretty harmless. You could wait for him there unless you want to spend the money on a room." She said giggling as she spoke.

"No...No that's fine. I wouldn't mind at all. But what would your boyfriend think of you brining some strange guy home?" Rico said fishing for her living status.

"Okay, first, I don't have a boyfriend. And second, I love to help people. Besides, your kind of cute." She said biting her bottom lip.

She helped Rico to the car and they left. During the ride, they made small talk to loosen up the moment. They pulled up to the apartment complex where the girl lived. She helped Rico out and they went inside. Rico looked around the small one-bedroom apartment. It was nothing he was used to, but it was a hideout. She gave him the phone and told him the address, so he could let his people know where he was.

Once he talked to Carlos, Carlos called Juan and the wheels were set in motion. "Rico should lead them to the diamonds and this will be over in a day or two at the most." Carlos thought to himself.

Around 10:30PM Nora and Rachelle landed at the airport in San Antonio. The only thing on Nora's mind was Rico. She had to get to him before Juan did.

Rachelle had already called in advance for a car to be waiting on them. They got off the plane and the driver was waiting.

"To the University Hospital, please." Nora said.

"Which one, ma'am? We have two." The driver informed her.

She looked at Rachelle with confusion in her eyes. "Which one?..." She asked.

"Let me make a call first." Rachelle called the police number back she called earlier and got the info they were looking for. "B.A.M.C." She said and they were off.

Upon the arrival at B.A.M.C., Nora's only thoughts were on Rico and if he was okay. They checked in and were escorted upstairs to the room where he was being held. Security checked their ID's and let them into the room to see Rico. When they walked in, Nora broke into tears to see the bandages all around his face and the tubes through him.

"Oh, my God, what have they done to him?" She said to Rachelle as she cried.

"I don't know, but I'll leave you two alone. I'll try and find some info on his charges and his condition. If you need me, I'll be at the front desk." Rachelle told her.

"Okay, and thanks again Rachelle." Nora said as she held Rico's arm.

"I would say no problem, but I know your father is going to have my ass for this." Rachelle said to her about disobeying Carlos.

"No, he won't. I'll take full responsibility." Nora said.

"That's cute." Rachelle said then she laughed and left the room.

Juan called Cola from the plane. He told him the change of plans. He was to now go to San Antonio to the address Rico gave, get him and hold him until Juan's plane landed in San Antonio. "Bring all the stuff in my treasure chest," Juan told Cola.

Cola loaded up all the weapons in the chest. Austin was only 45 minutes from San Antonio, so he'd be there in no time. Once on the road he headed straight to the young girl's apartment.

Rico and the young girl talked for a while and she decided to take a shower. "Would you like to join me?" She joked with Rico.

He said no, he was married, but it was a nice gesture. When the girl went to the back to take her shower, Rico went into the kitchen and grabbed one of her knives and placed it in his waistband. He felt the hair on the back of his neck stand on end and he didn't know why. So to be safe, he armed himself.

The girl called out to him, "Hey, are you sure you don't want to come in? I don't bite." She yelled from the restroom.

"No, I'm fine, thanks." He thought to himself, damn cute girl, so desperate. I thought girls back home were easy.

An hour passed and they heard a knock on the door. "Oh, that must be your ride." The girl said to Rico as she strut around in a tank top and low cut shorts. She looked out the peephole and saw the big guy standing there. "Who is it?"

"I'm here to pick up my friend, Rico. Is this the right apartment?" Cola asked in his deep Hispanic accent.

"Yes, just a minute." She said.

Rico got up off the couch and went to the door. He said thanks and left out. Cola looked at him and smiled. "Long time no see, old friend." He told him.

Rico smiled and shook his head. When they got in Cola's truck he called Juan. "Hey, I got him, what do you want us to do?" Cola asked Juan.

"I'll be there in 2 hours. Go rent a room and keep him out of sight." Juan told Cola.

"Gotcha." Cola said then they hung up.

"Perfect." Juan said to himself.

Adams couldn't leave Solis, so instead of going home, he went down to the parking lot to get some fresh air. On his way down, he decided to go check Rico's room.

When he arrived, it was guarded by two patrol officers, through the observation window, he could see Nora beside the bed talking to the body.

"Who is that?" He asked.

"That's his wife and the attorney went downstairs…" One officer replied. Adams just looked, then he walked away.

On the fourth floor, MAK told Vanessa and the girls he was going to get a cab to take him to drop the clothes off and he'd be back later.

On his way downstairs he ran into Adams. They went outside and started to talk. Adams told him he'd give him a ride to the house, just give him about 30 minutes to take care of some paperwork. MAK agreed, so they talked a while longer and Adams went in to do the papers.

At the motel, Cola and Rico sat quietly waiting on Juan's call and it finally came. "Hola." Cola said on the phone.

"I'm here. Come get me." Juan said and hung up.

"That's our cue. My boy, let's go, you've relaxed long enough." Cola told Rico.

They got up and left to the airport to get with Juan. Juan was standing out from when the truck came through the terminal parking lot. He got in the back seat and hugged Rico.

"It's been a while, my friend. Are you ready?" Juan asked him.

Rico looked at him and smiled, no words. Juan knew how Rico was, so he kew what the unspoken words meant. They pulled away and headed for the hospital.

"Now, look, I can't go in, so I'll describe the kid and his girl. The rest is up to you. There's fuckin' police who's taken special interest in the kid, so watch him." Rico told them. Rico gave Juan and Cola perfect descriptions of MAK and Vanessa and Adams. That should make ID easy.

They pulled up to the hospital. Juan told Cola to stay with Rico, he'd go in. He went inside the hospital and asked the front desk for the floor for surgery.

"the fourth floor, sir, but it's packed. So be ready to wait long." The receptionist said with a smile.

Juan smiled and headed for the elevator. When he exited the elevator, he saw all he needed to in the hallway. MAK was sitting in the hallway chairs with some bag between his legs. One female was with him, but it wasn't Vanessa. It was Sara.

MAK and Sara sat outside Vanessa's room talking. MAK told her all about the diamonds. He told her about the rest stashed at the factory and that he's the one who killed the truck driver. She just looked, but never judged him for his confession.

"Here Sara, take this bag until I get back. The diamonds are in there under these clothes. I don't want to take them with me. That detective is going to make me to the house, so I don't want him to know I still got them." MAK told her handing her the bag.

Sara took the bag and went back into Vanessa's room. MAK got up and headed back downstairs. Juan got up and followed him to the elevator. He got on his phone to text a photo to Cola's phone to show Rico. Rico confirmed the photo. When the doors opened, they stepped off but to the left Juan saw Nora and Rachelle. So he ducked back in the elevator.

"What the fuck are they doing here?" He said to himself. Nora had come down to get something to drink. She stopped and talked with Rachelle for a minute and was on her way back upstairs.

MAK sat and waited on Adams to come down to the lobby. Juan called to Cola and told him to ask Rico, "What the fuck was Nora and Rachelle doing here in San Antonio and at this hospital?"

"Oh, shit they must be looking for me." Rico said surprised. "Let me see your phone." Rico told Cola. Cola told Juan they didn't know. So Juan said he'd work around it.

Cola gave Rico his phone and Rico called Rachelle.

"Hello, Rachelle Benson, may I ask who's calling?" She said.

"It's me, Rudolfo. What are you doing in San Antonio with my wife?" Rico said to her.

Rachelle looked at her phone before speaking again. "Rico? How can this be Rico? Rico is in the hospital. His wife is looking at him." Rachelle said feeling confused.

"No, Rachelle, it's me. I escaped. I'm outside in the parking lot. Tell Nora that's not me. We are here to get something. Then we're headed to see Carlos." Rico told her trying to get her to listen.

"Who is 'we' Rico?" Rachelle asked.

"Me, Juan and Cola." Rico told her.

"Rico, Carlos sent Juan and Cola to kill you. That's why Nora and I are here to try and get to you before they do." Rachelle told Rico.

"Are you serious, Rachelle?" Rico asked, looking at Cola.

"Yes, Rico. I was supposed to take her to Carlos, but she insisted on coming to save you." Rachelle told him.

"Okay, well, get her out of there. I'll be okay." Rico said.

"Rico...Rico..." It was too late, he hung up.

Inside the hospital, Nora went back upstairs to Rico's room. While in there, she went to give Rico a kiss, she moved the bandages from his lips and noticed the reddish-brown goatee. Rico's hair is jet black and he's always clean shaven.

Rachelle ran for the elevator to warn Nora. When the elevator door opened, the crowd came rushing out the doors and Juan was in the mix. She never saw him exit. As he walked out, he saw MAK sitting in the lobby alone. He spoke to MAK and kept going outside.

Through the window, he waved his hands to get MAK's attention. MAK looked around and was the only one he could be talking to, so he got up and went to see what he wanted. Once outside, Juan started small talk.

"Hey, you smoke homeboy?" Juan asked MAK smiling friendly.

"Yeah man, but I don't got shit on me right now." MAK said, thinking he was talking about weed.

"I'm talking about cigarette's man." Juan said breaking out into a fake laugh.

"Oh, yeah. I smoke cigarettes." MAK said laughing back.

"You look like you need one. You've been stressing over something, bro?" Juan told him as if he was a mind reader. "Hey, I understand. My grandmother is on the support machine, dude." Juan lied to gain MAK's trust.

"Damn, sorry to hear that bro." MAK said feeling sorry for Juan.

"I left my cigarettes in the car. Want to walk with me? I'll give you a few. I know how it is to need and not have." Juan said.

MAK laughed and they walked to the truck.

Nora ran out the hospital room and told the officers. "That's not my fuckin' husband. Where is my fuckin' husband?" Her loud voice brought attention to the room.

"Ma'am calm down please. What's going on?" One officers said trying to calm her.

"What's going on is my husband has black hair. Whoever is in that bed has redish brown facial hair." Nora shouted waving her arms around her chin.

"Miss, are you sure?" The officer asked looking back at the body in the bed.

"I just saw his fuckin' hair! Where is my husband? Is this some kind of joke?" Nora yelled looking all around.

The nurses came in the room and checked the body lying on the bed. "What happened in here? His face wasn't affected." One nurse said.

"Get the Chief on the line." One officer said.

The nurse unwrapped the face and Nora went crazy. "That's not Rico! That's not Rico! Where is Rico?" Nora began yelling.

Just then, Rachelle came running to the room. "Nora, come with me please, it's important." Rachelle grabbed her pulling her in her direction.

Nora was crying but Rachelle pulled her to the elevator. At the elevator, she told her what Rico just said. Right then, she hugged Rachelle and they jumped on the elevator. Not knowing the officer saw the strange change in emotion.

Chapter 13

Rico had to get his plan together fast. He knew Juan would make good on his word for Carlos. Juan already had MAK to the killing point. They were on their way back to the truck. Juan was a master at his job "By any means necessary" was his code in this area. Rico was hit in the leg, so a hand on hand battle with Juan and Cola was definitely out of the question.

"This kid knows my face." Rico told Cola. "He'll panic if he sees me and I'm supposed to be in the hospital." Rico said trying to plan carefully.

"So what do we do?" Cola asked.

"Call Juan and tell him to stall for a few seconds." Rico told him.

Cola called Juan. Juan looked at his phone and picked it up. "Hola." Juan said turning his back to MAK.

"Rico said to stall for a few, because the kid knows his face and he might try and run if he sees him." Cola told Juan hoping he'd listen.

Juan hung up in Cola's face and looked back at MAK. They never stopped walking to the truck.

"What did he say?" Rico asked Cola.

"Shit, he hung up on me." Cola said to Rico.

"Damn." Rico thought to himself. As they approached the car, Juan swung and elbow that caught MAK off and right in the chin area. Not quite on the button. It was intended to knock him out, but it only made him stumble.

Inside the hospital, the police were in a frenzy over this Rico situation. The word got upstairs to Adams and he bolted out the chair down to the room where Rico was supposed to be and started barking out orders.

"Lock this place down! Nobody leaves these premises!" He yelled at the offices. "All call in back up now!" Adams shouted. The officers began lock down preparations immediately. An alarm blared loud through the hospital in which all officers knew that was going on.

Adams contacted Sgt. Little and told her what just happened. She freaked out and grabbed her stuff. "Where is Vanessa and John?" She asked Adams.

"God damn it! John is waiting for me downstairs and Vanessa, oh shit! I'll call you back." Adams said hanging up on her.

He ran to Vanessa's room, where he found the girls sitting making jokes.

"Hey, Detective Adams, I never got to…" Vanessa was beginning to say.

Before she could finish her sentence Adams yelled, "Where's John? We have a problem."

"What kind of problem?" Vanessa asked with worry in her face.

"Rico is not in his bed. Somebody else in is it. He's gone." Adams broke the news to her.

"GONE?" All three girls said simultaneously. "What do you mean?" Tiffany squeeled.

"I mean gone. Not here. Not there. Gone. Now get your stuff and come with me." Adams shouted at them.

"He said he was going to the house and he'd be back." Vanessa said beginning to tear up again.

Sara looked worried and she knew how dangerous Rico could be and she knew if he got away, he wouldn't leave without those diamonds she was holding in her bag... Someone else can get killed over these, she said to herself.

"I know what he wants. I have it right here." Sara said with her head down. Everyone turned to her and looked at her in confusion.

"What! Who wants?" Adams said to her looking annoyed.

"Rico." She said. "He's after these diamonds." She said reaching in the bag and she pulled the bag out filled with diamonds.

In the parking lot, MAK surprised Juan by not passing out. MAK kicked Juan's leg with all his might. When Juan fell, MAK jumped up and ran for the hospital entrance.

"Damn it!" Juan yelled, then broke into full stride after MAK.

Cola jumped out the truck and joined the chase. Juan caught up the MAK and kicked the back of MAK's foot, causing him to stumble and lose balance. At the speed he was running he slammed into the back of one car in the parking lot very hard. So hard, it knocked the wind out of him.

Juan's foot came crashing into his head. The impact knocked him to the ground and into a roll. He used that momentum to roll under the car.

"Come here, you son of a bitch!" Juan said looking under the car. "You got something I want." He told MAK.

"What the fuck are you talking about, dude?" MAK said in confusion.

"The diamonds, motherfucker!" Juan told him.

When MAK heard the words, he almost vomited under the car. Juan reached and MAK grabbed his arm then pulled hard. It yanked Juan up against the side of the car. MAK repeated that 4 or 5 times. Then he rolled to the other side of the car for a quick get away, but was met by Cola. Cola stomped him repeatedly.

Sar told them on their way downstairs how MAK told her he's the one who really killed the truck driver and stole the diamonds and some drugs. "He said there are more diamonds at the Butter Crust factory." She told them.

Adams, Tiffany and Vanessa couldn't believe what they were hearing. Adams's took the diamonds from Sara and said, "Look, if he wants these, he can have them. We have to save John. Those guys are going to kill him for sure now."

Vanessa passed out cold in the elevator. When the doors opened they were trying to wake her.

"Get some help! Hurry!" Adams yelled through the elevator doors to the passer bys.

A nurse came and took her to a chair for support. Just then, a lady came into the lobby yelling, "Hey officers, some guy is getting mugged in the parking lot."

The officers ran out of the door. It clocked to Adams – John – then Rico. He jumped up and ran out the door with them. Sara caught the clue late and she yelled, "Oh, shit! MAK!" Her and Tiffany ran out the door. Sara was not as fast, since she had a fresh wound.

The officer's yelled at Juan and cola to stop the assault on MAK. The both looked in surprise. Cola pulled his pistol and started shooting. Everyone scrambled for cover.

MAK swung and hit Cola in the private area and he tumbled over like a sack of potatoes. Juan grabbed the gun and started to drag MAK to the truck. Rico saw everything and grabbed the knife and cut off his wristband, and calculated his next few chess moves.

Tiffany and Sara were together behind an old minivan. Adams was behind a smaller car giving hand signals to the officers. He told them to call for backup. "Don't let those assholes out this parking lot." He demanded.

One officer got on the radio and radioed in, "Officers, need assistance, front parking lot – shots fired and possible hostage situation in progress." He shouted.

The call went out and all the officers headed for the parking lot.

"Get the fuck up." Juan yelled to Cola as he sent cover fire for him.

"I'm going to kill that fucker. You just hold him." Cola said referring to MAK for hitting him in the sack. They ran to the truck.

Cola popped the back and pulled out the weapon he brought from Austin. He pulled out an M-16 with a mini-grenade launcher attached. He handed Juan his Rfavorite twin 9mm with extended clips. Juan grabbed two hand grenades for special precaution and tucked them on his waste.

Two shots came zipping by their heads. Cola let off a mad spray of bullets that sent the law running. Some ran back inside, the other dove for cover. He sent one grenade there way that blew up 3 cars. It sent the cars airborne.

"Who the fuck are these guys?" One officer yelled from his cover spot.

"Holy shit!" Another yelled.

"Surround them on all sides!" Adams yelled out. "Fire back! Fire back! But don't hit the kid!"

Rico looked in the back and grabbed a pistol of his own and got out of the truck.

"Hold your fire...Hold your fire!" Adams yelled to all officers. All officers held their fire. Then Adams yelled to Juan and Cola. "I have the diamonds. Do you hear me? I have the diamonds, not the kid. Take me."

"What the fuck are you doing? They'll kill you!" Sara yelled to him.

Cola fired more shots. "Stop, stupid, he has the diamonds." Juan told him. "No trade. Give me the diamonds or we turn this parking lot into a police graveyard." Juan yelled as he stepped out into the open. "Now show me the diamonds!" Juan said to Adams.

He looked as Adams raised up from his spot. Cola took aim at the ready position. "Say when. I got him." He said to Juan looking at Adams through the rifle's scope.

Adams help up the diamonds and Rico's eyes lit up like light bulbs. This is the first time he's seen the diamonds since he placed them in the truck days ago.

He came around the truck from the back and shot Cola twice in the head before his body knew what happened. The blood sprayed everywhere. The shot surprised Juan and MAK. They both jumped. The Rico grabbed MAK and pointed the gun at Juan's head. "Drop it or I'll kill you, Juan." Rico said aiming directly between the eyes.

"What the fuck are you doing?" Juan shouted to Rico. As he pointed the twin 9MM at Rico and the other one aimed at MAK's stomach. He's been in these situations before, so to get Rico, he'll shoot MAK in the stomach. And as he falls, fire a head shot at Rico.

Rico knew him all too well and quoted his moves. "Don't try it Juan. If you flinch, you're dead." The police took aim, so Juan shifted quick. Too quick for Rico to shoot. And like that, he was gone between the cars. Rico stood there holding MAK around the throat with the gun to his head. "Bring me those diamonds and tell your pals to back up into the hospital." Rico ordered Adams as he looked around for an exit.

"Where are you going to go, man? You're surrounded on all sides." Adams told him as he pointed.

"I got away from the hospital and plenty other places. Now, do what I said." Rico told him.

Adams gave the order for the officers to back off into the hospital. The officers backed off and Adams started towards Rico.

"Slow, copper. I'll kill you both." Rico told him squeezing MAK's neck tighter.

"I just want to get you your diamonds and get that kid safe." Adams told him.

"Okay, that's far enough. Take your weapon out and put it on the ground." Rico told him.

Adams undid his holster and discarded his weapon.

"Now, turn around and walk towards us slow." Rico told him as everyone silently looked on. As he walked towards Rico and MAK, Rico threw MAK to the floor and grabbed Adams. "Now, give me my diamonds." He said to Adams holding him in a throat lock.

"Not until the kid is safe." Adams said. He held the diamonds tight. "Run, kid." He told MAK. MAK got up but instead of running, he grabbed Adams gun off the ground and aimed at Rico.

"No, go kid, just run. It's okay." Adams told him.

"Okay?! That son of bitch is the cause of all this mess. He deserves to die, not Tim."

"You robbed my truck kid and you blame me for this?" Rico said as he took aim at MAK. Juan came up from the rear with both grenades in his hands with pins in his mouth. He threw one at MAK and the other between Rico's legs.

Rico's only reaction was to shoot, but it did no good. Juan ran past too fast and the grenade exploded. The blast blew him and Detective Adams to pieces. The windows of surrounding cars exploded, spewing glass everywhere. The two cars they were standing next to were thrown over on their sides.

The grenade that flew towards MAK hit the car next to him and exploded. The pressure knocked him 10 or 12 feet across the parking lot. Not enough direct blast to kill him, but he broke a few bones.

The officers and the rest of the people heard and saw the blast and they lost it. When they saw Adams and Rico explode they couldn't believe their eyes. It saddened and drove people hysterical. They ran to the parking lot with fire extinguishers and yelling for medics, but it was no use. There was nothing left of either one of them. Rico nor Detective Adams.

Rachelle and Nora came running out the hospital, but were stopped by the officer holding back onlookers. Sara and Tiffany were hysterical. They saw the explosion that killed Adams and Rico followed by the second that killed MAK, so they thought.

As the police started to surround the area and block things off, Juan slowly made his getaway undetected. On the ground he saw two diamonds, so he pocketed them and dialed Carlos.

"Hola, Juan. Tell me something." Carlos said.

"I have bad news, Carlos." Juan told him.

The call went out all over the radios and the TV stations got wind of it. Explosions at the B.A.M.C. Hospital – Kidnapper escaped Police Custody and Blew up Hospital.

Things had officially hit the roof in San Antonio. Sgt. Little heard over the radio that Adams was dead. The tears flowed uncontrollably Chief Garza came to see the horror in the parking lot. He couldn't believe his eyes as he pulled up through the police barricade.

"How did this happen?" He shouted to no one in particular. No one could understand what just happened here today. They all stood like mannequins with their mouth wide open and eyes full of tears.

The EMS rushed to check for any survivors or innocent bystanders, who may have been caught in the blast or the gunfire. They canvased the area and one medic found a foot. One found parts of a torso others picked up pieces of body parts until one saw MAK's body halfway under a car. He came to the body and noticed shallow breathing.

"Hey, I got one alive. Hurry over here. He's still breathing." The medic yelled for help.

MAK's lower half was crushed under the car. He was unconscious and barely breathing. Another medic yelled, "I found one over here." She was referring to a dead Cola.

The medics and firefighters rushed to assist with trying to get MAK from under the car. His face was very badly burned and two of his fingers were missing. Glass was implanted in his face from the explosion. The officers held everyone back as they all rushed the line to see who it was that could have survived those two blasts.

News cameras were everywhere by now along with plenty of spectators. They got the car up enough to slide his body out. They rushed him inside with armed officers leading the way.

When Sara and Tiffany saw them carrying him, they screamed. "Oh my God! Is he alive?"

"He's still breathing." One medic said. The crowd began clapping and cheering. Vanessa was on oxygen when they came through with MAK. She jumped up from the chair, still in a slight daze.

"Is he alive?" Vanessa yelled.

"Please, ma'am. Move back." One officer told her.

"That's my boyfriend. Is he going to live?" Vanessa demanded.

"Ma'am, please." The medic shouted. They ran past her to rush MAK into surgery. Sara and Tiffany came running in behind them crying.

"What the hell happened?" Vanessa pleaded for someone to give her answers. They couldn't even get it together to tell her.

"Don't tell me any bad news, Juan. I'm not in the mood to hear bad news." Carlos told Juan, cursing in Spanish and slapping a bottle off the table.

"Well, that's what I have for you and it's all your daughter and that fuckin' attorney's fault." Juan told him arrogantly.

"What do you mean my daughter and the attorney?" Carlos shouted. "They're on their way here!"

"No, they're not boss. They're here and they told Rico what was going on. Shit went haywire, but Rico's dead." Juan told Carlos.

"Where is my daughter and the attorney?" Carlos said in a calmer but sinister voice.

"At the hospital." Juan told him.

"Where are my diamonds?" Carlos asked.

"They were blown up with Rico. Cola dropped a grenade on Rico and the kid and some detective. The detective had the diamonds and the explosion blew them everywhere." Juan said using Cola for a scapegoat.

"Don't come back here without my fuckin' daughter and take that attorney out." Carlos shouted.

"Can I do what I want with her?" Juan asked.

"I don't care. Just do it and get Nora back here." Carlos said.

Juan always told Rachelle her head would look good on his trophy case, so now he has his golden opportunity. From his spot across the street, he could see the hospital and all the people. They were too small to make out faces, so to find Nora and Rachelle he'd have to return to the scene of the crime. One thing he hates to do.

He knew he had to complete the mission. Carlos would use all the extent of his power to get Juan if Nora isn't back in reasonable time. Rachelle must be eliminated in the process.

He cocked both guns and walked towards the hospital with one purpose, get Nora and Rachelle by any means necessary.

In the parking lot, people were finding diamonds everywhere. Nora and Rachelle only looked as the medics scrapped together pieces of her husband.

"Let's go Rachelle. I can't take this anymore." Nora said through tears and despair.

"Okay, let me get the car driver on the phone." Rachelle told her. Nora walked into the hospital to have a seat and saw Vanessa, Sara and Tiffany crying and discussing what happened. She listened to the details and found out that MAK was Vanessa's boyfriend, which was the other guy involved in the explosion. The one who survived.

Rachelle walked in and sat beside her. "The car is on the way." She told Nora. While they waited, she told Rachelle what she just heard. Rachelle wanted to know what the hell she got into, so she decided to strike up an info session.

"Excuse me ladies, we couldn't help but hear your conversation." She said getting their attention. "This is the wife of one of the victims of the explosion." She told them.

That caught the girls' attention quick. "Can you explain to us what's going on? We're sorry about your boyfriend miss." Nora chimed in.

Vanessa looked at Nora and began to speak, but her voice broke. Sara decided to speak up. "From what we were told, my friend's boyfriend came into some diamonds that belonged to your husband and now your husband has killed her brother and a lot of innocent officers over those diamonds." Sara said rolling her neck and eyes as she spoke.

Nora looked concern, but she knew Rico was a gangster when she married him. "I'm sorry about your brother, miss." Nora said sincerely.

GREED

"My name is Vanessa and I'm sorry about your husband too." Vanessa said still crying.

Outside, Juan stalked the crowd like a wild animal looking for Rachelle and Nora. Once he made his way through the crowd, he walked past the front entrance and saw them in the body sitting with the girls.

"Bingo." He said to himself. "I'll wait here until they walk out and then take them." He said to himself. He sat in the outside smoking section and waited.

Sara asked Nora about the diamonds. "What's so special about those diamonds? Your husband went through a lot for them, ma'am."

"It was worth 50 million dollars." Nora told her. The amount shocked everyone, even Rachelle.

"Are you fuckin' kidding me?" Tiffany said.

"No, I don't kid. My father is in the diamond trade, illegally of course." Nora told her.

Sara sat and couldn't believe her ears, because she and MAK were the only ones who knew that. That it wasn't 50 million dollars worth of diamonds that blew up in the explosion, it was 25 million. MAK told Sara everything that includes the hiding place of the other half of diamonds.

"What would your father pay for the diamonds?" Sara asked Nora curiously.

Everyone looked at her with a strange confusion. "My father is money hungry. If he could get them for free, he would. But he will pay for them, if he thought he could win something off of it. Why do you ask?" Nora asked her.

Sara looked at the girls and thought about all they've been through. Might as well get something out of it. "That wasn't all the diamonds." She said to them all quietly.

The group got very quiet. "What do you mean?" Tiffany asked her looking anxious.

Nora looked at her and said, "Look, my father is not someone to play with or make deals like that with. It's too much at stake. He sent hitmen for Rico and that's his son-in-law. You're nobody to him." Nora explained.

"Yeah, but he wants the diamonds and we need money after all they've put us through. Tell him give us 10 million and I'll give him the location to the other half of those diamonds." Sara said to her looking at Tiffany and Vanessa.

"Are you kidding?" Tiffany said.

"Yeah! Are you kidding her?" Vanessa chimed in. "Look, there is no time for this game. I was told by MAK that he stashed the other half of diamonds and I know where." Sara told them again.

Nora didn't want to deal with her father at this point. She knew he would be furious that she came to San Antonio instead of following his orders.

"Okay, look, I have an idea if you're serious." Nora told her.

"I don't believe what I'm hearing. Your husband is dead and my boyfriend is almost dead and you two bitches are trying to make deals with the same diamonds that got them both where they are? That same greed is going to kill you all." Vanessa said shaking her head.

Nora looked at her and felt the pain, but she knew without Rico she had nothing and she refused to stay with daddy forever.

"What else do we have? We've all lost everything. I know all of Rico's connections. I can make calls and we can split the money. I have nothing against any of you. We can all go our ways after, and this is my lawyer, she can keep us safe until we make a deal." Nora said to Vanessa.

"I'm game." Sara said.

"I'm game." Tiffany said.

Vanessa looked at them and shook her head. "I don't believe you all. I don't want no part of this shit." Vanessa said turning her head.

"Well, if she's not down, I'm not down." Sara retracted.

"Me neither. But Nessa, I really wish you would think about it." Tiffany said.

"Think about your baby. MAK is messed up. He won't be able to work if he lives." Sara said.

Vanessa thought hard then looked at them all. Just then Rachelle's phone rang. It was the driver letting her know he was outside. "Look, that's the car. What's going to happen here? We need to go." She said.

They looked at Vanessa and said, "Let me just go see MAK one last time before we go." They all smiled and Tiffany helped her upstairs, the others went to the car.

Outside, Juan sat patiently waiting on Rachelle and Nora. He saw the limo out front, but didn't think anything of it until they walked out the hospital doors along with Sara. Rachelle pointed at the car, but they stood at the door waiting for Tiffany and Vanessa.

Juan got in motion. He headed for the car with his head down, so not to be seen by either of the girls. He walked to the passenger side window and knocked on it. The driver let down the window and Juan pointed the gun at him. He hoped the driver cooperated. It was too many police out there to have a tussle or shoot him.

"What do you want man?" The driver said – all the while looking around for help.

"If you comply, you'll live. You don't, you die. Now unlock the doors." Juan said acting as casually as possible. The driver unlocked the doors and Juan got in the backseat and closed the door back.

"Look man, I don't have money." The driver said looking in the rear view mirror."

"I don't care about your money. I want the car asshole. Now take your jacket and hat off and give it to me." The driver gave him the jacket and hat then Juan told him to get out, duck down and walk straight forward and don't look back. The girls were in conversation and didn't notice too much.

The driver got out the car and walked away. He was just happy this guy didn't kill him, so he never looked back. Juan climbed over the seat to the driver's seat, put on the hat and jacket and waited.

Vanessa and Tiffany couldn't see MAK due to the emergency surgery, so they decided to leave. "You know we're going to hell for this." Vanessa said, while they went back downstairs. They stepped out the hospital and met the others at the door.

"Ready?" Nora asked them.

"Yeah, ready to go to hell." Vanessa said.

They walked to the car not knowing trouble was in their next few steps. They got to the car and all climbed in the back. "Where to?" The driver said in a Hispanic accent which drew Nora's attention. She blew if off and they all looked at Sara.

"Where to, little lady?" Nora asked her.

Sara gave directions to the old Butter Crust Factory and they pulled away. They made small talk about Nora's father as Juan listened. Once out of the area and no police were around, he pulled to the side of the road, rolled down the divider window, locked the doors and stuck the pistol through the window and took the hat off. The girls screamed and tried to get out, but he shot Tiffany in the head.

Blood sprayed everyone. Her body slouched over into Vanessa's lap. They screamed and yelled, "What do you want?" Nora and Rachelle recognized Juan and panicked. They knew this was Carlos' work.

"What do you want Juan? Rico is already dead. Isn't my father happy yet?" Nora shouted to him.

"No, he isn't. He wants you back and her dead." He said pointing at Rachelle.

"You know this motherfucker who just killed my friend?" Vanessa said.

"Yes, I know him. He works for my dad and he's no good." Nora told them.

He pointed the gun at Nora, but she never flinched. "You know, if you me Juan, the rest of your life my dad will haunt you." She said grinning at him.

"I can't shoot you, but my orders are very clear for this one. Kill her." Juan laughed. Vanessa and Sara looked in terror as they shot comments and insults back and forth.

Nora told him, "You can't kill her. She knows where the diamonds are." All the girls looked at her in sudden panic.

"What the hell do you mean I know where the diamonds are?" Rachelle said surprised at the comment. Rachelle was angry, but had no idea, Nora just saved her life or at least prolonged it.

"We know that's what you came for, isn't it?" Nora asked him.

"You're telling me a lie. The diamonds were blown up. I saw them." Juan told her, remembering Adams holding the bag.

"Those were fake. The police were trying to bust Rico. The real diamonds are stashed and only she knows where. So if you kill her, you'll be in big trouble, because I'll tell my father you lost our only link to the diamonds." Nora told him hoping he bought it.

The other girls were looking and listening to Nora's story and wondered what she was up to. Was she setting them up to get her father's diamonds back for him or what?

Juan thought about what she said. Then thought about how pleased Carlos would be if he brought back Nora and the diamonds, killed Rachelle and Rico all in one day. So he said, "Show me where or I start shooting these bitches." He told her.

"The factory." She said.

While the limo was pulling away from the hospital, the real driver looked and notified the police. While he was telling them what happened, the Chief and Sgt. Little were walking by.

"Hey, Chief, come here this." The officer said. "What is it now? I have a lot going on." Chief told him.

"You might want to hear this." He said to the Chief with the look of urgency in his eyes. "Tell the Chief what you told me." The officer said to the limo driver.

"Okay, I was called by Mrs. DeLuna's attorney to pick them up. Once I got here, I called and let her know I was here. Some guy walked to my window and pulled a gun and took my spot. He took my jacket and hat and he just sat there like he was sitting for them. I saw them come out and get in the limo, but they had three other females with them." The driver said nervous and confused.

"Where were they headed?" Chief asked.

"I don't know." The driver said still nervous from having the gun in his face.

"Chief, he said one of them was pregnant." The officer reinterated.

The Chief didn't say anything for a moment. The name DeLuna rung to him. Rudolfo DeLuna? "Rico… Damn it. That's Rudolfo's wife and pregnant girl…"

"Oh, shit." Sgt. Little said. "Vanessa."

"What does this limo look like?" Sgt. Little asked.

"A black stretch Lincoln Town Car." The driver said.

"Call it in and get all units on it ASAP. Call the night bird and get a road block up to 5 miles." Little said. "How long ago did they leave?" She asked.

"Around 10 to 15 minutes ago." He replied back.

"Shit… Chief, I know this is about those diamonds. If Rudolfo came for the diamonds, not that he's dead, his wife must've found out Vanessa could know where they are." Sgt. Little told the Chief.

"But who took his car at gun point?" Chief asked.

"I don't know, but I know this has something to do with those diamonds." Then she ran into the hospital.

"Where is she going?" The officer asked.

"I don't know. She gets these hunches and runs with them. Most of the time she's right. So follow her and assist her in any way she needs because I feel she's going to need assistance."

Sgt. Little ran to the elevator where they took MAK. She was about to enter and was met by the officer who was outside.

"Chief told me to follow you and help in any way." He said, scaring her a little. They got to the emergency floor and saw the armed officers standing guard outside on the doors.

"Move out the way. I have orders from the Chief to see the guy in there." She yelled at them.

"He's in pretty bad shape, Sgt." The guy said.

"I have one question for him." She said.

"He just got blown up. He's not talking. He can't talk." The guard said.

Little pushed past them and looked into the room. There were tubes everywhere. MAK was out cold.

"Where are they headed?" She thought out loud. "Think, think." She kept repeating. Just then her phone rang. "Hello?" She said.

"We just got a call for a body on the side of the road. A passing car saw the body get shoved out of a limo. Get your ass down here or I'm leaving you." Chief told her.

She ran to the elevator down to the first floor and the Chief was waiting in a patrol car. "We have the helicopter searching the area where the body was dumped. We should have something in a minute." Chief said.

They headed towards the area the body was dumped.

Over the ride to the Butter Crust factory, the girls exchanged looks.

Juan made Sara get in the front and drive, since she knew the way. He held the rest of them at gun point, one on them and one on her.

The factory came into view and they pulled in. There was police tape there from the shootout. Juan got out and made the girls get out the car.

"Now, take me to the diamonds." He said to Rachelle as he pointed a gun to her head. Nora jumped in front of her.

"No, you have to promise you won't kill them once you get the diamonds." She said to him.

He grabbed Nora by the hair and was about to shove her to the floor, but she kicked him hard in the shin area then attacked him. "Run," She told the others.

They all ran in different directions into the factory. He was scared to harm Nora, due to Carlos, but he hit her with an open palm to the chest and knocked her to the floor and he opened fire. The bullets whizzed by Rachelle's head, but one hit her in the back.

She fell into the wall at the entrance of the factory door. Vanessa ran through to the other side, up some stairs and into an office to hide. Sara tried to help Rachelle up, but Juan fired shots to make her back.

"Look, little girl, just leave her. She's dead once she gives me those diamonds and if you get in the way, you'll die too. So don't make this hard." Juan told her in a spooky voice.

Sara felt so bad, because she knew Rachelle knew nothing. "Run… Help your friend." Rachelle told Sara.

Without thinking, she reached out and grabbed her hand and began to pull Rachelle in. Juan dragged Nora by her hair towards the entrance where Rachelle's body lay before Sara helped her.

Sara couldn't get the body far. Rachelle was heavy due to the dead weight. Juan walked through the door and yelled, "Come out or she's going to pay." He said and he punched Nora in the face repeatedly.

"Go." Rachelle told Sara aggressively.

Juan saw the blood trail from where Sara dragged Rachelle around the corner. "I only want the lawyer, little girl. I'll let you and your friend go, if you leave now. You have my word." Juan told her.

"Please, go." Rachelle pleaded with Sara.

"Sara, Vanessa, please just go. We'll be okay." Nora said through bleeding teeth.

Sara crawled away from Rachelle. When she was far enough, she got up and tried to find Vanessa. As she came to the stairs, she saw the office Vanessa was in. She went in. She and Vanessa sat there for a while scared to death, not knowing what to do.

There was a window on the other side of the office. Sara went to it and noticed it had a way out to the lower level outside the factory. She and Vanessa crawled out the window down to the outside and to the side of the building.

Inside the factory, Rachelle and Nora played with Juan's mind by telling him lies about the diamonds. He wanted them so bad he started to beat both women trying to get answers.

Sara and Vanessa went running down the street. They got to a house where a lady and her daughter were outside the porch. They asked if they could use the phone to call their father for a ride home because their car was broken down.

"Sure girls, come in. You're pregnant, you don't need to be walking this late at night." The lady said.

Sara dialed 911. When the dispatcher picked up she asked to be transferred to Sgt. Little.

"What's your emergency, ma'am?" The dispatcher said.

"Tell her it's about the explosion at the hospital." Sara said.

"Please hold." The transfer went through.

"Hello, this is Sgt. Little. Who is this?" Little said.

"Little, this is Sara. Vanessa and I are down the street from the old Butter Crust Factory. Tiffany is dead and Rico's wife and the attorney are about to get killed. Please hurry!" Sara told her hysterically.

"What's going on?" Little asked.

"Some guy kidnapped us from the hospital trying to find those diamonds." Sara told her.

"Did he find them?" Little asked.

"I don't know. We ran away through the window." Sara said trying to catch her breath.

"You stay where you're at. We're on our way." Little told her.

"No, go to the factory and save those girls." Sara said.

"Okay, just stay put and what's the address where you're at?" Little asked.

The old lady gave them the address and they hung up.

"Chief, that was Sara and Vanessa. They're at the old Butter Crust Factory. I told you it was about those diamonds." Little told him.

"Let's go." Chief said.

They arrived at the factory and Juan was still searching for the diamonds. Rachelle was dead and Nora was unconscious both side by side. The Chief went around back. Little and the other officer came through the front. When they saw the bodies, Little rushed to see if any of them had a pulse. Nora had one, Rachelle didn't.

Sgt. Little called for an EMS unit and the other officer walked around looking for Chief.

"Chief, where are you?" He asked.

"Over here. I got him." Chief told them.

"Yeah, you got me, Chief." Juan said as he eased step by slow step back towards the Chief.

"Get on your fuckin' knees and put your hands on you head now." Chief said.

Juan kneeled down, but instead of placing his hands on his head, he grabbed for his waistband. Chief fired two shots into Juan that knocked him over dead.

Little and the other officer heard the shots and came running. They saw Juan lying dead and the Chief over his body checking his waist. He found the gun Juan was going for and pulled it out.

"Call it in." He told Little.

"I already have." She said.

They came to the front of the factory and waited for the EMS units to arrive. Sgt. Little sent a unit down the street to get Vanessa and Sara. Once everything was wrapped up, they took the girls to the station and promised them protection.

"Look, we're going to transport you girls to a witness protection house in DeSoto. We'll transport John there as soon as he's out of surgery, is that okay?"

"Yeah, that's cool, but what about Nora?" Vanessa asked.

"What do you mean?" Little asked.

"Well, her dad is the one who did all of this. She's trying to hide from him." Vanessa said.

"Well, we'll talk with her, but for now we have to get you two safe out of San Antonio."

Several hours later, they arrived at the safe house in DeSoto. Sgt. Little gave them a key and they secured the house.

"No one knows you girls are out here, so you'll be safe here. I'll be at a motel a few miles down the road. Call if you need anything." Little told them. They hugged and went into the house.

GREED

It was nice three-bedroom furnished house. They sat on the couch and Vanessa looked at Sara and said, "Thank you for everything."

"No problem girl, hopefully we can sleep tonight." Sara told her then laughed.

Vanessa told her, "Hey, girl, when we were at that factory I ran into that room I was looking for a hiding spot and look." She said with a smile. She pulled out the bag of diamonds from inside her pants. Sara stared at the diamonds and started to laugh. Then Vanessa started to laugh.

"We're rich, soon as Nora gets out here, girl." Vanessa said.

They sat up for a while longer. Then they got sleepy. The TV was still on when they passed out.

THE END

www.ingramcontent.com/pod-product-compliance
Lightning Source LLC
LaVergne TN
LVHW021705060526
838200LV00050B/2514